# GINA WASHINGTON SLEPT HERE

*Also by Katherine Bolger Hyde*

*Crime with the Classics*

ARSENIC WITH AUSTEN
BLOODSTAINS WITH BRONTË
CYANIDE WITH CHRISTIE *
DEATH WITH DOSTOEVSKY *
FATALITY WITH FORSTER *
HANGING WITH HUGO *

*Novels*

THE DOME-SINGER OF FALENDA
AFTER HE'S GONE *
THE VESTIBULE OF HEAVEN

*Other titles*

LUCIA, SAINT OF LIGHT
EVERYTHING TELLS US ABOUT GOD
A TASTE OF PARADISE
BRAVE, FAITHFUL, AND TRUE

* *available from Severn House*

# GINA WASHINGTON SLEPT HERE

Katherine Bolger Hyde

SEVERN
HOUSE

First world edition published in Great Britain and the USA in 2024
by Severn House, an imprint of Canongate Books Ltd,
14 High Street, Edinburgh EH1 1TE.

severnhouse.com



*British Library Cataloguing-in-Publication Data*
A CIP catalogue record for this title is available from the British Library.

ISBN-13: 978-1-4483-1187-3 (cased)
ISBN-13: 978-1-4483-1188-0 (e-book)



*All Severn House titles are printed on acid-free paper.*

FSC www.fsc.org
MIX
Paper from
responsible sources
FSC® C013056

Typeset by Palimpsest Book Production Ltd., Falkirk,
Stirlingshire, Scotland.
Printed and bound in Great Britain by TJ Books Limited,
Padstow, Cornwall.

# Praise for Katherine Bolger Hyde

"Hyde knows how to hook the reader"
*Publishers Weekly* on *Fatality with Forster*

"A complicated plot, well-drawn characters, warm-hearted moments juxtaposed with heart-stopping action, and a satisfying ending"
*Booklist* on *Hanging with Hugo*

"Emotionally satisfying"
*Kirkus Reviews* on *After He's Gone*

"As heartbreaking as it is shocking"
*Booklist* on *Fatality with Forster*

"Effectively blends romance and mystery"
*Booklist* on *Death with Dostoevsky*

"An engaging start to a series"
*Booklist* on *Arsenic with Austen*

# About the author

**Katherine Bolger Hyde** has lived her life surrounded by books, from teaching herself to read at the age of four to majoring in Russian literature to making her career as an editor. She lives in Washington State with her husband and is the author of six Crime with the Classics mysteries, including most recently, from Severn House, *Hanging with Hugo*, and the standalone thriller, *After He's Gone.*

www.kbhyde.com

*To my mother, Charlotte*
*for all the good times and beauty we shared*

# ONE

Erin crawled her Subaru along the narrow lanes of Pacific Grove, California, peering at the street signs as she listened to the bossy, superior voice of the GPS on her phone. Must be time for new glasses. Nearsightedness was an occupational hazard of being a reference librarian.

Who laid out these streets, anyway? They seemed to change names with every curve and intersection. Maybe the uneven coastline and hilly terrain were to blame – hard to create a regular grid around those features. Presumably she'd find it picturesque if she ever managed to get to her B&B and relax.

What a way to begin a getaway that was supposed to be an antidote to stress – a chance to unwind and catch up with herself after all the frantic activity of arranging her father's funeral. A chance, perhaps, to get beyond the shock of his death and begin to grieve.

She was an orphan now. Being orphaned at thirty-two didn't carry quite the poignancy associated with parentless children. But she had lost her mother at age twelve, so she sort of qualified as a child orphan as well. Losing her father felt less like a new abandonment and more like the completion of a process that had begun long ago – a process that had been woven into her destiny from the time of her birth. She had always been meant to be alone.

The annoying nasal voice of the GPS announced, 'You have reached your destination.' Erin came to with a jerk and hit the brakes. Fortunately there were no cars behind her.

What destination? To her right was the ocean, to her left a forest – no building in sight. Oh, but there, hiding among the eucalyptus trunks and partially overshadowed by their drooping leaves, was a sign next to a gravel driveway: *Seafarer's Rest.* That was the name of the B&B she'd booked for her long weekend.

She'd stopped a few yards beyond the turn, so she honked to

signal any cars that might be coming around the last bend, backed up carefully, and turned into the drive. After a hundred yards, the eucalyptus and Monterey pine parted to reveal a grassy clearing around a large Victorian house.

Erin paused to admire the house before continuing to the parking area. A true Painted Lady, worthy of the older neighborhoods of San Francisco. Turrets, gables, porches, balconies, gingerbread – the works. The base color was a dusty peach while complementary tones of pale yellow, mint green, lavender, aqua, and cream ran riot on the trimwork. Mumsie would have loved this place.

A pang deeper than any she'd felt since her father's death ran through her. Erin's grief for her mother was twenty years old but no less intense for all that. It was hard to 'find closure,' as the psychobabble went, when one's mother disappeared without trace. Well, with one trace, which Erin had discovered before she knew her mother was gone. After showering on that fateful morning – the first morning of her motherless life – she'd read in the steam on her mirror:

*Always remember I love you. Mumsie.*

At the time, she had only smiled, not suspecting this quirky note was meant for a final goodbye. Mumsie was always leaving her unexpected notes – in her shoe, in her lunchbox, taped inside the cover of a textbook. It was their private game. With no siblings and with Father away so much as an airline pilot, Erin and her mother had been essentially a family of two, bonded in a love that was too free and playful, too deeply respectful on both sides, ever to feel suffocating.

How could one ever cease to grieve a loss like that?

Erin shook herself back into the present and continued up to the entrance, where the drive widened to allow parking for half a dozen cars. She pulled her overnight case and messenger bag out of the car, paused once again to admire the inn's façade, and mounted the dozen steps to the glass-inlaid front door.

In the hall, filtered light from the stained-glass windows gleamed off the polished wood of the walls, the carved walnut reception desk, and the grand staircase that curved upward at one side. A mild breeze wafted through open transoms. Erin took a deep breath of eucalyptus, lemon-scented wood polish, tantalizing odors from the kitchen, and peace. She'd come to the right place.

The friendly, matronly receptionist – possibly the owner? – greeted Erin and slid an old-fashioned guest register across the desk for her to sign. She handed Erin a real brass key on an engraved copper fob and directed her to her room: 'Left at the top of the stairs, second door on your left. You're in room nine, the north tower.' Better and better.

Refusing the offer of help with her bags, Erin mounted the wide, curving staircase, her sensible shoes sinking into plush carpet with each step. She found her door, unlocked it, and gasped.

The two straight walls gave way to a broad semicircular sweep of lace-curtained windows above a cushioned seat that ran all the way around. A small table with a couple of straight chairs faced the view of treetops parting to reveal a tantalizing glimpse of the sea. She set down her bags and made a circuit of the room. A four-poster bed with a mountain of pillows and a fluffy down comforter. An antique inlaid wardrobe, cedar-lined, in which she could almost sense the ghosts of the ball gowns of decades past. A spacious bathroom with a deep clawfoot tub. Original watercolor seascapes of decent quality on the walls. Nothing electronic, not one piece of standard hotel furniture or mass-produced art to be seen. She might have been in 1903, when, according to the sign by the front door, this inn was built.

When Alex, her colleague at the library reference desk, recommended this place, urging her to splurge and treat herself for once in her life with her father's insurance money, she had balked. Spending money on herself – frivolously at that – was not something her usual principles, or resources, allowed. But he had persisted, reminding her of how much it meant to her to have beauty in her life, of how much she needed this break after years of the slow drain of caring for her dying father and the final burst of energy required to lay him to rest. At last she had capitulated. And now, sitting on the window seat and looking out toward the sea, she was deeply glad and grateful that she had.

After a while, she checked her watch, her stomach reminding her of those tempting odors from the kitchen downstairs. Five past six. The dining room was open. She turned toward the bed where she'd dumped her bags, feeling this setting warranted a slightly more formal outfit for dinner than the jeans and light sweater she had on. As the bed came into view, she felt a sudden chill wash over her. She turned to close the windows, but the chill was gone as quickly as it had come. She left the windows alone and changed into a skirt and sandals.

After a delicious solo dinner of seafood Rockefeller with a delicate Riesling and a good book, Erin returned to her room, intending to write in her journal, read for a while, then soak in the inviting tub before going to bed. But she found herself yawning already. Must be the sea air. She ran a bath and dozed in it until the water went cold, then went to bed.

She slept deeply for several hours, until the full moon rose and shone straight through her windows. She didn't wake fully then but moved into a dreaming phase of sleep. Mumsie was there – not unusual; Erin often dreamt of her mother as if she were still alive. But this time she was *here*, in this room, though the furnishings were subtly different – sheer curtains instead of lace, pastel floral bedclothes instead of pure white, prints of old masters rather than original watercolors on the walls. Even in her dreaming state, Erin marveled at the detail with which she saw all this. It wasn't vague and unstable like an ordinary dream; it felt like a real scene in which she was present as a disembodied observer.

Erin called out to her mother, but she didn't seem to hear. Mumsie moved about the room preparing for bed, closing the windows, checking the lock on the door, turning down the comforter and moving some of the pillows to one side. She got into bed and stared upward for a few minutes, her lips moving as if in prayer, then made the sign of the cross over herself and settled on her side to sleep.

But moments later, Erin heard a scraping at one of the windows. She darted a look at her mother, but Mumsie slept on. As Erin watched in frozen horror, the window creaked outward and a man climbed in over the seat. The figure was grainy and faint in the moonlight, dressed all in black, including gloves and something covering his face and head.

The man crept up to the bed, lifted one of the spare pillows, and brought it down over Mumsie's face. She lay still for a moment, then flailed and thrashed as the pillow pinned her head. Erin cried out, tried to pull the man away, but she was not an actor in this scene; she could change nothing. She could only watch in agony as her mother's life drained away.

Suddenly it was Erin herself in the bed, gasping for breath. She threw out her arms to push the attacker away, but her arms met empty air. No pillow covered her face, but her heart pounded and her mouth was dry. She threw off the bedclothes and ran to the windows, opened one and leaned out, gulping huge breaths of fresh night air and willing reality to reassert itself.

At last her heartbeat slowed its frantic pace and she fell back on the seat, staring once again at the empty bed.

That had been no ordinary dream.

When she'd returned to a shaky version of normal, Erin checked the clock by the bed. Three twenty. She could hardly rouse the house at this hour, but neither could she go back to sleep. She turned on a lamp, closed and locked the windows, checked the lock on the door, and took a quick look in the empty bathroom. Then she took out her journal and settled at the small table to clear her mind by channeling her thoughts through her pen.

She wrote everything she could remember about the day of her mother's disappearance and the harrowing weeks and months that followed. Her frantic search through the house for clues – what clues, she had no idea – while her father paced distractedly, arguing on the phone with the police, who refused to act until her mother had been missing for twenty-four hours.

The next day, Father finally persuaded the police to come to the house. When Erin revealed that a suitcase and some of Mumsie's things were gone, along with her car, the detective became even more recalcitrant. 'She's an adult, Mr Washington,' he said in slow and patient tones, as if talking to a child. 'It looks as if she left of her own accord. We've checked the hospitals, and she doesn't seem to have been in an accident. There's not much more we can do in a situation like this.'

Father loomed over the seated detective, hands on hips, piercing him with the glare that always made Erin cower. 'My wife has not left me,' he forced out through gritted teeth. 'She would never do that. She'd certainly never leave her child.' He grabbed Erin by the shoulder and pushed her forward as if she were an exhibit for the defense. 'Gina and Erin are extremely close. There's no way Gina would go anywhere voluntarily and leave her daughter behind. Especially not without leaving word.'

The detective – Carver, his name was, the name carved in her memory along with every other detail of that awful day – turned to Erin with a smile that tried to be kind although it held out no hope. 'She didn't say anything to you? Leave you some sort of note?'

Erin hesitated with a sidelong glance at her father. Answering that question felt like a betrayal. But surely the police could get nowhere without the truth. 'She wrote something in the steam on my bathroom mirror. I saw it when I showered yesterday. But I didn't think anything of it. She's always leaving me notes.'

Carver said gently, 'Do you remember what it said?'

She gave him a frown that said, *Of course I remember, I'm not a child.* 'It said, "Always remember I love you. Mumsie."'

Carver pooched out his lips, drumming his pencil on his notebook. 'That could mean anything.'

'Exactly,' Erin replied.

Carver stood so that his height matched Father's. 'I'd like to speak to your daughter alone for just a minute, sir,' he said, his voice infused with authority.

Father shot a glance from Carver to Erin to the silent policewoman standing by the door, then reluctantly left the room. Carver sat back down and gestured Erin to a chair across from him.

'So you and your mother are pretty close, then?'

She nodded. 'We do everything together. Except school and her work, of course. Father's away a lot, flying.'

'She works at . . .' Carver consulted his notes. 'The Cruikshank Gallery?'

'That's right.'

'Is she close to her coworkers?'

Erin shrugged. 'There's only her and Mr Cruikshank. I don't think she likes him very much. He's weird.'

Carver cocked an eyebrow at her and scribbled a note. 'When you and your mother go out, is it always just the two of you? Does either of you ever bring a friend along?'

'Sometimes my friend Jenna from school goes to a movie or something with us.'

'What about your mother? Does she ever bring a friend? Or meet anyone when you're out?'

Erin thought back. 'Once we ran into her friend Wendy at the beach.'

'But never . . . a man?'

Erin frowned at Carver. He thought he was being so subtle, but she knew what he meant. She wasn't a child. 'You mean you think Mumsie was having an affair. That she's run off with some guy. No way. Not Mumsie. You obviously don't know her if you can think that. Father and I are her whole world.'

'I understand that, but you said your father's away a lot. She must get lonely. Sometimes grown-ups do things they wouldn't normally do just because they're unhappy.'

'But she wasn't lonely or unhappy. She had me.' The grown-up Erin recognized how naive this statement was, but at the time she'd believed it implicitly. She and her mother were a unit, complete within itself. There'd been no need for anyone else.

Carver had left it at that. He told Father to let him know of any developments and left.

But nothing had ever developed. Father had called everyone her mother knew, and no one had anything to tell him. Erin had bused all around Santa Cruz County, visiting all their favorite haunts – the library, the museum, the movie theater, the beach, the redwood forest, the marsh walk, the funny little upstairs coffee shop in Capitola, the yarn shop where they were taking knitting classes together, the place where you could paint your own pottery, the art store where her mother bought her painting supplies. Nobody had seen her in any of those places. She'd left no more hidden notes, no clues of any kind.

Hope faded day by day until finally – Erin could never say exactly when – its last tiny flame was snuffed out. She learned to live as a motherless child.

# TWO

By the time Erin finished writing, the first glimmer of daylight shone through the bank of windows. She pulled back the curtains and gazed out toward the sea. She still wasn't sleepy. It was only six o'clock – too early for anyone to be available to attempt to answer her myriad questions. She took a long hot shower to banish the ghosts, dressed in jeans and sneakers, and headed out for a walk.

Erin walked quickly down the drive to the main road, hugging her sweater around her. The sun had not yet penetrated the woods, and even on this June day, the breeze was chilly. When she came to the main road and crossed to the ocean side, she paused to orient herself. The Monterey Bay lay around the tip of the peninsula, to her right; she faced the Pacific Ocean in all its untamed glory. The beach beckoned, but the scramble down to it from here daunted her; she wasn't sure she'd be able to get back up. The wind bit through her light sweater, and her stomach growled. She'd save finding a way to the beach for later in the day.

Back up the drive she went, pausing to admire the multicolored bark of the eucalyptus trees. When she and her mother were taking knitting classes, Mumsie had become fascinated with the process of dyeing yarn using natural materials. She'd collected a grocery bag full of eucalyptus bark along with a jar of onion skins and a basket of wildflowers, and the two of them had experimented. Ultimately they produced a couple of hanks of wool speckled with earthy greens, yellows, browns, and purples, with which they'd made matching scarves. Erin still had hers somewhere, assuming the moths hadn't gotten to it. But after her mother disappeared, she didn't have the heart to go on with either knitting or dyeing. The scarf was her first and last project.

Now she stopped at one tree whose colors were particularly vivid – layers of pink, yellow, and aqua beneath the peeling brown. *You would have loved this one, Mumsie*, she thought. And quick on the thought came the answer: *Yes. I did.*

Erin froze. Had she really just heard her mother's voice? No, not with her ears, but it was still ringing in her mind – *in* her mind, but not *from* her mind. Mumsie had spoken to her.

*Explore the tree, my love.* Again, the words were clear.

Erin took a deep breath to steady her nerves and her hands. Then she ran her fingers up the trunk toward a low branch, and a flash of brightness caught her eye. Something sparkling was caught deep in a crevice near her own eye level. She peeled the layers of bark away and pried out an emerald drop in a gold setting that might once have been part of an earring.

An earring she recognized. Her mother had just such a pair. Her favorites – she wore them frequently, despite their value. Mumsie had believed nice things should be enjoyed rather than hidden away and protected. The emeralds brought out the green of her eyes and made her smile every time she caught a glimpse of her own reflection. Erin had loved them as well.

She stood immobile, unable to tear her eyes from the earring. Her vision unfocused until all she could see was a field of sparkling green. A feeling of her mother's presence enveloped her, stronger even than the voice had been, so strong that for a moment she forgot to breathe.

Then the feeling faded, her focus returned, and she was left with an unshakable conviction: That dream was no coincidence. Her mother had been here. She stayed at this inn; she lost an earring brushing – or being pushed? – against this trunk. And possibly she died here.

Erin pocketed the emerald and ran the rest of the way up the drive. Surely the inn staff must be up and about by now. It was nearly seven.

The lobby was deserted, but she heard clinking from the dining room. Inside, the matronly woman who'd signed her in was setting out the last of the utensils on the buffet while a few early guests queued up to fill their plates. Erin hurried up to her, breathless.

'Excuse me,' she said. 'I'm sorry to bother you so early, but were you here about twenty years ago?'

The woman turned to her with startled eyes. 'Why, bless you, yes, I was. I own this place – been running it since my parents passed away. I've been here – oh, going on thirty years now.' A little crease appeared between her brows. 'Why do you ask?'

Erin glanced at the eager breakfasters already helping themselves to eggs, bacon, and French toast. 'Do you have a minute? Could we talk somewhere more private?'

The woman – her name tag read *Elise Jenkins* – gave the buffet a once-over and appeared satisfied. She nodded to a young girl just coming out of the kitchen as if to say, *You take over here*. 'Yes, all right. Come into my office.' She led the way through the lobby and behind the reception desk to a swing door that opened onto a tiny room – more of a nook, really – filled with shelves and cubbyholes that bulged with papers, envelopes, and odds and ends. Erin's eye fell on a row of leather-bound registers similar to the one she'd signed the night before.

'It's hard to explain, but I have reason to think my mother may have stayed here at some point about twenty years ago. Do you still have your guest registers from that time?'

Elise's baffled expression intensified. 'Ye–es,' she said, 'but I don't normally show them to people. It's a matter of confidentiality, you see.'

Erin's heart was racing as if she'd had three cups of espresso. She must get this woman to understand. She seemed like an understanding sort of person.

'I realize that, but it is twenty years ago. Surely it couldn't hurt at this point.' Elise's expression remained skeptical, so Erin forged ahead. 'It's important. My mother disappeared twenty years ago. We never found out what happened to her. So if she did stay here, that could be a vital clue. It would give me a place to start.'

Elise's eyebrows rose to her hairline, then drew together in concern. 'Oh, you poor thing. To know nothing all this time – that must have been awful for you.' She turned to the row of registers. 'I have one book per year. Do you mean twenty years exactly – 2001?'

'Yes. My mother was last seen on June twenty-first, 2001.' Erin realized with a start that was twenty years ago to the day.

Elise pulled out a hefty volume and laid it on the small desk. 'Here you are.'

'Thank you so much.' Erin sat in the straight oak chair and opened the register, her fingers tingling with anticipation.

Elise hovered for a moment, then said, 'This is likely to take a while. I'll leave you to it – lots to do at this time of the morning.'

Erin met her eyes. 'I can't tell you what this means to me.' She smiled, and Elise smiled back – the smile of a true kindred spirit. Then she bustled out, and Erin settled to her work.

She skimmed the pages for the end of June, looking for either her mother's name or her handwriting. She'd concluded long ago that her mother must have had some compelling reason not to want to be found at the time, or Erin would have found her. If that had been the case, she surely would not have signed a guest register with her real name.

Nothing in June. She moved on to July, August, September, her quaking forefinger passing down each column with no result. That took her long enough that she wished she'd at least gotten a cup of coffee before she began.

As if reading her mind, Elise appeared in the doorway with a steaming mug in one hand and packets of cream and sugar in the other. 'I thought you could use some coffee,' she said. 'Any luck?'

Erin took the mug, beaming her gratitude. 'Not yet. I've looked through September – on to the last quarter.'

'I hope you find something. But if you need another volume, you know where they are.' She gestured to the shelf.

'Thanks again. For everything.'

Elise smiled and left. Erin added cream to her coffee and took a sip – strong, dark, delicious. She turned to the beginning of October and ran her finger down the page.

She was about to move on to the next page when one name caught the corner of her eye and pulled her back. *Anne S. Blythe*. The married name of Anne Shirley of Green Gables fame. That was her mother's handwriting, all right – she looped her Ys in a way Erin had never seen anywhere else. And trust her to choose the name of one of her favorite characters – one this inn might have reminded her of – but to disguise it so it wouldn't jump out to the casual observer.

Her mother had checked into room nine – Erin's room – at four fifty-three p.m. on October fifth. The time, date, and room number were written in a different hand, presumably the owner's since it matched the dates of other guests. But the checkout time and date matched neither the name nor the other numbers. Nine fourteen a.m. on October sixth. The nine and the six had full curves at bottom and top, respectively, and the one had a long tail leading up to the main stroke. She'd seen some Eastern Europeans write their numbers that way.

Quickly, she skimmed the rest of the two-page spread as well as the pages before and after. Those distinctive number shapes appeared nowhere else.

Erin sat back, digesting this. Perhaps Elise had employed a temporary assistant who only worked that one morning. Unlikely. Could her mother have been traveling with someone else? Erin had rejected that possibility years ago. Could Mumsie have decided on a whim to disguise her handwriting? But what would be the point when she'd already signed in with her normal hand?

She would have to ask Elise. The chances of her remembering one guest from twenty years ago were remote at best. But perhaps if the circumstances were unusual enough, they might have stuck in her memory. Erin picked up the open register book in both hands and carried it out to the desk, where Elise was on duty.

'I found something,' she said. She laid the book on the desk and pointed to the entry. 'That looks like my mother's handwriting. The name is false, of course.'

Elise peered at it, then laughed. 'Of course – Anne Blythe. I wonder why I didn't pick up on that at the time – we must have been busy. That would have been shortly before we started requiring ID to check in. She must have paid in cash – I would have noticed a different name on a credit card.'

'But look here – the checkout time was put in by somebody else. Can you by any chance remember what might account for that?' Erin gazed at Elise as if exercising mind control to bring her memories to the surface.

Elise frowned in thought. 'Let me see . . . October fifth, 2001 . . . Just a few weeks after nine-eleven. Everyone was on edge then, suspicious of anyone who looked the least bit Middle Eastern, though we didn't get too many of those around here . . .'

She stood a minute with her eyes closed, then popped them open. 'I do remember something from around that time. A man showed up – I remember him because he was dark-haired and kind of exotic-looking, and I was annoyed with myself for being uneasy around him. He said the woman in room nine – his wife, he claimed – had been taken ill in the night and had called him rather than rousing the staff. He said he'd taken her straight to the hospital, and now he'd come back for her things. He must have entered the checkout time.'

A dark-haired, exotic-looking man. Certainly not Erin's father – he was as blond and fair as they come. Not Detective Carver; his hair – what little there was of it – had been sandy brown. And not Mr Cruikshank from the gallery; his hair was dark, but his complexion was pasty pale and his features fleshy – hardly exotic-looking.

'You let him take the things?'

'I collected them myself – that's why I remember which room it was – then asked him to describe her luggage before I handed it over. He described it exactly. More exactly than the average husband would be able to, now that I think about it. Most men aren't that observant.'

Erin pulled out her wallet. 'Could this have been the woman in room nine?' She handed Elise the small snapshot she'd carried with her since before her mother disappeared. Erin had caught Gina with her Polaroid, walking on the beach in a colorful sundress that showed off her lovely figure, sandals in hand. She was laughing, her long dark hair blowing in the breeze, her green eyes sparkling. The photo was the essence of Mumsie as Erin remembered her.

Elise perused the picture. 'I can't say with certainty that was her, but I do believe I've seen this woman before.' She handed it back to Erin. 'It's not a face one would easily forget, is it?' Her eyes softened. 'You must miss her very much.'

Erin swallowed, blinking back tears. 'Yes. I do.' She stowed the photo carefully, then said, 'This man who claimed to be her husband. It certainly wasn't my father or anyone I can think of that she knew. Can you remember anything more about him?'

Elise screwed up her eyes. 'Hmm . . . He was tall – maybe about six feet? Athletic-looking. I think he was wearing a dark suit. And he had some kind of slight accent, but I couldn't place it. Not Latino – I would have recognized that.' She looked back at Erin. 'He was quite suave and charming. He made me mistrust my instinct that there was something wrong. Of course, now I can see I should have trusted that instinct. I should have called the police – but I was afraid of sounding like an alarmist. You know, seeing a terrorist in every foreign face.' Her eyes filled with concern. 'I'm so sorry, my dear. I hope nothing terrible happened because I failed to act.'

Erin shook her head briskly, dashing away an escaped tear. 'It's not your fault. I'm pretty sure the terrible thing had already happened.'

Her worst fears were realized. Her dream had been real, and her mother was dead.

# THREE

Erin took a photo of the register page and returned the book to the shelf. At Elise's insistence – not because she was hungry – she went into the dining room, put some fruit and a spoonful of eggs on a plate, and refilled her coffee. As she ate without tasting the food, she made notes of everything Elise had told her – on her phone for now; she'd transfer them to a proper purpose-bought notebook when she got the chance.

Without consciously considering the matter, she'd already made the decision to resume her long-abandoned investigation into what had happened to her mother. The passage of time was against her, but she now had a starting point – or ending point, depending on how you looked at it – and the resources of an adult with a master's degree in, essentially, research. And she was convinced that fate was on her side. How else could she account for the seeming coincidence of being led to this place and finding what she had found? Perhaps Mumsie herself was directing her steps from beyond the grave. She could find no other explanation for that dream, or for the overpowering feeling of her mother's presence when she found the earring.

She finished eating and looked at her watch. Eight twenty-five. A good time for that walk on the beach she'd promised herself. A walk that would give her a chance to think and plan. She pulled on her sweater and set off.

She'd reserved a room for three nights, but now she wondered whether she should cut her respite short. She felt instinctively that there was no more to be learned from Seafarer's Rest itself, but perhaps the neighborhood might provide additional clues. With only a week of her leave yet to run, she couldn't afford to waste any time.

On the other hand, what could her next step be? Having a trail to follow implied that one could somehow discern the next step. But she was working backward. Even supposing her mother had left deliberate breadcrumbs for her to follow – the earring, for example, and the name in the register – she would surely have expected Erin to follow them in the order they were created, not in reverse.

Her thoughts carried her along the drive to the highway, where she paused to look for an easy way down to the beach. She Googled 'beach access near me' and saw that Asilomar State Beach was a mere half mile down the road to her left, so she turned her steps in that direction.

The sand on the beach was white and loose, interrupted by grasses, low shrubs, and driftwood of all shapes and sizes. Wooden walkways traversed the low dunes with benches interspersed along their length. Erin walked until she saw groups of people in the distance, then chose a bench and sat. She needed to be alone.

She stared out across the dunes to the rippling gray-blue water until the chill breeze brought tears to her eyes. Down the beach, where the people were, she could barely discern a woman with long dark hair in a bright-colored dress, tossing a beach ball back and forth with a child.

The tears flowed now, and the breeze could not be blamed for all of them. Beaches had been some of their favorite places. They'd explored every one in Santa Cruz County and a few beyond. The less-frequented beaches were the best. Erin and Mumsie would hunt for shells, explore the tidepools, marvel at the varied forms of life that teemed in the water and the sand. They built elaborate sandcastles defended by moats that would fill with water as the tide came in. When she was little, Erin had invented a bakery game in which she would create an assortment of cakes, pies, and pastries formed of sand and decorated with pebbles and tiny shells, which Mumsie would buy from her with larger shells. The beach was their special place – Father never came along. He flew to Hawaii so often he claimed to be 'all beached out.'

Her mother's absence was an ache that had lain at the core of Erin's heart all these years, covered with thick layers of scar tissue but never healed. Now that scar tissue ruptured, and it all came pouring out through her streaming eyes – the memories, the anguish of unknowing, the loneliness, the anger, the deep conviction that her mother's disappearance must somehow be

Erin's fault. As an adult, she knew that last was logically unlikely, but the pain of believing it could not be dispersed by logic. Only if she learned the truth of her mother's fate could she ever be set free from that crushing burden of guilt.

When she had sobbed till her chest ached and cried herself dry, Erin heaved her body up off the bench and turned back toward Seafarer's Rest. She was no closer to knowing the next step on her quest, but she did know she would need help. At least from the police, useless though they'd been all those years ago. They had resources that she as a civilian would not be able to access; they could open doors that might be closed to her. The challenge would be to make them take her seriously – a grieving daughter demanding they reopen the twenty-year-old investigation into her mother's disappearance on the strength of little more than a dream.

But today was Sunday. Hardly the most auspicious day to put her case – the detectives would likely be at home, mowing their lawns, playing with their children, doing all the normal-people things that had seemed unreal and unattainable to Erin ever since she lost her mother. She and Father had certainly never been a normal family. He'd retired from flying and taken a desk job once Mumsie was gone, ostensibly to care for Erin, but in practice it was she who cared for him – cooking, cleaning, washing and ironing and starching his crisp white shirts. Listening to him wallow in self-pity when he drank the occasional full bottle of vodka; settling him on his side when he passed out on the couch so he wouldn't choke on his own vomit; preparing a hangover pick-me-up for him when he awoke. As a teen, she learned to drive so she could run all the errands. She even paid the family bills online. Through all this, she managed to keep up with her studies, including a local college and grad school, but she never had time for real friendships, let alone dating. But that was a blessing in disguise. She could never allow herself to get close to anyone lest they be snatched away as suddenly as her mother had been.

Erin looked around and realized that in her musings, she'd wandered onto a walkway that led inland instead of back to the road she'd come in on. Suddenly she was among substantial buildings of redwood and stone spaced about the hillside along winding lanes.

She knew this place. This was the Asilomar Conference Center. She and her mother had come here once for some sort of artists' retreat. That is, her mother had attended the retreat and Erin had tagged along. Mumsie had loved the place, both for its beautiful setting and for the architecture. The original buildings had been designed in the First Bay Tradition style by Julia Morgan, California's first female architect and one of Mumsie's heroes.

Erin felt a pricking in her thumbs that she interpreted to mean not 'something wicked this way comes,' but 'here I'll find a clue.' She spotted a sign with a map of the grounds and made her way to the Hearst Social Hall, where the reception desk was located.

She would need a strategy. A big place like Asilomar, run by the California State Park system, would hardly be as amenable to the entreaties of a grieving daughter as independent inn owner Elise had been. They'd be unlikely to let her look at their old registers, assuming they had them. They might be willing to look up a particular name for her, but she didn't know what name to give them.

What would her mother have chosen as an alias specific to this place? Something to do with Julia Morgan, no doubt. But that unaltered name would surely have raised red flags with the staff. Erin entered the empty social hall at the far end from the reception desk and strolled around the room, looking for inspiration. On one wall hung a portrait of Phoebe Apperson Hearst, mother of William Randolph Hearst and original patroness of this center when it belonged to the YMCA. Julia Hearst or Phoebe Morgan, perhaps? It was worth a try.

She approached the desk, behind which a shaggy young man lolled in a tipped-back chair with his Converse-clad feet up on a shelf, looking at his phone. When he caught sight of Erin, he guiltily ripped the earbuds from his ears and stood. 'Welcome to Asilomar. How can I help?' he said with a winning smile.

Erin put on her friendliest smile in return. It was too much to hope that she, in her current harried and windblown condition, would be able to charm this young man, who must be ten years her junior. But it couldn't hurt to try.

She glanced at his name tag. 'Good morning, Jason. I'm Erin Washington. I'm doing some historical research, and I wonder if you can help me. Is it possible to search your records for someone who may have stayed here about twenty years ago?'

Jason's eyebrows rose into his floppy blond bangs. 'Twenty years? Whoa, that's a long time. Almost my whole life. I don't know if the computer system goes back that far.'

Immediately Erin felt like a relic of the Paleolithic age. 'Of course I have no idea when this center started using computers, but don't you think they might have digitized their records up to that time?'

'Fair point.' He tapped around on the keyboard for a minute. 'Well, whaddaya know. Here it is – guest register for 2001. Can you narrow down the date at all?'

'Probably late September or early October.'

'Got it.' He tapped some more. 'And the name?'

'I'm checking on a couple of people.' Erin was willing to bet that Jason was a college student who'd taken on this summer job with little knowledge of the history of his place of employment. Chances were he'd never even read the name under Phoebe Hearst's portrait. But since this was the Hearst Social Hall, her mother would probably have chosen something less obvious. 'Try Phoebe Morgan. Or—' An inspiration hit her. Mumsie would have been amused. 'Maybe J.P. Morgan.' Which was both a combination of the initials for Julia and Phoebe, and the name of one of the great Gilded Age industrialists.

'Morgan, Oliver . . . Morgan, Rebecca . . . Yup, here it is. J.P. Morgan. Checked in September thirtieth, left October fifth.' He looked up at Erin, who beamed her gratitude. 'Want me to print it out for you?'

'Oh, yes, please. That would be wonderful.' Maybe she had a little charm left after all. She hoped Jason wouldn't get in trouble for this undoubted lapse of protocol.

The printer hummed, then he handed her a sheet of paper. *J.P. Morgan, Sept. 30–Oct. 5. Visitor's Lodge #23.* What a bonus – room number and all. Fate and/or her mother must truly be on her side.

'Thank you so much,' she gushed. 'I can't tell you how helpful this is.'

'Happy to be of service,' he said with a grin. He swallowed and looked as if he might be working himself up to ask for her phone number, so with a parting smile she scurried out.

On the way she passed a rack of brochures and picked up a folded map of the grounds and a brochure titled *Julia Morgan's Asilomar*. The latter might not prove useful, but it would at least be interesting to read.

The smell of coffee greeted her nostrils as she passed through the door onto the stepped terrace that looked toward the sea. Suddenly her hastily wolfed breakfast seemed eons ago. To her left she saw people entering a door marked *Phoebe's Café*. She followed them and, when her turn came, ordered a large white-chocolate mocha and a croissant, which she took back out to the terrace. As she consumed them, grateful for the warmth as much as the nourishment, she perused the map and brochure.

The Visitor's Lodge was one of the original Morgan buildings, apparently, and it was not far away if one followed the network of well-kept footpaths that meandered among the trees and connected all the structures. As soon as she'd finished her second breakfast, Erin set off.

Like all its sister Morgan designs, the lodge had a solid but graceful façade of natural stone topped by redwood shingles and punctuated by large multi-paned windows. Inside, a split staircase, also of redwood, led to the second floor. Erin took the left-hand flight, since left seemed to be the theme of the weekend. There before her at the top of the stairs was a door marked twenty-three.

How to proceed? She could hardly barge in on some guest. Even if the room happened to be empty, it would surely be locked. And darn it, she'd left her Young Detective's Kit with its handy lock-picks and magnifying glass at home.

But she could feel her mother urging her on. She approached the door, raised her hand, paused a moment, then knocked. The door moved under her hand – it was slightly ajar, so the lock had not engaged.

But that didn't tell her whether the room was occupied. Mid-morning, anyone who was here for a conference would undoubtedly be attending some class or lecture. Maybe they were running late and accidentally neglected to pull the door fully shut behind them.

With a trembling hand she eased open the door, so that if anyone were inside, they would have plenty of time to cry out so she could flee. But no one did. In a moment, she was inside an unoccupied room with no suitcase or personal items in sight. Fate or her mother's spirit had come through for her again.

With a sigh of relief, she closed the door behind her and took in her surroundings. The room was spacious and luxurious in a rustic way. The walls and ceiling were clad in redwood board-and-batten paneling. One large window looked out toward the sea, while a glass door on the intersecting wall led to a private balcony. Opposite that was a stone fireplace set between built-in cupboards.

Mumsie would have felt at home here. Erin could envision her playing the part of a visitor from 1916 or so, when the lodge was new – hair coiled atop her head, wearing a practical tweed suit with a high-waisted jacket and a narrow skirt that fell to the tops of her buttoned ankle boots, with a tucked and frilled white blouse peeking out between her lapels. Falling into the spell of that vision, Erin moved about the room as if staying there. She sat and bounced on the four-poster bed, examined the bathroom, looked into the cupboards, sat at the Mission-style desk under the window and opened the drawers.

Except for the top shallow one, which held brochures and a laminated card with helpful information, the drawers were empty. But the voice in her head whispered, *You're warm – look deeper.* She pulled each drawer fully out and examined their backs and undersides. The lower left-hand drawer caught slightly on the way out. She turned it over.

There, flattened against the underside of the drawer and held by one corner in the join between the sides and bottom, was a postcard. Wishing for tweezers, Erin teased it out as delicately as if it were a priceless parchment. She laid it on the surface of the desk and returned the drawer to its place.

The address-and-message side of the postcard was blank and yellow with age. But the picture side was still vivid. It showed one of the quaint little storybook cottages for which the town of Carmel-by-the-Sea was famous.

During that last summer – what little there had been of it before her mother was gone – the two of them had taken a self-guided walking tour to see as many of the Carmel cottages as they could find. Each of them had chosen a favorite, and the one on this postcard was Mumsie's. The sign on the mailbox said *Bucklebury Cottage*.

Coincidence? Hardly. Her thumbs were throbbing now. This was a breadcrumb that her mother had deliberately planted for Erin to find. It would mean nothing to anyone else – just a stray souvenir some guest had accidentally left behind. But to Erin, its message was as clear as if it had been written on the reverse of the postcard: *I was here, and before that I was in Carmel. Come and find me. Love, Mumsie.*

Erin checked her watch for the first time since she'd left the inn after breakfast. Eleven fifteen. She'd missed checkout time. But no matter. Carmel was only a short drive down the coast. She could explore there with the inn as her base. Some research was in order first.

She followed the footpaths back to the beach and then up along the shore to the inn. The walk was long, but she traversed it with a heart full of hope now rather than grief. She was on the trail; she had a mission. A mission that would lay her mother's ghost and prevent any recurrence of that horrifying dream.

By the time she reached the inn, guests were filing into the dining room for lunch. Erin dashed upstairs to change her sandy footwear and joined them. As she ate at a solitary table, she used her phone to look for any likely place her mother might have stayed in Carmel.

She found several storybook cottages that were run as B&Bs, but there was no telling whether that had been the case twenty years ago, well before the advent of Airbnb. A few of the town's many inns and hotels were built in a similar style and would be worth exploring. But as she considered her plan of attack, her broken night's sleep and morning of intense activity followed by a satisfying lunch caught up with her. Her eyes would insist on drifting shut. It seemed a nap was the most she would be capable of this afternoon.

When she awoke to the lowering sun streaming through her west-facing windows, it was past three o'clock – too late to begin an expedition to Carmel. But at least she could prepare for it. Erin drove to Lighthouse Avenue, the small, tourist-oriented business district of Pacific Grove, and found a stationery store that carried an assortment of blank books and notebooks.

This investigation called for something more than a standard spiral-bound notebook or composition book. After browsing for some time, she finally came upon the perfect thing – purse-sized, spiral-bound for ease of writing, with a hard cover on which was printed one of Mary Cassatt's paintings of a mother and child. She chose a new pen in a coordinating color as well. Everything must be auspicious for her quest.

Back at the inn, Erin transferred the memories she'd recorded in her journal the night before into her new notebook. Then she wrote a full account of everything she had done, thought, and discovered, beginning with the dream and ending with a list of promising locations in Carmel to explore the next morning. After dinner at her solitary table, she treated herself to a long hot soak in the capacious bathtub, then went to bed with a feeling of accomplishment and hope. Her sleep was dreamless and long.

# FOUR

On Monday morning, Erin was the first in line for breakfast. Immediately afterward she set off for Carmel.

Her instinct told her to go first to the cottage on the postcard. As far as she'd been able to find online, Bucklebury Cottage was now a private residence, whatever it might have been in 2001. It was not yet eight o'clock – rather early to be bothering strangers in their home. She'd try one of the inns first.

The nearest was the Cozy Cotswold Cottages off Ocean Avenue. She cringed at the somewhat contrived alliteration, but at least they hadn't changed all the Cs to Ks. According to their website, this place had been in business for almost ninety years, making it one of the oldest inns in Carmel.

As its name suggested, the inn consisted of a number of tiny cottages connected by flagstone paths lined with flowers. A small central courtyard boasted a fountain made of cascading shells. The cottages were not truly in the Cotswold style – square-built of the yellow limestone native to that region of Britain. Instead, they sported a modified version of the steep gables, curving rooflines, and fake half-timbering typical of Carmel's fairytale cottages designed by Hugh Comstock in the 1920s.

The cottage facing the street had the glass-paned door and display windows of an office, as well as a discreet sign, so she climbed the steep steps and went in.

A gray-haired man, possibly in his sixties, was filling some Thermoses with coffee at a table to the left of the reception desk. He turned as the bell dinged above the door. 'Good morning,' he said in a cheerful voice. 'Like some coffee? It's fresh.'

'I'd love a cup, but I'm not a guest,' Erin responded. 'I'm doing some research, and I'd like to ask you a few questions, if I may.' She'd decided the research angle was at once more official-sounding and less intimidating than a flat *I want to question you.*

The man's eyebrows rose, but he finished filling the Thermos, poured the last of the coffee into a ceramic mug, and handed it to her. ‘Cream and sugar?’ He gestured to a cow-shaped china cream pitcher and a bowl of sugar cubes. Nothing disposable here, Erin was happy to note. She wasn’t an eco-warrior; she just liked things authentic.

‘Thank you.’ She added a dash of cream and used a tiny silver spoon to stir it in.

The man moved behind the desk. ‘Now, what can I do for you? I’m Ernest, by the way. I own this place with my wife. Or more like it owns us.’ He gave a self-deprecating grimace.

‘Erin Washington. Pleased to meet you.’ She shook his hand, then sipped her coffee before pulling out her notebook. ‘I’m trying to trace the movements of a woman who may have stayed here in the summer of 2001.’

Ernest’s eyebrows rose higher this time. ‘Twenty years ago? That’s a long time.’

‘Yes, I know. But do you have records going back that far?’

‘We do, but . . . Well, that long ago, I guess it can’t hurt.’ He bent down for a minute, then rose with a register volume in his hand. ‘We didn’t have computers yet then.’ He laid the volume on the counter and opened it facing himself. ‘What name are you looking for?’

Erin hesitated. ‘That’s a bit of a problem. I think she was probably using a false name, but I don’t know what it was. Most likely something only I would recognize.’

Ernest cocked his head at her. ‘You have some connection to this woman?’

‘She was my mother.’

His brow crinkled. ‘Oh. I see.’ He frowned at the book for a minute, then said, ‘Can you be a little more specific than “summer”?’

If her mother had been leaving deliberate breadcrumbs, presumably she would have left them in order, meaning she would have stayed in Carmel immediately before moving on to Asilomar. ‘Probably the last week of September.’

He turned a block of pages, then flipped one at a time. ‘Here we are.’ He turned the book around and pushed it across to her. ‘September nineteenth to thirtieth.’

Erin flashed him her best smile. ‘Thank you so much.’

She skimmed the names from the end to the beginning, looking for her mother's handwriting, but no joy. So she went more slowly the other direction, reading each name. Just a bunch of perfectly ordinary names, along with some foreign or unusual ones, but none with any special significance that she could see.

'Do you mind if I go back one more page?'

Ernest hesitated, then shrugged. 'Go ahead.'

But the result was the same. Nothing.

Her heart sank into her toes. It was ridiculous for her to have hoped for success at the first place she came to, but there was such a warm atmosphere here, she had in fact expected this to be the refuge her mother would have chosen.

Still, she had to be thorough. She pulled out the photo she'd shown to Elise at the inn. 'Do you recognize this woman at all?'

Ernest took the photo and contemplated it for a minute. 'I'm afraid not. That's a face I wouldn't be likely to forget.' He handed it back with a commiserating smile.

Erin tucked the photo into the inside pocket of her notebook, where it would be handier than in her wallet. She made the note, 'Cozy Cotswold Cottages – nix,' then closed the notebook. 'Thanks so much for your help.' She raised the mug as if in a toast. 'And for the coffee. It was delicious.'

Ernest took the half-full cup. 'You're welcome. I hope you have better luck at your next stop.'

Back at her car, Erin paused to consult her list. The logical next stop was the Surf & Seagull, all the way down Ocean Avenue near the beach. It was only a few blocks, but since the hill was steep and she wouldn't need to come back this direction, she took the car.

The Surf & Seagull proved to be an inn built in the style of an English country pub, complete with faux-thatched roof and a wooden sign that depicted a goofy-looking seagull standing improbably on the crest of a wave. A broad plank gate led into a courtyard parking lot. Erin pulled in as close to the front entrance as possible and went in.

The door led into a deserted bar-cum-dining room. 'Sorry, we're not open yet,' a female voice called out from some recess.

'I didn't come to eat,' Erin replied, matching the voice's volume. 'I was hoping to talk to the manager.'

From behind a swinging door a young girl emerged, wiping her hands on her apron. 'I'm afraid the manager's not here right now,' she said. 'My mom's out getting supplies. Can I help you at all?'

'I hope so. I'm doing some research, and I wanted to ask about someone who may have stayed here in September of 2001.'

'Whoa. That's a long time ago.' The girl – who looked about seventeen – bit her bottom lip. 'We weren't even here then. My mom bought the place in 2010.'

Erin's heart sank. 'I see. I don't suppose you have any records from the previous owner?'

The girl made a doubtful face. 'Not that I know of. You'd have to ask my mom to be sure.'

Erin checked her watch. Eight thirty. 'Any idea when she'll be back?'

'An hour, maybe?' The girl shrugged. 'She goes all the way to Salinas for the produce.'

Erin huffed and ran a hand over her hair. She looked around at the artificially aged wood of the tables and chairs, the prints of fox-hunting scenes on the walls. This place smelled like a dead end.

'Maybe I'll come by later. Thanks.' She headed for the door.

'Come for lunch,' the girl called after her. 'We do a killer shepherd's pie.'

Erin waved without turning and continued out the door. Shepherd's pie would sit in her agitated stomach like a rock. She might be able to manage a salad, at most, when lunchtime came, but she couldn't even think about food now.

She'd arbitrarily decided on nine o'clock as the earliest decent hour to knock on the door of Bucklebury Cottage. Almost half an hour to go. She had one lodging place left on her list, which she'd limited to establishments that had some obvious Old World ambiance. Of course the town sported dozens of other hotels, inns, B&Bs, and rental cottages; it was a tourist mecca. But the postcard she'd found strongly suggested she would not have to look that far.

The remaining inn was the Tor House Lodge, on Scenic Road – the coast road – a few doors away from Tor House itself. She and her mother had once visited Tor House, the charming, eccentric owner-built former home of the poet Robinson Jeffers and his wife, Una. Erin had been enthralled with the hand-laid stone walls, the tiny, low-ceilinged rooms, and especially Hawk Tower with the child-sized secret staircase Jeffers had included for his sons. The winding stone staircase led all the way to the battlemented roof of the tower, which offered a panoramic view of the ocean and the coastline. Erin could have stayed there forever.

The lodge resembled Tor House only in being built partially of the same local stone, though Erin doubted its builders had hauled the stones one by one from the beach as Jeffers had done. This was a square two-story building that advertised a dozen guest rooms, a dining room serving three meals a day, and a 'salon' that claimed to host cultural and intellectual gatherings in the spirit of those the poet's wife, Una, had delighted in.

Erin entered the lobby, where archways to the left and right led to the dining room and salon, respectively. The reception desk was unmanned, but a dome-shaped bell sat next to a small sign that read *Please ring for service*. Erin tapped the bell.

'Coming!' a musical tenor-pitched voice rang out from the direction of the dining room. 'Be with you in a minute!'

The voice was followed in short order by the figure of a slender man of medium height and indeterminate age dressed in a dark olive suit with a paisley shirt and a bright orange knitted tie. He scurried up to the desk, adjusted his already straight tie, and ran a hand over his perfectly smooth, glossy black hair before turning to Erin with a bright smile. 'Welcome to Tor House Lodge. How may I be of service?'

Erin introduced herself and gave him her now-standard line about research. 'Do you have guest records going back to 2001?'

The man – his name tag read *François*, but Erin suspected his birth certificate read simply *Frank* – made a worried moue. 'Oh, dear, I don't know about that. I mean, I think we do, but I couldn't possibly share them. Not without some official authority.'

'Is there anyone you could ask? Or are you the owner?'

He stood a little taller and primmed his mouth. 'My partner and I are the managers. We have complete discretion in these matters – the owner prefers not to be involved in the day-to-day running of the lodge.'

'I see.' Erin considered her options. So far she'd relied on sympathy and charm to gain cooperation, but François didn't seem terribly sympathetic and would almost certainly be impervious to her charm. 'I completely understand the need for discretion. Naturally I wouldn't dream of putting you in a difficult position. Perhaps you could consult with your partner and get back to me?'

She saw his nostrils flare and his chest expand. Oh dear. Apparently that wasn't the right approach.

'My partner and I are two minds with but a single thought. I'm sorry, but unless you have some sort of warrant, I'm afraid I won't be able to help you.'

Erin knew when she was beaten. If François's attitude was representative of the spirit of the place, she doubted her mother would have been comfortable here. But then, he might not have been working here twenty years ago. Perhaps the staff had been more sympathetic back then. If none of her other options panned out, maybe she could try again and hope that François's partner's thoughts were less identical to his than he believed.

She gave him a perfunctory smile. 'Thank you for your time.'

Outside, she checked the time again. Eight forty-five. Close enough. *Bucklebury Cottage, here I come.*

The cottage stood on a corner lot, surrounded by a beautiful garden in the profuse English style. It had been the garden as much as the house that had enchanted Mumsie all those years ago, Erin remembered now. 'I could do something like this at home, surely,' Gina had said as they inched their way along the borders of the property, lingering as long as they dared without being intrusive. 'The climate must be virtually identical.' She'd pointed at a clump of tall purple flowers, saying, 'There, Erin, take a picture of those. I'm not sure what they're called, but the people at the nursery will know.'

That had been only a couple of weeks before she disappeared. They'd gone plant shopping together, but the garden had never had a chance to grow.

Erin stood at the low white gate with its hand-lettered sign, remembering. This garden had changed somewhat – the tall purple flowers no longer grew under the front window – but it still reflected the same style. She was gathering her courage to approach the door when it opened and a slender, slightly stooped, white-haired woman appeared, watering can in hand.

Erin started and lost her nerve. She was about to turn away when the woman said, 'May I help you, dear? Did you want to look at the garden?'

Flummoxed by such friendliness from someone who must be overrun with tourists come to gawp at her unusual home, Erin flapped her lips like a beached fish. 'I – well, yes, I would, if you don't mind.'

'Come on in,' the woman said with a welcoming gesture. 'Don't be shy.' When Erin came close, she whispered, 'I don't let just anyone come in and trample on my flowers. I can tell you're the right sort.'

How on earth she could tell that, Erin had no idea, but she was grateful she'd made the grade. Emboldened by the woman's welcome, she introduced herself.

'Maggie McGregor,' the woman replied, shifting her watering can to her left hand and removing her gloves to shake Erin's hand.

'I've been here before,' Erin said. 'My mother and I stopped to admire this garden once about twenty years ago. Did you live here then?'

'Oh, my, yes. I've lived here forever.' Maggie beamed. 'Well, not quite forever, but since I was married, nigh on sixty years ago. My Henry's gone now, but I'm still here – rooted deep as that cherry tree. I've said more than once the only way I'll leave this cottage is feet first.'

'You don't take in guests, by any chance? Paying guests, I mean?'

Maggie laughed. 'Oh, no, dear. Never have. Not that the money wouldn't come in handy, but it's all I can do to look after myself these days. And I'm afraid I'm too much of a packrat to clear out a room to rent.'

Erin's stomach sank, but she retrieved the photo from her notebook and showed it to Maggie. 'This is my mother,' she said. 'Do you by any chance remember seeing her?'

Maggie stowed her gloves in one apron pocket, then pulled a pair of reading glasses out of another. She perched the glasses carefully on her nose, took the photo and studied it, then sorrowfully shook her head.

'I'm afraid not. She looks lovely, though.' She handed the photo back to Erin. 'You must miss her very much.'

Erin swallowed as her throat swelled. ‘Yes. I do.’

Maggie patted her hand. ‘I hope you find her, dear. Or find out what happened to her. That is what you’re trying to do, isn’t it?’

This woman’s insight was uncanny. Maybe living in a fairytale cottage for as long as she had done turned you into a fairytale character – not a witch, in Maggie’s case, but one of those wise old women whose kitchens are hung with braided ropes of herbs and who know everything worth knowing about everyone who crosses their path.

Erin nodded. ‘She disappeared not long after we came here. I found a postcard of this cottage and thought maybe she’d come back.’

Maggie shook her head with a sad smile. ‘I’m sorry, dear. But don’t give up. I’ll pray for your search to be successful.’ She crossed herself just as Mumsie used to do.

‘Thank you,’ Erin managed to utter before the tears overtook her. Then she turned and fled back to her car.

# FIVE

After that string of disappointments, Erin needed to regroup. She also needed refreshment, so she drove back downtown to the famous Tuck Box, the Comstock-designed tearoom complete with thatched roof and half-timbering. She ordered tea and scones and pulled out her notebook and pen.

The score for the morning so far was Carmel 4, Erin 0. She could proceed through every lodging place in the town that had been in business twenty years ago, but would the results be any better? She might spend days and achieve exactly nothing. Clearly she needed a different plan of attack than simply approaching people and asking for privileged information.

Fake François had mentioned a warrant. Perhaps it was time to involve the police. But which police? Would the Carmel police be willing to commit resources to follow the trail of a woman from another county who might possibly have stayed in their town, perhaps for only one night, twenty years ago? Erin couldn't imagine herself asking – she'd be dismissed as a crank.

What about Pacific Grove? That was where she believed her mother to have died. But with no clearer evidence than an earring, a couple of ambiguous register entries, a postcard, and a dream, they could easily dismiss the idea that a murder had ever occurred. She'd need a body or at least a fresh crime scene to get their attention.

A moment of doubt assailed her. In her fragile emotional state, had she allowed her grief to persuade her that a set of random circumstances held deadly significance? Was she in fact attempting to weave a solid case out of threads of gossamer that would dissolve at the slightest breath?

She took the photo of her mother and the postcard of Bucklebury Cottage out of the notebook pocket and laid them on the table above her plate, found the earring in the zippered pocket of her purse and set it alongside them, and pulled up the photo she'd taken of the signature *Anne S. Blythe*. The waves of meaning that emanated from these objects were just as strong as they had been at first. She could almost hear Mumsie's voice: *Don't give up, Erin. I'm waiting for you. Find me.*

There was only one possible response to that voice: *I'm coming, Mumsie. Show me where to look.*

She stowed the items back in their places and returned to considering her options. If she ruled out the police of Carmel and Pacific Grove, that left Santa Cruz, from where her mother had originally gone missing. What were the chances that Carver was still working as a detective there? As a child, Erin had been ill-equipped to judge adults' ages; he could have been anywhere between thirty and fifty when they last met. And if he was working now, would he welcome a chance to reopen a failed investigation? Would he be haunted by it, or would he have buried the memory deep, determined never to dig it up again? Would the evidence she'd found, such as it was, be enough for even him to take her seriously?

Only one way to find out. She scooped up the last crumbs of her scone and washed them down with the dregs of her tea, paid her bill, and headed back to Seafarer's Rest.

She reached the inn with barely enough time to throw her things in her bags before the eleven o'clock checkout time. When she handed in her key, Elise, the owner, said, 'Oh, you're leaving early? I'm so sorry. I'm afraid I will have to charge you for the three nights you reserved.'

'I understand.' Erin handed over her credit card. 'No problem.'

Elise ran the card and gave it back to her. 'I hope you managed to get some enjoyment out of your stay.'

'Oh, I did. But I got something much more important than that – I got my first lead toward finding out what happened to my mother. I've done all I can in this area now. I have to go back to Santa Cruz to pick up the trail.' Impulsively, she reached across the counter and touched Elise's hand. 'Believe me, that's the only reason I'm leaving. I love this inn. And I'm sure my mother loved it too.'

Elise blinked and swiped a hand across her cheek. 'Would you mind telling me your mother's real name? Just in case I remember anything else. And I already have your contact info.'

'Gina Washington.' Erin hadn't spoken that full name in years. It felt like an incantation. If only it would act to resurrect her mother – or at least to reveal her fate.

'Gina Washington.' Elise wrote the name on a notepad and tore off the sheet. 'Thank you. I wish you all the best in your search.'

Erin thanked her and made her escape before she dissolved in tears. Sympathy from a stranger only served to highlight the depth of her loss.

The midday traffic on Highway 1 was light, and Erin made it to the River Street intersection in less than an hour. She hesitated as to whether to continue straight toward home or turn left toward the police station downtown, but her stomach reminded her it was lunchtime – most likely for the detectives as well. So she stayed on Highway 1 as it merged into Mission Street, then turned left at Bay to make her way to her childhood home.

The house was in the area known as the Circles, just a few blocks from West Cliff Avenue, where a path popular with walkers and cyclists ran along the edge of the cliffs above the beach. Erin unlocked the door of the bungalow and stepped inside, only to have her legs accosted by her silver point Siamese, Miss Silver, and her nostrils assaulted with a mixture of odors reminiscent of a hospital – disinfectant with a barely perceptible undercurrent of human waste, overused cat litter, ocean-breeze-scented air freshener, rotting food, and death. She'd been so frazzled after her father's funeral, so anxious to escape this house that had been like a prison to her throughout his illness, that she hadn't taken the time to clean the room in which he had spent his final months. A wave of nausea washed over her. How had she lived with those smells for so long?

She set her bags down just inside the door and picked up the insistent Miss Silver for a cuddle. 'Didn't Alex clean out your litter box when he came to feed you? I'll have to have a word with that boy.'

She made the circuit of the house, opening every window as wide as it would go and turning on all the fans. When she got to the room at the back of the ground floor that had served as her father's bedroom during his illness, Miss Silver jumped out of her arms and ran for the living room. Her father had never allowed the cat in here, and their antipathy was mutual. Erin had to pull her shirt up over her face until she'd managed to pry open the windows, which her father had insisted on keeping tight shut. She took in a deep breath of outside air, then turned to scan the room.

Most of the odors emanated from here. The rumpled sheets on the hospital-style bed reminded her she'd never washed them after Father had been taken to hospice. She'd spent every free moment there with him for the week that elapsed before he died. And then she'd been so busy arranging the funeral, notifying all his friends and family, answering letters of condolence, and settling his affairs that she'd never thought to clean up this room.

Holding her breath, she yanked the sheets off the bed and hurried to dump them in the washing machine. She'd need to give the whole room a thorough going-over, but that would have to wait. She could not be diverted from her mission.

With the sheets in the washer, the bedroom door closed, and the litter box emptied, the smell abated enough that she thought she might be able to stomach some lunch. If, that is, she'd left herself any food in the house. But the smell from the kitchen garbage was almost as bad as those in the bedroom.

Miss Silver stood by her food bowl, yowling imperiously. Erin spooned a can of food into her bowl and filled her water before turning her attention to her own needs. The fridge yielded a smattering of condiments, some highly questionable takeout left-overs, a brick of moldy cheese, and half a bottle of white wine. She was tempted to scrape the mold off the cheese and wash the remainder down with the wine, but if she walked into the police station with alcohol on her breath and told her fanciful-sounding story, she'd be thrown out on her ear.

She swept the entire contents of the fridge into the garbage and hauled the bag out to the can, amending her mental to-do list to read: *Fast food, police station, grocery store, clean house, unpack*. In that order. And after that – well, that would depend on how things went with the police.

# SIX

After a quick lunch at the taqueria on Mission Street, Erin pulled into the small parking lot next to the police station on Center Street downtown. As she approached the stairs to the entrance, her steps slowed. The modern Spanish-style building was far from forbidding in itself – the façade might almost have belonged to an elegant hotel – but the memories it awoke in her were those of a frightened young girl whose world had just caved in on itself. She had to force herself to move forward into the lobby.

At the desk, she asked for Detective Carver, half expecting to hear that he had retired. But the officer took her name and picked up the phone. 'Detective Sergeant Carver?' she said, with a slight emphasis on 'sergeant' for Erin's benefit. 'There's an Erin Washington here to see you, sir.' She listened a moment, then said to Erin, 'Have a seat. He'll be right down.'

Erin sat on one of the hard plastic chairs that lined one wall. She took deep breaths to calm her racing heart, exhorting herself to remember that she was an adult now; all the drama surrounding her mother's immediate disappearance was far in the past. Her father with his antagonistic bluster was gone, and she could set the tone of the coming interview as one of sweet reasonableness. At least, as reasonable as a request to reopen a cold case on the strength of a dream could possibly be.

Carver did not keep her waiting long. A door opened and there he stood, looking shorter than she remembered him, his sparse hair considerably grayer and his face more lined, with a paunch hanging over his belt; but he was still recognizable. The sad smile with which he'd always addressed her spread over his face. 'Erin Washington. It's been a long time.'

She stood as he came toward her with his hand outstretched. 'I would have known you anywhere,' he said. 'You look so much like your mother.'

Erin blinked. That wasn't something she'd heard since she was a child. Her mother's family were all in England; she hadn't seen them since she and Mumsie had visited there when Erin was ten. Mumsie's friends had not kept in touch after the investigation petered out. She supposed it was difficult for them to know how to talk to her – impossible to ignore the tragedy that had destroyed her life, impossible to discuss it. And Father had never commented on Erin's appearance one way or another. To him, she was a sounding board, a housekeeper, an errand-runner, eventually a nurse. She doubted he had truly looked at her in the last twenty years.

She pulled herself together. 'Thank you for seeing me,' she said, shaking Carvers' hand. 'I wasn't sure you'd remember me.'

His smile faded, and a haunted look came into his eyes. 'Your mother's case is not one I could ever forget.' He blinked and cleared his throat. 'What brings you here today?'

She glanced around the lobby. The room was empty but for the officer at the desk, yet the large echoing space seemed unsuited to nuanced communication. 'Can we go somewhere else? It's . . . a little complicated.'

'Sure thing. Come on up to my office.' He held the door for her and led her upstairs.

His office was barely big enough to hold a desk and one visitor chair. A glass wall faced into the bullpen, where half a dozen officers, both uniformed and not, talked on phones, scribbled on whiteboards, or coaxed papers out of copying machines.

Carver motioned her to the chair and closed the door behind them, reducing the noise level but not blocking it out. 'Now. What can I do for you?'

Erin perched on the edge of the chair, her back ramrod-straight, and took a deep breath. 'I've come to ask you to reopen my mother's case.'

His eyes went wide for a moment. Then he tilted his chair back and ran both hands over his scalp. He blew out a noisy breath.

'Reopen the case? You do know how to stop an old man's heart.' He sat forward again, elbows on the desk, hands clasped. 'Based on what? You found some new evidence after all this time? 'Cause I have to tell you, we'll need some compelling reason. Cold cases are never a priority, understaffed and underfunded as we are.'

Erin swallowed and took out her notebook. 'I don't know whether you'll call it evidence, but I found some things that seem quite significant to me.'

Before she could launch into her account, a knock sounded on the office door. The door opened a crack and a woman's head appeared. 'Boss, you got a minute?' Then she noticed Erin. 'Oh, sorry, I didn't realize you had company.'

Carver waved her in. 'Since you're here, Cat, you may as well listen in. Grab a chair and join us.'

The woman, who seemed about Erin's own age, grabbed a plastic chair from a row against the wall of the bullpen and pulled it inside, barely managing to wedge it in alongside Erin's. Her ponytailed dreadlocks swung as she turned to sit down. She faced Erin with a professional smile.

Carver spoke before his colleague could introduce herself. 'Erin Washington, meet my junior partner, Detective Cat Herrera.' The two women shook hands. 'Cat's only been out of uniform a year, but she's as sharp as they come. Cat, Erin is the daughter of Gina Washington, the most puzzling missing person case of my career. Went missing twenty years ago and we never found a clue. Now Erin's come to ask us to reopen the case.'

Cat's brown eyes lit up. 'A cold case? Fascinating! We'll do it, won't we, boss? I've never had a cold case before.'

He held up a restraining palm. 'Hold on there, Cat. Let's hear what Erin has to say. I have to tell you, I'm going to take some convincing that this is worth investing the department's time.'

Cat rolled her eyes but sat alert, ready to take in Erin's argument. Erin shot her a tiny smile. She seemed like a possible ally against the entrenched institutional incredulity of the department.

Erin took a breath and plunged in. 'I was staying at a B and B in Pacific Grove over the weekend. Seafarer's Rest. My father just died and I needed a break.' Carver made a sympathetic face, but Erin hurried on before he could voice his condolences. 'While I was there, I took a walk in the grounds and found this stuck in a tree.' She dug the emerald out of her purse and laid it on the desk. 'It's a piece of an earring that belonged to my mother.'

Carver raised one eyebrow at her and picked up the emerald to examine it. 'How can you be sure? It doesn't even have the whaddayacallit, the part that attaches to the ear.'

'These earrings were unique.' Erin pointed to the gold setting that rimmed the stone. 'See that fluted pattern? They were handmade by a local artisan. The fluting is her signature. She never made the exact same design twice.'

Cat held her hand out for the emerald. 'May I?' She turned the stone over and peered at the back of the setting. 'I think there's something engraved here. Got a magnifying glass, boss?'

Carver opened a drawer and handed her a jeweler's loupe.

'Yep, here it is. Just initials – L.R.' She shot a questioning glance at Erin.

'Luna Rose,' Erin said hastily. 'The artist. She always signed her pieces.'

'We should be able to verify that,' Cat said, returning both earring and magnifier to Carver. 'Assuming she's still around, that is. She might have a record of selling these to your mother. Or remember her.'

Carver broke in. 'That's all very well, but it doesn't prove anything. Even if the earring was Gina's, all it shows is that she was probably in that place at some time. Nothing to say when or under what circumstances. Could have been before she went missing.'

'True, but I have more.' Erin took out her phone and found the photo of the register page. 'See here?' She held it out to Carver. 'This is a page out of the guest register for Seafarer's Rest from October, 2001. That entry, Anne S. Blythe? That's my mother's handwriting. I'd know it anywhere. And the name is one of her favorite fictional characters.'

Carver screwed up his eyes. 'Even so . . .'

Erin rushed on. 'The owner remembers her. I showed her a picture of my mother, and she remembered her coming to stay. But she never checked out. Some man came by the next morning and said my mother had been taken ill in the night and gone to the hospital, and he'd come to collect her things.' She pointed again. 'See, that's his handwriting on the checkout date. The number shapes look Eastern European.'

Cat looked from Erin to Carver. 'That's got to be significant, boss. Why does she use a false name? Because she's running from somebody. And somebody caught up with her.' She turned back to Erin. 'Did you find anything to show where she'd gone from there?'

Erin shook her head. 'That's the end of the trail. My belief is that the man who came to collect her things had killed her in the night and removed her body.' She'd never put it to herself in such bald words until that moment, and the horror of it almost overwhelmed her. She held a shaking hand over her eyes and sat back in the chair.

She felt a touch on her shoulder and heard Cat's voice. 'This must be really difficult for you.' Her tone held real sympathy, not just the professional variety. 'But isn't it possible he'd just kidnapped her, not killed her?'

Erin looked up. That possibility had not occurred to her – but only because of her dream. She'd determined before coming in here that she would not bring up the dream. It would only make her sound even more irrational than she already did.

'I . . . I suppose it's possible. But why not take her things at the same time? Why come back for them and draw suspicion on himself?'

Cat frowned into midair. 'Don't those questions apply just as much if he killed her? Oh, wait, I get it – if he had to manage a body, he wouldn't be able to handle the luggage at the same time.' She shot a glance at Erin. 'Sorry.'

Erin shuddered at the image but shook it off. 'And if he did kill her, leaving her things behind would excite even more suspicion than coming to get them. Luggage without a guest screams missing person, right?'

Carver, who had been listening to the two of them in skeptical silence, now sat forward with his palms on the desk. 'Let me stop you right there. This is all pure speculation. For one thing, we can't be sure this mystery guest was really Gina Washington. Handwriting can be copied or just be similar by coincidence. Face memories from twenty years ago are completely unreliable. And as for the mystery man – it's entirely possible his story was true. This woman, whoever she was, could have been taken ill and gone to the hospital in the middle of the night. It could all have been perfectly innocent.'

For half a moment, Erin's confidence was shaken by this rational explanation. But her deep conviction held. 'But that's not all. I have more.'

'I thought you said the trail ended there?' Cat put in.

'It does, going forward, but I found some things that point backward.'

Now Cat and Carver exchanged a baffled glance. Erin pulled the postcard out of her notebook pocket.

'I went to the Asilomar Conference Center. It's just down the coast from Seafarer's Rest, and I knew it was a place my mother loved – we'd been there before. Their guest records are digitized, so I couldn't get a photo, but somebody calling herself J.P. Morgan stayed there in the days just before Anne S. Blythe checked into Seafarer's Rest.'

She looked into two blank faces. 'J.P. Morgan? The famous Gilded Age industrialist? I think she was playing off Julia Morgan, the architect who built the original buildings at Asilomar, and the initial P for Phoebe Hearst, who financed it.'

Even Cat looked skeptical at that. 'That seems like kind of a stretch.'

'You don't know how my mother's mind worked. She was always making connections, playing around with words and whatnot. It's absolutely typical for her. Anyway, the guy gave me the number of the room where she'd stayed. I found it unlocked and poked around, and I came across this stuck in the back of a drawer.' She laid the postcard on the desk, photo up.

Carver spoke slowly, as if to a child. 'A postcard.' He picked it up and looked at the back. 'Nothing written on it.' He gazed at Erin with a mixture of sympathy, exasperation, and condescension. 'What makes you think this is in any way significant?'

Erin tried to swallow her desperation, but her shaking voice and quivering hands betrayed her. 'That cottage. It's my mother's favorite of all the fairytale cottages in Carmel.' She darted her eyes between the two detectives. 'Don't you see? She left it there for me to find. It's a breadcrumb. Just like the earring and the false names. She wanted me to follow her trail.'

As soon as she'd spoken those words aloud, Erin realized how unbalanced they made her sound. What, after all, did she really have by way of hard evidence? Absolutely nothing. The only thing she had was her own conviction, based on a feeling and a dream. She'd never convince anyone else those things were real or should be taken seriously. She'd been a fool to come here. She would have to do this on her own after all.

Erin stood. She picked up the postcard, which Carver had laid back on the desk, along with the earring. 'I can see you don't believe me. I'm sorry for wasting your time.'

Cat stood to make way for Erin to reach the door. 'I'll walk you out.' She said to Carver, 'OK if I take lunch now?'

Carver nodded silently, but Erin shot a glance at him through the glass as she passed toward the exit with Cat at her side. His face had changed completely. His expression was nearly blank, unreadable, but there was something in his eyes that Erin thought might almost be fear.

# SEVEN

Outside the building, Cat said, 'Want to come to lunch with me? I'd like to talk about this some more.'

'I've eaten, but sure. Thank you.' Had Erin found a possible ally after all?

'There's a taqueria around the corner. Not quite Abuela's cooking, but at least it's run by actual Mexicans.'

'Abuela? That's "grandmother," right? Didn't your mother cook?'

Cat gave her a sidelong glance and waved a couple of dreads in her face. 'Do I look full-blood Mexican to you? My mother came from Mississippi. She specialized in soul food.' Cat grimaced. 'Between Momma and Abuela, my waistline didn't have a chance.'

Erin laughed. Cat couldn't have been called svelte, but she wasn't fat, either – just solid. The physical demands of her job must be sufficient to offset all the carbs in her ancestral diets.

They'd arrived at the taqueria. Cat opened the door and stood aside for Erin to enter. 'Can I get you a drink, at least?'

'Sure, I'll take a Coke.' It had been a long and exhausting morning. A little extra sugar and caffeine couldn't hurt. Erin found a table and waited while Cat placed her order.

She told herself not to expect too much from this encounter. After all, what could a junior officer do without her superior's approval? But it surprised her how much better it made her feel just to have someone who seemed to be on her side.

She smiled as Cat sat down. 'Thanks for listening to me. I must have sounded a little crazy in there.'

Cat sat forward with intensity in her dark brown eyes. 'I know that kind of crazy. Way too well.' She closed her eyes and took a breath. 'My little sister disappeared when she was six. I was ten. She was never found, and I never got over it. My parents either, obviously. That's why I went into the police.' She sat back with a wry grin. 'I've had times when I would have snatched at anything that even smelled like a clue.'

Erin teared up for the umpteenth time that day. 'I'm so sorry. Such a young child. That must have been – well, just about the worst thing that could happen to a family.'

Cat cleared her throat. 'Let's not play "Who's had the worse time of it?" Safe to say we both lost our childhoods to a missing family member. Right?'

Erin nodded. 'Right.' She met Cat's eyes, and they exchanged a sad sisterly smile.

'Right. Now.' Cat sat up straight, about to go on, when the server appeared and laid a plate of enchiladas in front of her. She smiled at him with a '*gracias*,' then turned back to Erin. 'I want to help you. Partly because of my sister, partly because I love a tough puzzle. And this one looks about as tough as they come.'

'But won't you get in trouble? Going behind Carver's back?'

Cat tucked into her enchiladas. 'Possibly. But I'm willing to risk it. And anyway, I might be able to get him on board.'

'How? He seemed pretty resistant.'

A mischievous light came into Cat's eyes. 'That postcard.'

Erin blinked. 'What about it?'

'Fingerprints. Assuming you and the boss haven't destroyed them all by handling it. Glossy finish on the postcard would have held them.'

'Oh! I never thought of that. They'd only be my mother's, though, right?'

'Not the perp's, no, if that's what you're thinking. But if we found hers, it would prove it really was your mother who left the postcard in that room. And that would go a long way toward making the rest of your story credible.'

'Of course. Why didn't I think of that?' Erin laid her notebook open on the table with the postcard peeking out of the pocket, now afraid to touch it lest she destroy this slim shred of possible evidence.

Cat pulled a small evidence bag out of her jacket pocket and used it to extract the postcard, then sealed it up. 'I'll process this unofficially for now. If we get results, I'll put it to the boss.'

Erin's heart leapt, then fell with a thud. 'But what can you compare the fingerprints to? My mother's wouldn't be on file, would they? She wasn't around during the investigation – that was the whole point.'

'They would have retrieved some from your house at the time. Along with something that had her DNA.'

'Ah, of course.' Erin remembered watching from an enforced distance as the officers who came with Carver moved around the house, dusting doorknobs and furniture with black powder that she later had to clean up, sorting through the bathroom and bedroom trash for discarded hairs from her mother's brush. And she and her father having their own fingers pressed to an ink pad 'for elimination.' Erin's prints could now be eliminated from the postcard as well.

The idea that she might have collected a bit of hard evidence in the midst of all her hunches and intuitions brought a new level of reality to the last few days, turning her quest into an investigation. The transformation was hopeful and disturbing at the same time. As long as she was going on instinct, her mother's death could remain in the realm of the not-quite-real. But if it were proven in terms the police – and even, ultimately, a court – would accept, she would never be able to deny it to herself again.

Cat spoke around a mouthful. 'So did you look into the postcard at all, or was that where you stopped?'

'Oh, I looked, all right.' Erin blew out a long breath. 'The cottage on the postcard is a private residence, but I checked with the woman who lives there and she's never rented out rooms. She didn't recognize my mother's picture, either. She was very sweet about it, though.' Erin smiled to herself at the recollection of Maggie McGregor's kindness. 'I also researched online the actual hotels and B and Bs that looked anything like a fairytale cottage or had any kind of Old World charm. I visited them all this morning.'

Cat examined her face. 'No joy?'

'No joy. Out of three places, one let me check his books, but I found nothing. The next, the owners hadn't been there that long. The last refused to give me any information.' Erin sat back, palms on the table. 'Even if the postcard pans out, I'm not sure what to do next.'

Cat chewed meditatively. 'You said one person refused to give you information?'

'Yeah. He said something about a warrant.'

'Hmm. An actual warrant would be tricky, but maybe flashing my badge would be enough to loosen him up.'

'I don't know, he seemed pretty tight. But it's worth a try.'

Cat finished her last bite and wiped her mouth. 'Tell you what. I'll take this' – she waved the postcard in its bag – 'back to the office and process it on the sly. Then when my shift's over, if you're up for it, we'll go back to Carmel and see if we can't do a little persuading. Sound good?'

Erin felt a broad smile spread across her face of its own accord. 'Sounds great.'

She'd been alone so long, she'd forgotten how good it felt to have someone on her side.

After saying goodbye to Cat at the station entrance, Erin worked on the rest of her plan for the afternoon – *buy groceries, clean house, unpack* – to which Miss Silver added *spend half an hour cuddling your beloved and completely exceptional feline*. Erin found herself at four thirty completely drained. Cat had said she would pick her up at six fifteen – time for a short nap and a shower. She felt as if she were starting another day, so she risked a cup of real coffee with her quick sandwich supper.

Cat arrived promptly driving a venerable Jeep. Erin opened the passenger door to see her hastily gathering trash from the cracked seat and the floor in front of it. 'Sorry, I don't get many passengers in my personal car.'

'No problem,' Erin replied. She kept her own car tidy, although she rarely had passengers, either. But it would take a lot more than a messy vehicle to offset her gratitude for Cat's help.

They drove through a burger place so Cat could get some dinner. Erin waited until Cat had wolfed her burger and they were crawling along in the southbound rush-hour traffic on Highway 1 before she asked, 'How'd it go with the postcard?'

Cat gave her a sidelong glance. 'I have good news and bad news. The good news is I did find some partial prints that are about an eighty percent match to your mother's. According to the fingerprint tech I bribed with the promise of a beer after work one day.' She made a face. 'I'll make sure that day's a long time coming.'

'But that's wonderful!' Erin said. 'Isn't it? What's the bad news?'

'The bad news is Carver says it isn't enough.'

'What?! Eighty percent isn't enough? That's crazy!'

'It would be enough if the postcard were one piece of evidence among many. Or maybe even if it pointed to an actual crime. But he says it's like the earring – all it proves is that Gina was there at some point. Probably. Not that anything particular happened to her.'

Erin digested this. Of course, Carver was right, if you looked at things from a strictly logical point of view. But even though Erin was normally a logical person, this investigation wasn't about logic for her. It was about love. And love worked by its own rules.

'So we're on our own. But you're on board regardless? I assume, or else we wouldn't be inching our way to Carmel at this hour.'

Cat shot her a grin. 'Yeah, I'm still on board. All the stuff you found – like Carver said, each individual detail could mean nothing. But all together, they add up to way too much to be coincidental. I don't believe in that kind of coincidence.'

'Neither do I. I make connections for a living.' Erin pondered a minute. 'You know, it just occurred to me – in a way, you and I do the same kind of work. I'm a reference librarian, so I work with books and computers instead of people, but we both do research and make connections to arrive at the truth.'

Cat gave a short laugh. 'You're right. I never would have thought of it that way. Librarian was about the last thing I ever wanted to be – too lonely, too sedentary. No offense, but too ivory tower.' She glanced at Erin, who made a dismissive gesture. She was used to this kind of stereotyping; it no longer bothered her. 'I wanted to live in the real world. But when you describe it that way, yeah, you are a kind of detective. I have a feeling we're going to make a good team.'

They exchanged a comradely smile, then lapsed into silence until the traffic thinned as they passed Watsonville. Then Cat said, 'So, I'm fine with making this trip just to talk to the one guy, if that's what it takes. But did you have any more potential places you wanted to visit?'

Erin kicked herself for this wasted opportunity. 'I had stuff I had to take care of this afternoon, so I haven't had time to do any more research. But there is that one place where the owners didn't go back that far. I only spoke to the teenaged daughter, so if the mother's there now, she might be able to point us toward some old records or the previous owner or something.'

'Sure, sounds worth a try. Which would we come to first?'

'That second place, the Surf & Seagull. It's at the bottom of Ocean Avenue, near the beach. Then we go south on Scenic Drive a ways to get to the Tor House Lodge.'

'Addresses?' Cat activated her GPS. 'I've never been to Carmel.'

'They don't do street numbers there. Weird, I know. You can exit straight on to Ocean Avenue, and then it's just downhill from there.'

Cat shook her head. 'Crazy. I knew Carmel was kind of a quirky place, but no street numbers? How do emergency services function? It'd be like my Mississippi great-grandpa giving directions.' She put on a thick Southern accent. '"Go pas' the duck pond and turn lef' wheah the Jenkinsons' ol' bahn use' to be." It's like they're stuck in another century.'

'I think that's the idea. The town was built in the nineteen twenties, but they wanted it to be like the land that time forgot. Which was what my mother loved about it.'

'Yeah? What kind of woman was your mother, anyway? She seems . . . interesting.'

'She was the most fascinating person I've ever known.' Erin allowed herself to drift into memories. 'She had an incredible zest for living. Sometimes that's code for being self-centered and pleasure-driven, but not my mother. She loved people, loved bringing beauty into their lives. If I had to name one thing that defined her, that would be it – she was all about beauty. Enjoying and creating it in every possible form.'

'Was she an artist?'

'She dabbled in painting, among other things, but she didn't consider herself good enough to sell her work – though I loved everything she did. She worked in an art gallery, where she could help other artists – “real” artists, she called them – succeed. And she loved turning ordinary people on to serious art. They’d come in looking for something to match their sofa, and she’d end up selling them a piece that would enrich their lives for years to come.’

Cat smiled. ‘I wish I could have met her.’

‘Me, too. I wish the whole world could have met her. It would be a better place.’

# EIGHT

Around seven thirty, they turned off the freeway onto Ocean Avenue, and Erin guided Cat to the Surf & Seagull. As she passed the goofy seagull sign and pulled into the courtyard, Cat said, 'OK, now I'm not just in another century, I'm in another country. Midsomer County, I think. Bodies should start popping up any minute now.'

Erin laughed. 'I'm surprised a cop would watch that show. Isn't it like the least authentic police work ever portrayed on TV?'

'Just about. But that's what makes it feel like fun instead of work. We get a bunch of cops together to watch it and make snarky comments all the way through.'

They pushed open the heavy oak front door to enter a busy room full of diners. Erin spotted the girl she'd spoken to that morning among the wait staff dashing about with full platters of fish and chips and shepherd's pie. 'Crap,' Cat muttered under her breath. 'Dinner rush. We'll never get anyone to talk to us at this rate.'

A middle-aged woman in black slacks and a white shirt approached them, menus in hand. 'Two for dinner?'

Cat flashed her badge. 'Actually, we were hoping to talk with the manager.'

'Ah. That would be me.' The woman swept a glance around the bustling room. 'What's this about? I can give you five minutes, no more. Unless you'd like to come back in an hour or so.'

Cat and Erin exchanged glances. 'Five minutes might do it,' Cat said. 'Is there someplace quieter we can talk?'

'Come into my office.' The manager led the way through a stair hall to a door on the other side. She unlocked it, and they entered a windowless little room whose uncluttered modernity presented a stark contrast to the rest of the pub. A metal desk with a computer, one filing cabinet, and two chairs comprised its furnishings.

'Now, what can I do for you?'

'We're checking on the movements of a woman who may have stayed here in 2001.'

'Oh, in that case I can't help you. I've only been here since 2010.'

'The previous owner didn't leave any records behind?'

The manager shook her head. 'They'd never computerized. I didn't want a bunch of old papers and ledgers cluttering up the place, so I scanned the essential stuff and recycled the rest. Old guest registers didn't seem essential.'

'Any idea how we could contact the previous owners?'

'Only with a séance. They passed away a few years ago.'

Erin shot Cat a *we're done here* look. She was more convinced than ever that the Surf & Seagull would not have been her mother's cup of tea. Or glass of beer, in this case.

'Thank you for your time,' Cat said. 'We'll let you get back to your dinner rush.'

Outside, Cat and Erin looked at each other and burst into laughter. 'I guess Midsomer is only skin deep after all,' Erin said.

'Yeah. At least that might keep the body count down.' Cat sobered suddenly. 'Sorry. I guess that was pretty insensitive under the circs.'

Erin sighed. 'Don't worry about it. I'm kind of hardened to such things at this point. And besides, in my heart I'm not looking for a body. I know Mumsie must be dead – in fact, I'm sure of it – but I'm still looking for the living, breathing woman I loved. And that's who somebody somewhere in this town must have seen.'

Cat put a sympathetic hand on her shoulder. 'On to the next place, then?'

'Right. Tor House Lodge and Mister Snooty-Pants Fake François. Or maybe we'll be lucky and meet his partner instead.'

'Fake François?'

'His name tag says François, but if that's the name he was born with, I'll eat my chapeau. Plain Frank is my guess. But I don't want to spoil him for you. Let's go.'

They drove south on Scenic Drive, past impressive houses on both sides, with patches of ocean flashing between those on their right. 'There it is,' Erin said as the two-story rough stone building hove into view.

'Back to Midsomer?' Cat said with a raised eyebrow.

'Not so much. More like a pretentious attempt to mimic artsy twenties Carmel.'

They entered the lobby to see an empty reception desk. A subdued clatter of cutlery and buzz of conversation issued from the dining room to the left. Erin tapped the bell but doubted it could be heard beyond the lobby.

Cat moved to the right-hand archway and peered into the empty salon. 'Hello?' she called. 'Anyone here?'

'Half a mo,' came a distinctly British-sounding voice from somewhere in the recesses of the building.

Cat moved back toward the desk, and Erin whispered, 'We're in luck. That is definitely not Fake François.'

'Could be Midsomer, though?'

Erin gave her head a decisive shake. She knew her accents, both from Mumsie's expert imitations and from years of watching British TV. 'This guy's not country. He's London. And not trying very hard to hide it.'

Just then, a large, florid, fiftyish man in an open-necked checked shirt over wrinkled khakis strode through the arch and slid behind the desk. 'What can I do for you ladies? Dinner's almost over, but we can squeeze in a couple of weary travelers if need be. Rooms are another matter – we're crammed to the gills at the minute.'

'We don't need food or beds, thanks all the same.' Cat flashed her badge. 'But we could use some information.'

The man, whose name tag read *Jackie*, raised his eyebrows. 'Now that's something we don't see every day. Coppers in my lodge! Wait till I tell Frankie. He'll flip.'

'I talked to François this morning, actually,' said Erin. 'He wasn't terribly forthcoming.'

Jackie waved a fleshy hand. 'Oh, that's just Frankie. They don't make arses any tighter than his. Now, what do you need to know?'

Cat handed the ball to Erin with a glance. 'I'm trying to trace the movements of a woman who may have stayed here in 2001 – probably toward the end of September. Do you have records going back that far?'

'Absolutely.' Jackie opened a discreet laptop on the lower part of the desk facing him. 'All digitized from the minute we took over, back in 1999. What name are you looking for?'

Erin bit her lip. 'That's the tricky part, I'm afraid. You could search for Gina Washington, but I'm pretty sure she would have been using a false name. Possibly something connected with Tor House – Una Something, maybe? Or Somebody Jeffers, or Jefferson?'

Jackie whistled. 'You don't 'alf know how to stump a bloke, do you? All right, 'ere we go.' He tapped the keyboard. 'No Gina Washington. No Jeffers – I think we'd have noticed that. Not so common – likely to be a relative of the brave Sir Robin.' He glanced upward to indicate the portrait of Robinson Jeffers that hung on the wall behind him. 'Here's a Jeffer*son* – no, that's from oh-three. Trying Una now . . . That's not common either, but it might have slipped by. Here we go – Una Call. That was her maiden name, his nibs's wife.' He jerked a thumb to indicate the portrait again.

Jackie peered at Erin. 'She must have been on the ball, this Gina Washington. Not many people would know Una's maiden name.'

'Yes,' Erin replied, her pulse racing at having picked up the trail once again. 'She had a bit of a fascination with the Jeffers family. Do you have the dates she stayed here?'

'Let's see . . . September twenty-seventh to thirtieth, 2001. Paid cash up front, apparently.'

'Yes, that's what I would've expected.' Erin gathered her courage. 'Any chance I could see the room she stayed in?'

Jackie made a regretful face. 'Sorry, love. Like I said, we're all full up. Can't barge in on a guest.' He turned back to the screen and clicked. 'Room seventeen . . . That guest is due to check out tomorrow. If you want to come back between eleven and three, we might be able to let you have a squint.' He leaned forward and spoke in a conspiratorial whisper. 'Be sure to ask for me, though. Frankie'll send you packing in a hot minute.' He winked.

Erin grinned back. 'Thank you so much. We'll be back.' She glanced at Cat, who was making a doubtful face. Of course, Cat would be on duty at that time. 'At least I will – if that's all right? Without the police presence?'

Jackie waved a hand. 'What's a warrant card more or less between friends? Sorry, it's *badge* over here, right? Anyway, no worries. I'll be expecting you.' He darted his eyes toward the dining room and whispered again. 'Best come during lunch. You-know-who will be busy in the dining room then.'

'Got it. And thanks again.'

Outside, Erin's excitement boiled over and she gave Cat an impulsive hug. 'I can't thank you enough. I'd never have had the gumption to go back there without you.'

'No problem. I'm only sorry I can't come with you tomorrow. Carver would hit the ceiling if I did any of this on the clock. Or, for that matter, if he knew I was helping you at all, since he rejected that fingerprint.'

'I'll be fine. I'll let you know if I find anything, and maybe we can take it from there?'

'Damn right we will. You're not getting rid of me now.'

By the time they got back to Santa Cruz, Erin was regretting having given up her room at Seafarer's Rest. But at least the next day, Tuesday, she'd be able to make the drive to Carmel and back without encountering rush-hour traffic.

She was puttering about the house Tuesday morning, filling time with leftover cleaning tasks until ten forty-five, which she'd told herself was the best time to leave, when her phone rang. Alex. She'd never let him know she was home. Which meant he'd probably come by to feed Miss Silver the previous evening, while she was out with Cat. Double dinner score for one crafty Siamese.

She put on a tone of voice that was brighter than she really felt. 'Hey, Alex, how are you?'

'The point is, how are *you*? How is Seafarer's Rest? I hope I'm not interrupting your packing.'

'No. Actually I left a day early. Not that there was anything wrong with the place – it's everything you said it would be. And more.'

'But you just couldn't allow yourself to relax and be pampered for three whole nights.' His tone was bantering, but there was genuine concern underneath.

'It isn't that. It's . . . complicated.' Erin had come to an unexpected fork in the road far sooner than she'd bargained for. To share or not to share? Alex was the closest thing to a best friend she had. She knew he was trustworthy and had her best interests at heart. And his research skills could be valuable in her quest, as he had tech magic at his fingertips that far surpassed her own.

But telling him all about this journey she was on would mean letting him much deeper into the private areas of her life than she had ever allowed him – or anyone unconnected with the case – to go. She didn't know if she was ready for that.

'Complicated?' His tone changed, its bantering note becoming forced. 'Don't tell me you met someone?'

'Nothing like that.' She would have to tell him something. And knowing his talent for winkling things out of her, it would ultimately have to be the truth. But not now. Not on the phone. 'I can't talk about it right now. I'll tell you when I see you.'

'Then that'd better be sooner than when you come back to work next week. Lunch? The Buttery? My treat.'

The Buttery was her favorite bakery-cum-café. She rarely allowed herself to go there because their mouthwatering pastries would be the death of her figure if she overindulged. But if she waited till after lunch to head to Carmel, she'd risk being stonewalled by Fake François.

'I'll have to take a raincheck, Alex. I have plans for the middle of the day that can't flex.'

'Dinner, then? Laíli?'

Her favorite Middle Eastern place. The thought of their juicy, perfectly spiced lamb shank was making her mouth water even now. 'All right. I should be able to manage that.'

'Meet you there at six fifteen. Deal?'

'Deal. Oh, and obviously, no need to come by to feed Miss Silver today.'

'Too bad. Tell my little girlfriend I'll miss her.' That was their standard joke. Miss Silver adored Alex; Erin did not exist for her when he was around.

Erin sighed as she ended the call. She'd done it now. Alex could get around her carefully constructed defenses better than anyone.

The drive to Carmel seemed half as long today, not just because of the lighter traffic but because her thoughts were so occupied with what she might find there that she barely noticed her surroundings as she drove. Thank God for that part of her brain that could keep navigating the vehicle safely while her active mind was elsewhere.

She pulled up in front of Tor House Lodge at eleven forty-five a.m. Even if there were few lunchers as yet, she could reasonably hope Fake François would be busy preparing for those to come. As she passed the dining room on the way to the front door, she sneaked a peek in the window. Yes, there he was – this time in a dark plum suit with a lime-green shirt and fuchsia tie – fussing about the tables, making sure each utensil was perfectly placed.

She pushed open the front door quietly, so as not to alert him, and was relieved to see Jackie on duty at the front desk. His eyes widened and he put a finger to his lips, like a child on a hunt for secret treasure, as he lifted a key from the rack and beckoned her to follow him up the wooden staircase that rose on the salon side of the lobby. The sight of his bulky form literally tiptoeing up the stairs nearly destroyed her composure, but she managed not to make a peep until they had safely reached the top.

Jackie let his heels down at that point and led her to the right to a corner room over the salon, facing the ocean. 'Here we are,' he said, unlocking the door. 'Though what you expect to find after twenty years, I can't imagine.'

'Neither can I, really,' Erin replied. In a rush of gratitude for his assistance, she told him. 'I think the woman who called herself Una Call was my mother. She disappeared in June of 2001, and I've only recently been able to pick up a trail that led me here. The clues I've found so far have been the kind that wouldn't mean anything to anyone but me, so I'm hoping to find something like that here as well.'

Jackie's eyes threatened to pop out of his head. 'Well, tickle me pink. What an adventure for our little lodge! I wish you all the luck in the world, love. I'd best pop back down to the desk – you'll let me know if you need anything else?'

'I will.' She gave him her best smile. 'And thanks again.'

Jackie shut the door behind him. Erin scanned the room. It was furnished in the Arts & Crafts style, more or less, with a sleigh bed and somewhat mismatched wardrobe, desk, dresser, and nightstand. The bedding, curtains, wallpaper, and rugs were all in green-based knockoffs of William Morris prints.

Unfortunately the prints did not quite coordinate, and the effect was rather overpowering. If her mother had been entrusted with the decoration of this room, she would have replaced the busy floral wallpaper with something more monochrome, such as a fern design.

Tearing her attention from irrelevant details, Erin began a methodical search of the room, beginning with the desk – although it wouldn't be like Mumsie to choose the same hiding place twice in a row. No joy in the desk, wardrobe, or dresser. All were pristinely clean and empty.

Next she turned to the nightstand. Its single drawer held only a local phone book. Erin rifled through it just in case but found nothing. She replaced the phone book and shut the drawer.

Uncertain what to do next, she sank onto the bed and let her eyes travel around the room. What hiding place could be missed in twenty years of cleaning and redecorating? The walls had been repapered; the rugs were somewhat worn but not as old as twenty years. Each item of furniture would have been moved and returned to place a dozen times, revealing anything that might have been hidden behind it.

But the wardrobe was quite high, its carved pediment nearly reaching the ceiling. A cleaner would have to be pretty dedicated to bother dusting behind that pediment, and conceivably the piece could have been moved without dislodging a small item from its top. On the other hand, something left there would have to have been hidden deliberately. It wasn't a place anything could be left by accident.

The voice in her head whispered, *Go and look.*

Erin pulled the straight wooden desk chair over to the wardrobe and cautiously climbed onto it. Even standing on the chair, she was tall enough to reach the pediment but not to see over it. Wishing for gloves in case of possible spiders and inevitable dust, she ran her fingertips over the hidden surface, starting as far back as she could reach and moving forward.

Right at the front, up against the back of the pediment, she felt something – something flat but with a different texture from the dust-covered wood. She felt around and found its edges. A rectangle about the size of a card. She got her fingers under it and tugged. One corner seemed to be stuck in a join.

She yanked harder and instantly regretted it as she heard the paper tear.

But the card came free. She lifted it over the pediment and shook off the thick layer of dust, along with a tiny spider that had mercifully evaded her probing touch. The torn corner was small; all the writing, which was on the clean underside of the card, was still intact. She turned it right side up so she could read it.

This was an invitation card, engraved in gold on elegant cream stock. Not to a wedding, but to the opening of an art gallery right here in Carmel. Raymonds-by-the-Sea on San Carlos Street between Ocean and Seventh Avenue. The date of the opening was September 29, 2001.

# NINE

Erin stowed the invitation in her notebook and ran down the stairs. She tossed a hasty goodbye-and-thank-you to the startled Jackie and was about to fly out the door when he called her back.

'Wait! Leave me a contact number, why don't you, in case I find out anything else?'

Of course – why hadn't she thought of that? She scribbled her name and number and 'Una Call' on a page of her notebook and tore it out. 'Thanks for all your help, Jackie.'

He lowered his voice to a conspiratorial whisper. 'Did you find any clues?'

'One. Possibly. Have to follow it up. But it could be a good one.' She paused and said with a little smile, 'Oh, and you might want to have someone dust the top of that wardrobe.'

He grinned back. 'Good luck to you, love.'

She hurried out. She had something far better now than a merely geographical indicator of a place her mother had stayed. This invitation was undoubtedly significant. Not only was it for a gallery opening – an event within her mother's own professional sphere – but Raymond was the first name of Mr Cruikshank, Erin's former employer.

She had to force herself to stay within the vicinity of the speed limit as she raced back up Scenic Drive to Ocean and the few blocks to Seventh Avenue. Fortunately on a Tuesday the downtown area was less crowded than on weekends, or she would never have been able to park anywhere near the gallery; as it was, she managed to find a spot on the same block.

And there it was, on the opposite side of the narrow street – Raymonds-by-the-Sea. Trust Cruikshank to leave out the apostrophe. He was far from being an uneducated man, but as her mother used to say of him, the only rules he acknowledged were aesthetic ones. He would undoubtedly have judged that an apostrophe so close to a hyphen was not an appealing look. And of course he had to use the hyphens to echo the town's full name of Carmel-by-the-Sea.

Erin crossed the street and paused outside the large gallery windows, shaded by a broad awning to keep the sun from damaging the art displayed therein. Among the expected assortment of watercolors, acrylics, and engravings by local living artists was one small oil whose style Erin immediately recognized. She looked closely, and there indeed was the signature: Elliot Forbes.

Forbes was the most distinguished of the artists who had migrated to the then tiny and obscure village of Carmel in the 1910s and 1920s, in search of solitude, inspiration, and a modicum of fellowship with like-minded intellectuals. He, along with a select set of locals and visitors, had gathered regularly at Tor House in Una Jeffers' salon. Since his death in the fifties, the value of his work had skyrocketed – not into the rarefied atmosphere of world-renowned masters like Rembrandt and Van Gogh, but well into six figures. It was unheard of to see any Forbes painting offered for public sale in a gallery; on the rare occasions they changed ownership, it was usually by auction. But then, Cruikshank was a wheeler-dealer if ever there was one. If he managed to get hold of a valuable painting, he would take whatever route he thought would maximize his profit in its sale.

Shaking irrelevancies from her mind, Erin entered the gallery. 'Good afternoon,' sang out a woman's voice from behind a desk. 'Let me know if I can help you at all.'

Erin sized up the voice's owner. She was smartly dressed in a gray suit and heels with blond hair in a French twist. Erin judged her to be only a few years older than herself – too young to have worked here at the time of the opening on the invitation.

'Good afternoon,' said Erin, suddenly conscious of her distinctly off-duty appearance. Since she was on vacation, she'd dressed in black yoga pants and a gray T-shirt with her hair roughly scooped into a ponytail. Definitely the look of a window-shopper rather than a person with the means to pursue a serious interest in acquiring art. But on the other hand, even the fabulously wealthy Steve Jobs had never worn anything but jeans and a black turtleneck. She could be a billionaire incognito.

'I was curious about the Forbes in the window,' she said,

summoning the air of a woman with enough money to expect her requests to be taken seriously. 'I assume it is for sale?'

French-twist Lady (this gallery was far too upscale for name tags) looked her over, a tiny smirk playing about the corners of her mouth. 'I believe it may be promised to someone,' she said. 'I'll have to check with Mr Cruikshank, the owner.'

Before Erin could protest, French-twist Lady had lifted a handset and punched a button. 'Mr Cruikshank? There's someone here who wants to look at the Forbes.'

The last thing Erin wanted was a face-to-face meeting with Cruikshank. What if he recognized her? It seemed unlikely, since he had last seen her when she was twelve, but she had spent a fair bit of time in the Santa Cruz gallery back then, so it wasn't out of the question. Not wanting to explain what had really brought her here, she hastened to construct a cover story.

A figure emerged from a back room. Erin would have known Raymond Cruikshank anywhere, if only by the cut of his Italian-made charcoal pinstripe suit. He'd put on a few pounds and his black hair had threads of gray, but it was still slicked back from a flawless part, and his signature mauve handkerchief still poked out of his breast pocket, matching his narrow mauve tie. If he'd worn a T-shirt proclaiming *Art Is My Business*, the message could not have been more clear.

As soon as he came within sight of Erin, Cruikshank stopped dead. His naturally pale face went pasty white, and he swayed slightly on his feet. He breathed a word that might have been 'Gina.'

So much for being incognito. Apparently Carver was not the only one who thought Erin looked just like her mother.

'It's me, Mr Cruikshank. Erin. Gina's daughter.' She watched his face closely as he blinked rapidly, bringing his eyes back into focus, and a tiny bit of color returned to his cheeks.

'Erin!' he said with forced enthusiasm, coming up to take her hand in both his own. His palms were clammy, and Erin withdrew her hand as soon as she decently could. 'How wonderful to see you! It's been – let's see – you weren't even a teenager when I saw you last. What brings you here?'

'It's been twenty years. Almost exactly. Since my mother disappeared.' She let that sink in, noting the bobbing of his

Adam's apple in his fleshy neck. 'I just happened to be wandering around Carmel and saw this place. I couldn't help wondering whether it was yours.'

He put on a bright smile. 'Oh, yes, this gallery is my second child. The second is always brighter than the first.' He made an *oops, faux pas* face. 'Of course you wouldn't know about that, being an only child. All the family brilliance is concentrated in you.'

She didn't reply to that beyond raising one eyebrow. Cruikshank had always specialized in extravagant compliments, which seemed to go down well with his wealthier customers. Even as a child, Erin had rolled her eyes at such talk; now that it was trained on her, she could give it the full disdain it deserved.

'At any rate,' he went on, unfazed, 'I divide my time between the two locations now, but I spend most of it here. I bought a home in Carmel several years ago.'

This gallery must be doing well, then. Santa Cruz was one of the least affordable towns in the country, but Carmel's real estate prices were higher yet – with residents' incomes to match.

'This gallery certainly seems prosperous. I was surprised to see you have a Forbes for sale.'

'Oh, that?' He gave a false laugh. 'That isn't actually for sale. It's a little thing of my own. I just keep it in the window to draw customers into the shop.' Cruikshank darted a lightning glance at French-twist Lady, who put a hand to her hair and cleared her throat. Clearly she'd been about to protest. If the Forbes had genuinely not been for sale, why would she not have told Erin so when she asked about it?

'Well, it certainly is good to see you, Erin dear. Let me know if I can help you at all.' He paused, then added as if the words were being pulled out of him, 'I don't suppose you ever found out anything about what happened to your mother?'

'Nothing concrete, no. But I have just recently started looking into her disappearance seriously.'

He blinked rapidly. 'Why would you do that? I mean, why now, after all these years?'

Erin shrugged. She certainly wasn't going to let him in on the actual events and thought processes of her last few days. 'I suppose it must have been the twenty-year anniversary that set me off. On the ten-year one I was still in school. Also, my father died recently. I guess I didn't want to accept becoming a complete orphan.'

With obvious relief, his features formed into a conventional condolence face. 'I'm so sorry, Erin dear. That must be very difficult for you. May your dear father rest in peace.' He put out a hand toward her shoulder, but Erin stepped back. 'Do let me know if there's anything at all I can do to help you. I think about dearest Gina every day. Such a tragedy. And so painful for you to go all these years without knowing what became of her.' His brows drew together. 'Do you think there's a chance she might still be alive?'

Erin looked him steadily in the eye. 'No. I don't think there's any chance of that.'

Cruikshank mumbled his excuses and disappeared back into his office. Erin made a cursory circuit of the gallery, checking the artists' names to see if there were any paintings by the artist whose work had been featured in the opening on the invitation. Seymour Finnegan, his name was. At last she found one – an acrylic abstract, the lines and colors compelling, the paint applied with a bold and liberal hand. The painting was undated. If he was still local and still working, maybe she could look him up. No point in asking French-twist Lady for his contact info; that sort of knowledge would be closely guarded lest a potential customer attempt to purchase directly from an artist, thereby depriving the gallery of its substantial commission.

Finnegan's was one of only a few paintings of merit here among many that were purely decorative – but all with hefty price tags. Mumsie would have shaken her head in despair. This gallery clearly catered to people who wanted a painting to match their sofa.

Except for that Forbes. The small seascape in the window, with its inimitably masterful treatment of sunlight and water, would be overlooked by the ignorant but would draw the eye of the aficionado – who would find little else of interest inside. What was Cruikshank's game, really? And could it have anything to do with events of twenty years before?

* * *

Erin's stomach rumbled, reminding her that it was lunchtime. She popped into the nearest café – Carmel boasted almost as many cafés as art galleries – and ordered a sandwich. As she waited for it to arrive, she pulled out her phone and Googled 'Seymour Finnegan.'

She found plenty of information about his work. Apparently he did representational painting as well as abstract and had been commissioned for public and private murals all over the Bay Area. His subjects varied with the location and purpose of the mural, but all the photos she found shared his distinctively bold, almost raw approach to color and form. Erin found herself drawn to the images although they were dramatically different from her usual taste.

Personal information, however, was decidedly lacking. The internet admitted that Finnegan lived in Carmel but was uncharacteristically cagey about anything beyond that.

Sighing for the days (which she personally could hardly remember) when everyone had a landline and most were listed in the local phone book, Erin called Alex at work.

'Hey there,' he answered, cheerful as always. 'Change your mind about lunch? I'm just on my way out.'

'No, sorry, I'm eating now – in Carmel. But listen, I need your help with something. I'm trying to track down an address or phone number for an artist called Seymour Finnegan.'

Alex laughed. 'Sounds like a frustrated whale-watcher.'

He gave her a second to parse that – *see more fin again*. She gave an appreciative chuckle.

'You have any parameters for him?'

'Just that he's alive, and he lives in Carmel.'

'OK, I'll see what I can do. You need this right away, I take it?'

'If you can, yeah.'

'I'll get on it and call you back.'

Erin's sandwich arrived, and she tucked in. She'd finished the first half when her phone rang.

'Wow, this guy must really be a recluse,' Alex said. 'He's as unlisted as you can get in the Information Age. The only thing I could find is that he's a member of something called the Carmel Artists and Artisans Guild. I have an address and number for them if you want to try weaseling something out of them.'

She took the details down. 'Thanks, Alex. See you tonight.'

She doubted very much that the guild would give out its members' contact info, but perhaps someone there would be willing to call Finnegan and ask if he would consent to talk to her.

Erin finished her sandwich and checked the guild's address. It was only a few blocks away, so she left her car where it was and walked there, figuring she'd have a better chance of success in person than on the phone.

The address turned out to belong to a largish late-Victorian-style house that had been converted into several small offices. The Carmel Artists and Artisans Guild occupied the left-hand side of the main floor, up a long outdoor flight from the street. Erin tried the door but found it locked. Then she noticed the sign in the window: *Out to lunch. Back at 1:30 p.m.*

She checked her watch – one twenty-two. The ground floor of the building housed a small bookstore, so she ducked in there to pass the eight minutes or so until the office opened. Time always passed more quickly when she was surrounded by books.

Grabbing a random book off a shelf, she parked herself near the front window, watching the stairs to the main entrance of the building. At one forty, she finally saw an older woman with long gray hair, wearing a flowing, colorful outfit, climb the stairs and go in. Erin hastily returned the book to the shelf and followed her.

The door to the guild office was just closing as Erin reached it. She stopped it with one hand, and the artsy-looking woman's face appeared around it. 'Oh, hello,' she said. 'Were you looking for me?'

'Yes,' Erin said with a smile. 'I was hoping to get some information about one of your members.'

'Come in,' Artsy Woman said, opening the door wide and standing aside for Erin to enter. She closed the door after her and moved behind a desk. 'What sort of information? We don't give out personal contact details without the member's permission.'

'No, of course not. I was hoping to speak with Seymour Finnegan. I thought you might be able to call him and ask if he's willing to see me.'

'I could do that,' Artsy Woman said, looking Erin over from

top to bottom. 'But I have to warn you, he rarely talks to anyone. He's very private. If you're press—'

'Oh, no, nothing like that. This is purely personal.'

'Personal? Does he know you at all?'

'No. But we have acquaintances in common. Raymond Cruikshank, the gallery owner. And I think it's possible Mr Finnegan may have known my mother some twenty years ago. Gina Washington? She used to work for Cruikshank's, in Santa Cruz. My name is Erin Washington, by the way.'

Artsy Woman picked up a phone. With her finger poised over the keypad, she said, 'He's going to want to know what it's about.'

Erin hesitated, but what was the harm? 'I want to ask him about his opening at Raymond's gallery in September of 2001.' She mentally gave *Raymond's* the apostrophe it should have had on the sign.

Artsy Woman dialed and waited some time. 'He doesn't pick up if he's working,' she said to Erin. 'Do you want me to leave your number for him to call you back?'

Erin nodded and hastily scribbled her number on the notepad Artsy Woman held out.

Presumably Finnegan's voicemail came on, because Artsy Woman spoke without pausing for response. 'Hello, Finn, it's Becca from the guild. There's a girl here who says she wants to talk to you about your opening at Raymonds in 2001. Her name is Erin Washington. She says you might have known her mother, Gina. Her number is – oh, there you are. What's that?' Becca listened, then handed the phone to Erin. 'He wants to talk to you.'

Erin almost dropped the phone in her eagerness to grasp it. 'Hello, Mr Finnegan? I'm—'

'Shut up and listen. If you're Gina Washington's girl, I'll talk to you. Come to my studio. I'm at the end of Scenic where it turns into Carmelo. On the right. Stucco, red tile roof, top of the hill. Got it?'

'Got it. When shall I—'

'Right now. Quick as you can fly. I'll put the coffee on.'

She was about to say 'thank you,' but he had already hung up. So she said it to Becca instead and flew out the door.

# TEN

Within minutes she was standing on Seymour Finnegan's doorstep. The door opened before she could knock.

In the doorway stood a barefoot man clad in naturally holey jeans, as opposed to the pre-ripped variety, under an oversized shirt splattered with paint of all colors. He was probably in his early to mid-forties, but age was the last thing one thought of when looking at him. A shock of jet-black hair fell about his face in all directions, but it was the face itself that arrested her. It was all planes and angles intersected by crevasses like an Alpine landscape, covered in leathery tanned skin with a day's growth of beard instead of snow. Two banked fires burned where his eyes should be, so that she wondered how his thatches of eyebrows were saved from going up in flames.

As he loomed above her, the thought crossed her mind that superficially, at least, he could have matched the description of the mystery man at Seafarer's Rest – given a haircut, shave, wardrobe overhaul, and attitude adjustment. But when he spoke, his thoroughly Californian accent dispelled that impression at once.

'Well, come in, then, Gina Washington's daughter – I can see you are. Don't stand there gaping at me like I'm some freak in the zoo.'

He turned and walked away, leaving her to follow. She shut the door behind her and scurried to catch up.

Finnegan led the way through a cluttered studio to a filthy hole-in-the-wall kitchen, where he poured two cups of coffee and handed one to her without asking if she wanted it. Then he strode back to the studio, not offering cream or sugar. Erin gave a shrug of the eyebrows and sipped the brew. Black and strong, with the faintest hint of turpentine. But that was probably just in the air, not in the coffee itself. She hoped.

The artist waved vaguely in the direction of a derelict loveseat half covered in face-down sketches, himself perching on a rickety wooden stool. Erin slid a couple of sketches out of the way and gingerly sat, hoping the ancient springs and threadbare upholstery would support her.

Finnegan stared at Erin until the blood started to crawl up her neck. 'Wanted to paint her, you know. Your mother. I do the odd portrait. Not that I get many subjects worth my time.' He leaned forward half off his stool and reached around behind Erin, pulling the elastic off her ponytail. Before she could object, he fluffed her hair around her face, then sat back with a satisfied nod. 'I'd paint you.'

Erin was taken aback, not only by the abruptness of his manner but by the magnetism that seemed to roll off him in waves. Although she couldn't say she liked him, she hadn't felt this way in a man's presence since – well, possibly ever. But she was virtually certain the charisma was quite unintentional on his part. He was probably unaware of it, or at least couldn't turn it off if he tried.

'That's very flattering, Mr Finnegan—'

'Finn. Don't you dare call me Seymour. And I never flatter. You have your mother's bones, and those bones are worth painting. All there is to it.' He glared at her. 'She would never give me the time to do it properly. Always wanted to get back to her family. Which I suppose was you.' He took a long sip of coffee and crossed his arms. 'So you owe me a portrait in compensation.'

Erin swallowed. This conversation was not taking at all the direction she'd had in mind in coming here. But she couldn't swim against Finn's current. It was all she could do to keep her head above water.

'I don't have any money to commission you.'

Brisk shake of the wild locks. 'Not a commission. I'm asking you to pose.'

If that was what he called asking, she had to wonder what it was like when he *told*. But that raised another question. 'What sort of painting are we talking about?'

He gave a derisive huff. 'Worried about your maidenly modesty? I'm surprised at you, being Gina's daughter. But don't worry – it's your face I'm interested in.' He gestured to the sketches beside her on the loveseat. 'Just dug those out after you called. That's the kind of thing I'm talking about.'

She picked up the pile of sketches and turned them right side up, intending to leaf through them. But the first one arrested her and riveted her to the spot.

Yes, it was her mother's face – but as Erin had never seen it before. When Erin had looked at Gina when she was alive, she had looked as a child on her beloved mother. She saw kindness, patience, playfulness, enthusiasm, affection, pride, and a deep, deep love.

But in this face she also saw a woman. A woman whose eyes held a buried sadness along with a sensuality begging to burst forth. A woman whose potential for passionate love was obviously unfulfilled.

As a child, Erin had never thought much about whether her parents were happy together. Her father was so rarely around that it hardly seemed an issue. As she matured, she had occasionally looked back and acknowledged the probability that her mother, at least, had wished for something more in her marriage than what she had. But Erin had never considered her mother as a sexual being. One simply didn't think of one's parents that way. Yet in this sketch, she saw the naked physical longing of a woman who felt herself unloved.

She drew in a ragged breath, then feeling Finn's gaze on her, looked up at him, almost against her will. His eyes burned into her.

The words leapt out of her mouth without her volition. 'Did you sleep with her?'

Finn gave a bitter bark of laughter. 'No. I did not. But God, I wanted to.' Again he turned accusing eyes on Erin. 'She wanted me, too. But she refused to do anything that might jeopardize her marriage. Not because of *him* – your father – but because of *you*.'

He leaned forward, his eyes boring into her soul. 'So maybe you owe me more than just a portrait.'

Erin swallowed and pushed herself back into the loveseat as far as she could go. He frightened her, but it was a delicious fear. How could she, a modern, liberated woman, react like this to a savage and overbearing man? She was furious with herself, but the magnetism held. She imagined him leaping from his stool, pulling her to her feet, and smashing his sensuous mouth against hers – and her lips yielding. For a moment, it almost seemed real – the most real thing that had happened to her in years.

Then Finn released her from his gaze with a genuine belly laugh. 'Don't worry, little girl. I like my women riper than you. I do want to paint you, but I don't want to fuck you. At least, not until you wake up.'

She nearly gasped with the mingled relief and disappointment. He took a long swig of his coffee, giving her a chance to collect herself – which she did with difficulty, feeling as if pieces of her soul were scattered around the studio along with the brushes and canvases. Finn wiped his painty sleeve across his mouth, leaving an incongruous smudge of purple at the corner of his lip. She yearned to kiss it away – until she reminded herself it was probably acrylic paint, and therefore toxic.

'But you didn't come here for me to torture you,' he said. 'You had some questions you wanted to ask me. Ask away.'

With shaking hands, Erin took out her notebook and pretended to consult it, though in fact she'd made no preparatory notes for this conversation. She'd had no idea what, if anything, Finn would be able to tell her that could be of use. She certainly hadn't anticipated finding out that he'd been in love – or at least in lust – with her mother.

Willing her voice to steady itself, she asked without looking at him, 'Did you meet her – my mother – through Cruikshank's? In Santa Cruz, I mean?'

'Yeah, that's right. This "by-the-Sea" place wasn't open yet then. My thing didn't just open my exhibition – it opened the gallery, period.'

'Did you see my mother there? At your opening?'

He stared into the distance. 'Funny you should ask. I remember that night so vividly. I hadn't seen Gina for months – all summer, in fact. Cruikshank told me she was taking a leave of absence, wouldn't say where she'd gone.'

Erin looked up sharply. 'A leave of absence? He said that?'

'Yeah, why? Was he lying?'

'I'll say he was. She'd completely disappeared. My father and I never saw her after June twenty-first of that year.' She stared at Finn in disbelief. 'Are you saying you never knew? You never saw in the news that she was missing?'

His haunted eyes looked through her rather than at her. 'I don't do news. Distracts me from my work. Only way I would've found out was through him. Cruikshank.' He blinked as if coming out of a dream. 'That son of a bitch. Why would he lie to me like that?'

Why indeed. 'But she did come to your opening?'

'Yeah. Showed up in this big baggy coat, floppy hat, blonde wig. Sunglasses. High heels, which she never wore.' Gina – Erin couldn't think of her as Mumsie at the moment, after seeing that sketch – had always said she was tall enough without high heels, and she preferred to be able to move.

Finn went on as if Erin were not there. 'I asked her what was with the disguise – it wasn't supposed to be a costume party. She pulled me into a corner and begged me in a whisper not to give her away. Said she couldn't be seen or there'd be hell to pay.'

'Is that all she said? She didn't explain why?'

'Not a word. Insisted she didn't want to get me involved. Like she was in danger.'

Erin digested this. It fit with Cruikshank's behavior to her this afternoon, but apart from that, it made no sense whatever. What danger could be associated with an art gallery? The worst occupational hazard was nailing your thumb with a hammer when hanging a frame.

'Do you know if anyone else recognized her?'

'Not as far as I could tell. I could see through her disguise because I have an artist's eye.' This was presented as fact, not a boast. 'But I doubt anyone else could have. The wig covered her hair, the hat and sunglasses hid most of her face, the coat disguised her figure, and the heels changed her gait. Not much left to recognize.'

'I would have known her.'

She didn't realize she'd spoken the words aloud until he answered. 'Yeah, I imagine you would. The eyes of love see all.'

She blinked back an incipient tear. 'And you never saw her again?'

He shook his head, his face a mask of sadness and regret. 'Never. Never had a clue what had happened to her, either.

Eventually, months or years later, somebody told me she'd been given up for dead.'

They sat for a moment in the comradeship of grief. The charged atmosphere of the earlier part of the conversation had dissipated completely. Erin was startled as if from a dream when Finn said, 'So, are you going to sit for me?'

His half-grin brought the magnetism back in force. 'I–I don't know. I only have this week to try to figure out what happened to my mother. Then I have to go back to work.'

'You don't work twenty-four/seven, do you?'

'No, but – with the drive down here and all . . .' She was grasping at excuses not to meet this man again and have to deal with the way he made her feel.

'I'll come to you. Just tell me when and where.'

Maybe on her home ground she'd feel safer. Or maybe she'd feel even more invaded. 'I'll think about it.'

He rummaged in a drawer and produced a business card from Raymond's, on the back of which he scribbled a number. 'Call me.' He thrust the card toward her like a challenge.

She took the card. Whether she would accept the challenge remained to be seen.

# ELEVEN

After her ordeal with Finn, Erin was too drained and emotionally shaken to attempt any more sleuthing that day. She drove home, poured a glass of red wine, and then lowered herself into a hot bath.

This day had turned her ideas about her mother's disappearance completely on their head. She'd gone from having no idea what could have lain behind it to feeling it must have had something, however tangentially, to do with Cruikshank and his two galleries. And she'd gone from viewing her mother as a happy, contented woman who'd been forced due to circumstances beyond her control to leave her beloved family, to wondering whether Gina had loved her husband at all and whether she'd been ready to grasp at any excuse to leave him.

But not to leave Erin. No amount of marital discontent could have led Gina to abandon her daughter, especially when Erin had Finn's word that Gina had refused an affair with a man she desired. Of course, one could never completely trust a man's perception that a woman wanted him – but the sketches certainly seemed to confirm it. Finn might deceive himself, his words might lie, but she didn't think his pencil would. He seemed to have too much artistic integrity for that.

Erin could not begin to process the idea that she was attracted to the same man her mother had been tempted by. It wasn't the age factor that bothered her – Finn could easily have been a decade younger than her mother and thus would be only a decade older than herself. It was the idea of sharing a man with her own mother. Even though Finn and Gina's relationship had never been consummated, and though Erin herself bore no blood ties to Finn, the whole situation reeked of incest. The very thought made her skin crawl.

And yet the memory of the way Finn had looked at her brought on quite a different reaction.

She plunged her head briefly under the water, attempting to

wash away those feelings. Finn had told her everything he knew about Gina's disappearance; she need never see him again. Surely this discombobulation would fade with time.

When she surfaced, her phone beeped to tell her – in case she'd fallen asleep in the bath, as if that were possible – that it was time to get out and get ready for her dinner with Alex. The thought of Alex brought a smile to her face. Alex, the safe and comfortable. Alex, the sunny and bright. It would be a relief to let him in on everything she'd gone through the last few days.

Out of sheer gratitude for his friendship, she put on the red dress she knew he loved on her and put some effort into styling her hair. She even added a touch of lip gloss at the hall mirror before heading out the door. Miss Silver mewed her approval. Perhaps Erin did resemble Gina somewhat after all.

She parked in the Front Street garage and walked the few blocks to Laíli – a name that always reminded her of Kaíli, the goddess Leo McKern's character worshiped in the Beatles' farce *Help!*. She and her mother had laughed till their sides ached watching that film, which Gina would put on whenever either of them was feeling down. The restaurant was not quite as cheering, but it did provide more solid nourishment.

Alex was waiting outside. A huge smile spread over his broad-cheekboned face when he saw her. Alex got his looks from his mother's Russian side of the family, with the height and fair coloring that harked back to medieval Scandinavian conquerors.

He enveloped her in a hug that would have been appropriate if they'd been separated for a month instead of four days. Although Alex hadn't known her father, he'd come to the funeral the previous Friday for moral support, for which Erin had been grateful. With only a few old friends of her father's in attendance – he had no extended family living – she would have been quite forlorn without Alex.

Now he held her by the shoulders at arm's length and looked her up and down. 'You look fantastic! It sounded on the phone like you were going through some tough stuff, but I sure wouldn't know it to look at you. That dress brings out the roses in your cheeks.'

She smiled. The dress also brought out a soupçon of cleavage, but there was no need to mention that.

'Our table's ready – I just wanted to be out here to greet you. Hungry?'

'Starved.' She hadn't thought about it till that moment, but the sandwich she'd had for lunch seemed eons away.

They chatted about work and neutral topics until they'd ordered and their food had arrived. Then Alex said, 'So. What's this "complicated" thing you were going to tell me about?'

She drew in a long breath. At the time they'd made this dinner date, the situation had been complex enough. Now it was so convoluted she didn't know where to begin. The Caterpillar's advice to begin at the beginning, go on to the end, and then stop was hardly useful when all you had was snippets here and there. And besides, what *was* the beginning? The dream that had sparked her investigation, or her mother's disappearance twenty years ago? Or some other turning point she hadn't even found out about yet? After this day's revelations, Erin felt there was no fact or viewpoint she could count on not to shift under her feet.

She decided to go with chronology as she had experienced it over the last few days. But that meant starting with the dream that she'd vowed to herself not to reveal, because the fact that she took it seriously made her sound like a nutcase.

This was Alex, though. Not only was she convinced it would be impossible to make him think less of her, but he was half Russian and had been raised Orthodox Christian – and therefore was more open to the mystical and inexplicable than anyone else she knew. She might be safe telling Alex.

But first she had to let him in on the biggest secret of her life.

'You know how I've always told you my mother died when I was twelve?'

'Yeah.' He touched her hand in sympathy. Alex was close to both his parents, who were still alive and still married to each other. He couldn't begin to imagine.

'That wasn't a lie, but it wasn't the whole truth, either. In fact, she disappeared when I was twelve. And I now have reason to believe she died a few months later.'

'Whoa.' Alex sat back in the booth, his hands on the edge of the table. 'That's kind of a lot to take in all at once.' His eyes revealed a depth of hurt she knew he would never express in words. 'Why did you never tell me she'd disappeared? That's, like, *big*. Like don't-keep-this-from-your-friends-cause-you'll-need-their-support big.'

'I know.' Erin stared at her lamb shank as if it could help her through this, but it remained silent. 'It was just so painful, and I was so used to dealing with it on my own. I didn't feel like I *could* tell anyone.' She looked back up at him. 'And anyway, where's that magic moment in a friendship when you know it's time to start sharing your darkest secrets? It's been more of a continuum with us. The right moment never seemed to come. Until now.'

He nodded slowly. 'OK. I can accept that.' He leaned forward again. 'Just take my sympathy as read and go on with your story.'

She nodded. 'It all started on my first night at Seafarer's Rest. I had this dream.' She braced herself to relive the nightmare. 'I dreamt that I saw my mother staying in the very same room I was in, only the decorations were different, as they would have been twenty years ago. I watched her getting ready for bed and going to sleep. And then—' She closed her eyes to gather strength, but the dream was waiting behind her eyelids. She popped them open again.

'A man came in through the window while she was asleep. I couldn't see him clearly – he was all in black with something over his face. He went up to the bed and . . . he smothered her.' She looked up at Alex, willing him to understand what the dream had meant to her. 'Alex, it was all so absolutely real. I'm convinced I was seeing what actually happened.'

He reached across the table and covered her shaking hands, stilling them with his calm strength. 'I can see that was a traumatic experience for you.' He hesitated, then, 'Did you do anything to confirm at least that she had stayed there?'

Erin nodded. 'First, just by accident, if you can call it that, I found an old earring of my mother's stuck in a tree on the inn property.'

Alex tipped his head to one side, his brow puckering slightly.

'And then I got the owner to let me look at the guest registers from that year, and I found her.'

Now his face brightened. The excitement of the chase was beginning to grab him. 'You actually found her name in the register?'

'Not her own name, but a name she might easily have used – Anne S. Blythe. And it was definitely in her handwriting. She had a very distinctive hand. She checked in on October fifth, 2001. And she never checked herself out.'

'You mean the space was blank? That could have been an oversight, surely?'

'It wasn't blank.' She took out her phone and found the photo of the register page. 'It was written by somebody else. Someone not associated with the inn.' She showed him the photo. 'See? It's a completely different hand.'

'Yeah, you're right. Those numbers – that's the way my mother writes her numbers. All Russians do. I mean, those educated in Russia.'

Erin nodded. 'I think I've seen other Eastern Europeans write them that way, too. And here's the clincher: the innkeeper remembered a man coming by that morning and saying that his wife had been taken ill in the night and he'd driven her to the hospital. So he checked her out and collected her stuff. She described the man, and it didn't sound like anyone my mother knew.'

Alex sat back in the booth and ran a hand over his dark-blond hair. 'That's quite a story.' He glanced at her and quickly amended. 'I don't mean a made-up story. I mean it's intriguing. I believe you that it's all significant.' He leaned forward and looked into her eyes. 'There is such a thing as a prophetic dream, you know. But they don't happen often. Most dreams are just mental garbage disposal, but a prophetic dream can come either from God or from the devil. You need to be very careful here.'

Erin was taken aback. She hadn't thought of this dream in terms of good or evil spirits. 'I think the dream came from my mother. I believe she's guiding me through this. She left clues for me while she was alive, and now she's helping me find them from beyond the grave.'

Alex's eyebrows rose. 'Now there's a theory. I'll have to talk to Father Seraphim about that one. I don't know whether the dead can send dreams and guide people or not.'

Erin waved his reservations aside. She was not limited by his Orthodox beliefs; in her universe, anything that clearly *had* happened *could* happen. 'Just listen to the rest of it. You'll see. There's way too much to all be coincidence.'

She went through the whole list of the discoveries she'd made and the conclusions she'd come to, including her failure to enlist Carver and her successful collaboration with Cat. She related her encounter with Cruikshank at the gallery. She told Alex everything – up to her meeting with Finn that afternoon. At that point, she became rather more economical with the truth. What Finn had said about the gallery opening, she passed on. But Finn's feelings toward Gina, her own feelings toward Finn, the proposition he'd made about painting her – none of that was necessary to the investigation. That was all on a need-to-know basis, and Alex did not need to know.

By the time she'd finished, they were sipping their after-dinner coffee and spooning up the last of their dessert. 'Wow,' Alex said when she finally paused for breath. 'You have had a busy few days.'

'And I have a busy week ahead of me. I need to use the rest of my break as productively as possible – once it's over, I won't have time to be gallivanting around the country chasing down clues.'

'True. Well, consider me your behind-the-scenes research team. I'll do whatever I can to help. I could probably manage some time off myself if I need to – I must have some PTO owing by now.'

True. Erin couldn't remember Alex taking a sick day, personal day, or vacation in the five years they'd been working together. 'I love my job,' he'd say when she asked him about it. 'Why should I take time off?' And yet he'd pushed her to take this vacation, although she loved the job as much as he did. Men. You could never expect them to be consistent.

'What's on the schedule for tomorrow?' he asked as he signed the bill. She'd offered to pay her half, but he waved her off.

'I'm not really sure. I need to check in with Cat, see if she has any ideas where to go next. She might be able to find out some background on a couple of people that could be helpful, too.'

'Keep me informed. And let me know what I can do. Yes?'

'Yes, I will.'

He walked her to her car, opened the door for her, and gave her another hug before she climbed in. 'Take care of yourself,

Erin.' He held her face in his hands for a moment. 'I mean it. All this was dangerous for your mother – it could still be dangerous for you.'

'I know. And I will.'

She started home, feeling as if she might be able to sleep peacefully now that she'd shared most of her burdens with a sympathetic but disinterested friend. She'd barely left downtown and turned onto Mission Street when her phone rang. She hit the Bluetooth button to answer it.

'Erin? Jackie here. From Tor House Lodge.'

'Oh, hello, Jackie. What can I do for you?'

'Ask rather what I can do for you.' He paused for dramatic effect. 'I found a second entry in the name of Una Call.'

# TWELVE

When Erin got home and looked at her phone, which she'd had turned off during dinner, she found three missed calls from Cat. She called her immediately, talking around the head of a Siamese who was quite put out at having been neglected all evening.

'Hey, sorry to be incommunicado. I was having dinner with a friend.'

'No problem. So did you find anything at Tor House Lodge?'

'I did indeed. And beyond.' Once again she related the events of her day – finding the invitation, her conversation with Cruikshank, tracking down Finn. But with Cat she was a little more open about the details of that last encounter.

'I think he was in love with my mother. Or at least in lust with her. And apparently she returned his feelings, though she refused to go to bed with him.'

Cat made a derisive noise. 'You trust a guy telling you a woman had the hots for him? And a painter, to boot? Sounds like he has an ego the size of one of his murals.'

'I don't know . . . He didn't really strike me that way. He didn't go on about his own genius or give me that guff about artists being above morality. He is genuinely talented, and he doesn't downplay that at all. And he doesn't seem super fond of people. But it's less about ego than . . . well, just being committed to his art. I think.'

Cat huffed. 'Sounds like he managed to charm you.'

Erin barked a laugh. '"Charm" is hardly in his repertoire. And yet there is something about him . . .' She could feel herself blushing and was glad Cat couldn't see. 'He wants to paint me – can you believe it? He says I owe it to him because he never got to paint my mother. He did a bunch of sketches, but I guess she disappeared before he could get down to the actual painting.'

'Forget that shit,' Cat said, her voice gruff. 'You have more important things to do with your time. Like finding your mother's killer.'

'I know, and I told him that. But he's willing to wait. He even offered to come up here for the sittings.'

'Huh.' Cat's monosyllable held a world of disdain. 'He didn't invite you to look at his etchings, by any chance?'

Since she'd actually been alone with the artist in his studio, this remark was nonsense, but she knew what Cat meant. However, admitting to Finn's teasing proposition and her own reaction to it was a bridge too far in this nascent friendship. 'Don't be silly. He wants to paint me. My face. Period.'

'Well, it is a face worth painting.' Cat cleared her throat. 'Just be careful, OK? This guy sounds dangerous to me. Not might-have-killed-your-mother dangerous, necessarily, but . . . hazardous to a woman's heart.' She paused. 'Like most men.'

Erin felt a burst of compassion for her new friend, wondering what could have happened to Cat to make her reach that conclusion. She herself didn't find men hazardous so much as alien, on the romantic level at least. But that was a conversation for another time.

'So, can you do a background check on Cruikshank for me tomorrow? I kind of doubt you'll find any criminal record, but my gut tells me there's something shady about that guy.'

'Sure thing,' Cat said. Erin thought she heard her mutter 'and Finnegan too' under her breath.

'Oh, and I almost forgot – Jackie from Tor House Lodge called me tonight, right before I called you. He found another entry for Una Call, an earlier one. So I'm heading back there tomorrow lunchtime. Different room – could be another breadcrumb.'

Cat's voice brightened. 'Great! I'll be standing by for your report. Maybe we can discuss progress in person this time? Over dinner, if I get off at a decent hour?'

'Sure. I'll call you when I get back to town.'

Erin spent most of Wednesday morning catching up on normal life – more cleaning, paying bills, doing laundry – and updating her notebook with everything she'd done and discovered the previous day. Once again, she timed her arrival at Tor House Lodge to coincide with the beginning of the lunch rush.

Jackie was waiting for her, his fleshy face alive with excitement. He pushed a printout across the desk to her and stage-whispered, 'Look – Una Call, room twelve, June nineteenth to twentieth, 2001.'

Erin stared at the printout in disbelief. 'But–but that was before she disappeared. She went missing on June twenty-first.'

'She wasn't away overnight just before that?'

Erin closed her eyes and leaned her brow on her hand, begging her mind to remember. The time immediately before her mother's disappearance had always been a blank to her. She must have known what was happening at the time, must have told Carver whatever she knew, but at this distance, the trauma of finding her mother gone overshadowed everything else in its vicinity.

She shook her head, defeated. 'I can't remember. But I'm sure Una Call is her – I found something in the other room she stayed in that led me straight to people who knew her.' Maybe Cat would be able to find something in the case files – something from her own or her father's statements at the initial police interview. 'Can I look at room twelve?'

'That you can, love. They checked out this morning.'

Room twelve was on the street-facing end of the inn, overlooking a rather ugly mansion on the opposite side of Scenic Drive. This room too was decorated in competing Arts & Crafts-style prints, but here the wardrobe had no decades-old stories to tell. The drawers and cubbyholes of the furniture were likewise devoid of any message from beyond the grave.

Erin finished her search and stood in the middle of the room, hands on hips, scanning the walls. 'Why did you bring me here, Mumsie? What's the point if you left nothing for me to find? I guess just the fact that you were here two nights before you left for good should tell me something. But I have no idea what.'

Her eyes fell on a couple of bookshelves above the desk. Perhaps if she rifled through all the books, something would fall out.

She began at one end of the lower shelf, picking up each book and shaking it upside down. A few random bookmarks fell out, but they all proved to be either receipts dated well outside the relevant time period, or innocuous brochures for local attractions, or actual cardstock bookmarks bearing the logos of bookstores.

None of them held scribbled messages. None of them made her thumbs tingle.

She started on the upper shelf. A few volumes in, she came to a hardcover whose dust jacket was yellowed and brittle with age. As she eased it from the shelf, her thumbs gave a faint anticipatory throb. Maybe this was the one.

She held the book in her hands, feeling its weight. She turned back the cover, peeled off the jacket, then paged through the whole volume, finding nothing. She turned the book upside down and shook it as she had done with the others, but no telltale slip of paper fell out. She peered into the space between the sewn binding and the spine, again employing her flashlight. But the shaft was innocent of any intruder save a dead gnat.

Yet she was certain this object held some clue. She restored the jacket and closed the book, holding it in both hands. As a physical object, this volume could tell her nothing. But perhaps the point was in the content of the book rather than its form.

She looked properly at the cover for the first time. *Shakespeare and Company*, by Sylvia Beach, with an illustration of people in 1920s clothing walking past the distinctive turquoise front of the famous English-language bookstore in Paris.

Her thumbs throbbed as if to say, *This is it, dummy! It's right in front of you!* Yet still she puzzled. She'd heard of Shakespeare and Company and its founder, the author of this book. In fact, she'd probably heard of them from her mother, though she couldn't specifically remember doing so. But Gina had carried a running list in her head of bookstores she wanted to visit someday, and Shakespeare and Company must have been at the top of the list.

Was it possible her mother had gone to Paris? Could one have flown out of the country in the summer of 2001 without leaving a trail the police would almost be obliged to follow, even in an investigation as lackadaisical as Carver's had been? She couldn't be certain, but she believed ID had been required to fly internationally even before 9/11. No false names allowed.

Something – possibly her thumbs, rolling their eyes impatiently – told her she was on the wrong tack. She set the book down on the desk and Googled first 'Shakespeare and Company,' then 'Sylvia Beach.'

Immediately a listing came up that made a whole handbell choir ring in her mind. The Sylvia Beach Hotel.

Now she remembered. Gina had told her about the unique small hotel in Newport, Oregon, where all the rooms were named for authors and decorated to reflect their eras and interests. She and Gina had talked about going there together now that Erin was old enough – the hotel did not allow young children. Neither did it have a single television – but it did have an extensive library where guests could lounge at their leisure.

If Gina had felt the need to escape, the Sylvia Beach Hotel would certainly have been a place she might have chosen to escape to. Seven hundred miles from home, obscure enough to be known only to book lovers, and a congenial retreat where she could pass her exile in spiritual as well as physical comfort.

That settled it. The Sylvia Beach Hotel would be Erin's next stop.

It was too late in the day to begin such a long trip, and anyway, she would need to make some preparations. After thanking Jackie once again for his help – and obtaining his permission to take the book away with her as evidence – she drove back to Santa Cruz and called Cat.

'Can you talk?'

Cat spoke in an undertone. 'Yeah, give me a sec to duck outside. You go ahead.'

'It turns out my mother stayed at Tor House Lodge a couple of nights *before* she went missing.'

Cat whistled. 'That's a twist. Can you account for it at all?'

'No, and it's driving me crazy. I can't remember much of anything from around that time – it's all a fog of confusion, anxiety, and pain.'

'Yeah, I know what that's like.'

'So I was wondering if you could maybe check the case files – see if my father or I mentioned anything about it to Carver at the time.'

'Sure, I can do that.' Erin heard noises suggestive of Cat fumbling for her notebook and pen. 'Just a sec.' Presumably Cat had to put the phone down to jot herself a reminder. 'Got it. Anything else?'

'Yes. I found something that makes me think she may have gone to Oregon.'

'Oh, yeah? What was that?'

Erin hesitated. Cat had traveled with her thus far on this strange journey, but would she be able to swallow messages Erin had received from her thumbs? Oh, well, she could but try.

'It's a book. I was looking through all the books in the room, in case there was a note or something in one of them, and I just got . . . a feeling when I came to this one. The author is Sylvia Beach, and my mother and I always talked about going to stay at the Sylvia Beach Hotel in Newport.'

Cat was silent a moment. 'That seems like kind of a stretch.'

'I know, but I'm sure it's right. I can't explain – I just feel intuitively when I'm onto one of these breadcrumbs. I know in my bones' – that sounded a little more credible than *thumbs* – 'that's where she went when she first disappeared.'

She could almost hear Cat shrug. 'It's your investigation. Anything you need from me besides the records search?'

'Not at the moment. Did you find out anything about Cruikshank?'

'Yes and no. He's never been arrested, but his name has come up in a couple of investigations into art fraud. Like a forged painting was hung for sale in his shop, but he claimed to believe it was genuine, and nothing could be proved against him. And there was a complaint once that he'd bought a painting by some prestigious artist for a pittance from someone who didn't know what they had – then he sold it on for tens of thousands.' Cat made a disgusted noise. 'It was clear he'd really done that. But unfortunately, it's not illegal. *Caveat emptor* and all that. Or, in this case, *seller emptor*, whatever that is in Latin.'

'I think it would be *caveat seller*, but I don't know either. *Caveat vendor*, maybe. Anyway, I can't say I'm too surprised to hear that. Even as a child I thought he was creepy, and my mother didn't much care for him, either.'

'But she still worked for him? Did she need the money?'

'I'm sure she had her reasons – she loved being around art and artists, for one thing. I don't think it was a question of money. My father made a good living as an airline pilot, and my mother had an inheritance socked away that she never touched. Come to think of it, that must have been how she paid for all these upscale hotels and whatnot. She wasn't exactly going for Motel 6.'

'Want me to pursue the money angle at all?' Cat said. 'I'd think Carver must have at least tried to follow her financial trail. Bank withdrawals, that sort of thing. Looks like she used cash to avoid being traced through a credit card, but she had to get the cash somewhere.'

'Yeah, that's an interesting point. Do look into that, please.'

'Right. I'll check on all this stuff and report back tonight. Things are quiet, so I should be able to get away at a decent hour.'

Erin had forgotten about their dinner plans. 'Oh, shoot. Listen, Cat, I've got a lot to do tonight to get ready to drive to Oregon tomorrow. I need to make reservations, pack, check in with work, find someone to feed my cat – oh, and my car's overdue for an oil change. Can I give you a raincheck?'

'You have a cat? I love cats. My blasted landlord won't let me have one. I'd be happy to feed it for you.'

'Well . . .' Would Alex be offended at not being asked again to care for Miss Silver? Would Miss Silver accept a carer other than Alex? Too bad for both of them. After backing out on dinner, Erin didn't feel she could deny Cat this small compensation. 'All right, thanks.'

'I'll pop by after work and you can introduce us, show me where the food is, give me a key. Won't take five minutes.'

'OK. See you then.'

# THIRTEEN

The first order of business was to attempt to reserve a room at the Sylvia Beach Hotel. Erin knew this was a long shot – the rooms tended to book up well ahead – and she could always stay somewhere nearby if it didn't work out; but staying in the hotel would give her a much better opportunity to find out about her mother's time there than would simply inquiring at the desk.

The hotel did not take online reservations, so Erin called directly. 'I know this is fantastically unlikely, but is there any chance you might have a room available for tomorrow night? Or any night this week?'

'Well, aren't you the lucky one!' the receptionist responded. 'I call this positively providential. We have just this minute had a cancellation for the Virginia Woolf room for Thursday through Saturday. Will that suit you?'

'Admirably.' She gave the woman her contact info and credit card number. 'I'll be driving up from California, so I may get in quite late. Is that all right?'

'No problem, dear. We'll be sure to have someone here to greet you. It won't be past midnight, will it?'

'Oh, no. Maybe ten at the latest.' Erin had already done her calculations. If she took the fast but boring route up I-5, she could be there in eleven hours, not allowing for traffic or stops. Traffic could add an hour or more on a weekday morning, stops maybe two hours. She'd leave at six just to be on the safe side.

Her reservation taken care of, Erin called her mechanic, Jorge. Yes, he could squeeze her in that afternoon. She dropped the car off, and Jorge himself drove her home, for which she rewarded him with her best smile.

She made a quick list and whipped through her packing, thanking the gods of small things that she'd had the foresight to do laundry that morning. She had to remove Miss Silver from her suitcase only three times before the cat stalked off in indignation to groom herself on the windowsill. By the time Erin had assembled everything and was ready to load the car, Jorge was at her door.

'Special delivery!' he said, beaming up at her with a toothy smile. She was several inches taller than he. She took the keys he held out to her and started to move toward the driveway, but he held up a palm. 'No need to drive me back – Manuel came with me.' He pointed to a classic Mustang parked in front of her house. 'I know you're in a hurry getting ready for your trip. You can pay me when you get back.'

'Thanks, Jorge. You're a star.' She made a mental note to give him an extra tip when she paid the bill.

She was carrying the last load to the car when Cat's Jeep pulled up. The detective emerged from her vehicle with a plastic takeout bag in one hand. She lifted it with a sheepish smile. 'I brought dinner. Figured you had to eat, even if you can't take time to go out.'

True enough. She hadn't wanted to avoid Cat's company, only the risk of getting to bed too late to be fresh for an early start the next day. 'Thanks, Cat. That's great.' She locked the car and led the way to the front door. 'Come on in.'

Cat set the bags down on the kitchen table. 'I don't know much about your tastes yet, so I went to the taqueria. I hope that's OK.'

'Perfect. I haven't eaten since morning, so I'm starved. Hope you got plenty.'

'Jumbo chicken burrito do you? And I asked for extra chips and guac.'

Erin poured white wine for them both. Wine wasn't the best fit with Mexican food, but she didn't care for beer and didn't have any in the house. Cat didn't seem to mind.

Miss Silver chose this moment to make her appearance, no doubt lured by the smell of food. She slinked up to Cat's chair and took a preliminary sniff. Miss Silver was not averse to strangers, but they did have to pass her smell test.

Cat turned at the touch of a damp nose on her hand. 'Oh, you beauty!' To Erin she said, 'Will she let me pick her up?'

'You'll have to ask her. But she's quite susceptible to flattery, so I'd say your chances are good.'

Cat scratched Miss Silver's head. The Siamese waited a

moment, then jumped onto her lap. 'I guess the answer is yes,' Cat said with a grin.

The two Cats indulged in a brief lovefest before the human one said, 'Why do you call her Miss Silver? Just because she's a silver point female?'

Erin raised an eyebrow. 'I'm a bit more creative than that. I named her after Patricia Wentworth's detective.'

Cat looked blank.

'British Golden Age mystery writer? No?'

Cat shook her head. 'I'm more into American noir.'

'Well, Miss Silver is a retired governess turned private detective. She's a Victorian holdover who goes nowhere without her knitting bag, but she's amazingly astute. Her young police sergeant friend, Frank Abbott, says that to her, the human race is glass-fronted.' Erin smiled at her pet, who was now calmly bathing herself on Cat's lap. 'And I've always thought my Miss Silver was just the same. She seems to know exactly what I'm thinking, and she has no trouble distinguishing between friends and potential foes.'

'Maybe you should take her with you when you're out sleuthing. She might be able to spot the bad guy before you do.'

'I'm sure she would. Unfortunately, she detests car rides. She always suspects there will be a vet visit at the end of the line.' Erin unwrapped her burrito. 'Speaking of bad guys, did you get any information for me?'

Cat nodded around a bite of burrito and pulled her notebook from her back pocket. The maneuver disturbed Miss Silver, who leapt off her lap with a glare.

'I checked the files like you asked. In your father's initial interview with Carver, he did mention she'd been gone overnight a couple days before she went missing. Said she'd been visiting a college friend who was going through a rough time – didn't say who or where.'

'So either he was lying – but why would he, if he wanted her found? – or she gave him that cover story because she didn't want him to know why she was going to Carmel.' Erin pondered as she chewed. Could Gina have gone to visit Finn? And gotten a hotel room so she wouldn't be tempted to stay over with him? She could ask Finn if he remembered seeing her at that specific time, but she doubted he paid much attention to trivia like times and dates. Although he might remember the last time he'd seen Gina before she vanished for a period of months.

Erin glanced at Cat to see her staring at her. 'Any thoughts you'd like to share with the class?' Cat asked.

'Oh, sorry. I was just wondering if my mother might have seen Finn – Finnegan – on that trip. I'll have to ask him about it when I get back.'

'Or I could interview him while you're gone.'

Erin grimaced. 'Something tells me he'd be unlikely to cooperate with the police.'

Cat shrugged. 'Whatever. Doesn't sound crucial. About the money trail – I found something there as well.'

'You did?'

'It seems Gina withdrew several large sums from a savings account over a period of a couple of weeks. An account that was only in her name. She cleaned it out.'

Erin stared. 'But why didn't Carver tell us? Why didn't he do anything with that information?'

Cat spoke hesitantly. 'It looks like he did tell your dad. And to your second point, my guess is, because it suggests she left voluntarily. And in a case like that, we cops have nothing to do. There's no law against a woman leaving her husband. Or even her child, as long as the child is cared for.'

Even though she'd already concluded her mother must have left home of her own volition, Erin was momentarily stunned at being confronted with the reality. Her mother had left her – her beloved daughter, center of her universe – of her own accord.

But then she reminded herself of the other thing she knew in the deepest part of her heart: Gina would only have done that if Erin's welfare – her life, even – had been at stake. Erin had to figure out exactly what those stakes had been.

Cat had just said good night when Alex called. 'How's the investigation going?'

'Moving along. In fact, I was going to call you – I found another breadcrumb. This one leads to Oregon. And I'm going to follow it there.' She told him about finding the book.

He whistled. 'So you're driving to Oregon because you found a book?'

'Because of what the book means, yeah. I have to – it's the only clue I haven't followed up.'

'It'll have to be a pretty quick trip – aren't you due back at work on Monday?'

'I was, but I called in and got my leave extended another week. I have plenty of hours saved up. And what am I ever going to do that's more important than this?'

'Yeah, I see your point. So I guess that means I'll be having more quality time with Maudie?'

Maud was the fictional Miss Silver's first name, and Maudie was Frank Abbott's irreverent nickname for her. 'Actually – I hope you don't mind, but my police helper, Cat, offered to feed her before I asked. She seemed so eager I didn't like to say no.'

'Oh.' Alex's monosyllable sounded a bit forlorn. 'Oh, well. I guess I could still stop in and say hello, right? If I promise not to overfeed her majesty?'

'I'm sure she'd appreciate the company.'

Alex was silent a moment, and Erin had time to wonder what was going through his mind. If only Miss Silver could tell her, since the cat undoubtedly knew. 'You will keep me posted, won't you?' he said finally, his tone wistful. 'I'd love to come along, but it would mean leaving the library awfully shorthanded, and on short notice, too.'

Erin had a moment of hypothetical panic. Company on this trip was the last thing she wanted. 'Not to mention the hotel only has the one room open.'

He cleared his throat. 'Yeah. There is that.'

'Don't worry,' she reassured him. 'I'll be fine on my own. And I'll be back soon. Maybe as early as Saturday, if nothing pans out.'

'Right. God be with you, m— Erin.'

She wondered what he had been about to say.

Erin set off at six the next morning only to find she'd miscalculated about the traffic. Silicon Valley commuters already zoomed in impatient droves over the steep and treacherous Highway 17 from Santa Cruz to San Jose, like a herd of metal antelope pursued by cheetahs – only instead of cooperating as a real herd would do, here each animal was out for itself. And that was only the beginning – for three hours, all the way to the far northeastern side of the San Francisco Bay, she alternately raced to keep ahead of the predator cars and crawled from mile to mile when the herd got too impacted to run.

At Vacaville, where the traffic finally dispersed, she stopped for gas and breakfast. She supposed there must be an actual town somewhere nearby, with homes and churches and parks and schools, not to mention pedestrians; but the portion of Vacaville that was visible from the freeway seemed to exist only to serve the traffic that flowed along it. Restaurants, gas stations, and shopping centers lined the parallel streets on either side.

A few miles past her pit stop, Erin emerged onto I-5 North. The long stretch of straight, flat, tractor-trailer-dominated highway that ran from Dunnigan to Redding constituted the most tedious driving she had ever experienced. She perked up when the Central Valley gave way to the Shasta foothills, and the road began to climb and wind through forested slopes, affording occasional tantalizing glimpses of the many branching fingers of Lake Shasta and eventually of Mount Shasta itself. She stopped in the town of Shasta for lunch so that she could feast her eyes on the mountain's majestic and self-sufficient beauty without the distraction of driving.

This place represented another item on the list of adventures she and her mother had planned but had never accomplished: renting a houseboat on Lake Shasta for summer vacation. It would have been just the two of them, of course; Father never got enough consecutive time off for such a stay. They'd talked in the spring of 2001 about doing it that summer, but when the school term finally ended, Gina had put Erin off, saying she had things she had to take care of at home first. Had she been planning her exodus even then? Or had she begun to be caught up in whatever it was that eventually forced her to flee?

Erin tore herself away with reluctance and continued her journey, down from the Shasta foothills onto the dry plain that lay between them and the Siskiyous at the Oregon border, then up once more into breathtaking mountain beauty that she could not fully enjoy while navigating the car. In Eugene, when the landscape had become flat and unremarkable again, she stopped for dinner before turning off I-5 to head toward the coast.

At around nine o'clock, having gotten slightly lost in the winding country roads that led over a final range of mountains from Albany to Newport, Erin finally pulled into the tiny parking strip of the Sylvia Beach Hotel. From the entrance, the long, narrow blue-shingled building hardly looked large enough to contain all the rooms advertised on the website. But she was far too tired to explore the hotel tonight. She unloaded her bags, checked in, found her room, and fell into bed. Tomorrow would be plenty of time to journey into the past.

# FOURTEEN

Erin slept late, for her, awaking just in time to dress and catch the tail end of the breakfast hour in the dining room downstairs, which afforded a panoramic view of the ocean and beach with a lighthouse beckoning from a far point. Inside, an impressive buffet of fruits and pastries was supplemented by the entrée of the day, which this morning was a cheese soufflé topped with berries and cream. She hadn't eaten so well in ages. She could almost wish she were here for a simple vacation instead of a mission to solve the great mystery of her life.

After breakfast, she explored the hotel. Since she had plenty of time, she'd decided to see what she could find out on her own before directly approaching the management about their guest records from 2001.

The Sylvia Beach Hotel was long and narrow, rising four stories from a hillside that climbed up from the beach. The lowest floor, built partly into the hill, held only the dining room and offices. The entrance was on the first floor and boasted a gift shop in addition to the reception desk. Several guest rooms, including her own Virginia Woolf room, lined a hallway stretching back toward the street.

A broad staircase led to the second floor, which contained only guest rooms, and a narrower one ascended to the third floor, home to more guest rooms as well as the famous library. Most of these rooms shared the same beach view as the dining room. A few guests had departed early, and a staff member encouraged Erin to peek into any of the empty rooms.

She did not merely peek but explored, not only searching for breadcrumbs but alert to the telltale tingling in her thumbs. In the spacious Mark Twain and Agatha Christie rooms, in the Shakespeare, Steinbeck, Jane Austen, and Emily Dickinson rooms, she found nothing suggestive and felt only the same mild awakening that had been with her since she checked in. It was not until she returned to her own room that her thumbs truly came alive.

Had her mother stayed right here, after all? She might easily have chosen it; she loved Virginia Woolf's work, especially her paean to feminine independence, *A Room of One's Own*. Erin couldn't be certain whether this room was modeled at all on Woolf's study, but it seemed unlikely, since most of the space here was occupied by a queen-size bed. She wasn't even sure if the colors of the room – terracotta walls, mustard ceiling, cornflower bedding and upholstery – were authentic to the Bloomsbury aesthetic. But that was not her primary concern.

She made a slow circuit of the room, waiting for the tingling in her thumbs to escalate into a throb. When she reached the nightstand, she felt an increase in intensity, so she sat on the bed and opened the drawer.

Inside was a Gideon Bible. Surprised to find this relic of a bygone age, Erin picked it up and riffled the pages, thinking her mother might have left a note inserted there. She found no note, but some flashes of yellow highlighter caught her eye.

> Luke 21:21: 'Then let them which are in Judaea flee to the mountains; and let them which are in the midst of it depart out; and let not them that are in the countries enter thereinto.'
>
> Proverbs 6:16–19: These six things doth the Lord hate: yea, seven are an abomination unto him:
>
> A proud look, a lying tongue, and hands that shed innocent blood,
>
> An heart that deviseth wicked imaginations, feet that be swift in running to mischief,
>
> A false witness that speaketh lies, and he that soweth discord among brethren.
>
> Psalm 125:5: As for such as turn aside unto their crooked ways, the Lord shall lead them forth with the workers of iniquity: but peace shall be upon Israel.
>
> 1 Samuel 13:6: When the men of Israel saw that they were in a strait, (for the people were distressed,) then the people did hide themselves in caves, and in thickets, and in rocks, and in high places, and in pits.

Taken in the proper sequence, these all seemed to make sense with what had happened to Gina: some dire situation had forced her to flee and hide herself. That flight was in some way caused by someone's deceit – which could ultimately lead to the shedding of innocent blood. And the mention of 'crooked ways' – could Gina have been referring obliquely to Cruikshank? She had been known to play on his name, calling him 'Crooked Leg' or reciting the nursery rhyme:

*There was a crooked man, and he walked a crooked mile,*
*He found a crooked sixpence against a crooked stile;*
*He bought a crooked cat which caught a crooked mouse,*
*And they all lived together in a little crooked house.*

All very suggestive, but it didn't take her much further than she had already come. However, she did feel justified in taking these highlights as confirmation of her hunch that Gina had been here.

Now she only needed to confirm it with a name in a register.

As she walked the short distance to the reception desk, she entertained herself with wondering what sort of name her mother might have chosen to use in this place. Something suggestive of Virginia Woolf or her Bloomsbury set, perhaps, but not too obvious since she was dealing with well-read people here.

The desk was staffed by the same woman who had checked her in the night before – a matronly type wearing a hand-knitted shawl around her neck, which the constant cool breezes of the Oregon Coast would make comfortable even in late June. Knit Lady paused in her current knitting and smiled a greeting. 'I hope everything is satisfactory so far?'

'Oh, yes, completely. But I have a favor to ask of you.' In this bookish atmosphere, Erin felt she was among friends; the personal approach would be the best. 'My mother disappeared twenty years ago, and I'm looking into her movements after she left the Santa Cruz area.' Knit Lady's sympathetic expression encouraged Erin to go on. 'I have reason to believe she stayed here – possibly in the same room I'm in. Is there any way you could check on that for me?'

'Hmm,' Knit Lady said. 'I suppose I could look in our old registers. Normally we wouldn't disclose that kind of information, but since she was your mother, and it was so long ago . . . What was her name?'

'Her real name was Gina Washington, but I don't think she'd have used it. She was on the run from someone or something, I believe, so she would have used a false name. She loved books and wordplay, so I'm guessing it might have been something suggestive of Virginia Woolf or one of her set.'

Knit Lady's eyebrows went up and a smile touched her lips. 'She sounds like an interesting person, your mother. This could be fun.' She turned to a bank of file drawers behind her and pulled one out. 'We're looking at 2001, yes? First or second half?'

'Second. Probably late June.'

Knit Lady extracted a hefty volume and set it on the desk. 'Let's see . . . Shall we start with June fifteenth, or . . .?'

'Let's start with June twenty-first.' Gina might have driven directly here upon leaving home.

'All right. Let's see . . . These all look pretty normal . . . Ooh, how about this: *Georgia Galloway*. Georgia could be a play on Virginia – they're both states, you know – and Galloway is just one letter off from Dalloway, the protagonist of one of Woolf's novels.'

That sounded promising. 'May I see the handwriting?'

'Just a moment.' Knit Lady pulled out two sheets of notepaper and laid them over the top and bottom of the page so that only the one name was showing. Then she turned the book to face Erin.

Erin's heart gave a leap. 'Yes, that's her handwriting. I'd know that Y anywhere. And she stayed in the Virginia Woolf room?'

'That's right.' Knit Lady pointed to the letters 'VW' in the *Room* column. 'Checked in June twenty-first and stayed three nights.'

'Oh, that's wonderful! Thank you so much.' Erin beamed at her.

Knit Lady closed the register and moved to put it away. 'Is there anything else I can help you with, dear?'

Erin gave a little laugh. 'Only if you happen to know where she went when she left here.'

'Oh, we don't keep records like that.' Knit Lady's expression grew thoughtful. 'Although . . . you could ask Geraldine. She's been here forever, and she's got a memory like a steel trap. She likes to chat with the guests, too. She might remember this Georgia Galloway.'

'Where can I find Geraldine?'

Knit Lady pointed to Erin's left. 'Normally you'd find her right over there in the gift shop. She's there ten to three, every day except Friday all through the year.'

Erin frowned in disappointment. 'You don't know where I could reach her today?'

Knit Lady shook her head firmly. 'She has a strict policy – her day off is her day off. No business remotely associated with Sylvia Beach Hotel.'

Erin sighed. 'I guess I'll have to catch her tomorrow, then. I'm here through Sunday anyway.' She ran her eyes over a rack of brochures advertising local attractions that stood at one side of the desk. 'Anything you'd particularly recommend to do around here?'

'That depends on what you like. There's a lovely beach, as you know, where you can walk, or wade, or sit with a good book. There are several bookstores in town, in case our library doesn't supply what you want. There's an aquarium, though that's likely to be pretty crowded with families. And lots of people enjoy the lighthouse up at Yaquina Head. Tallest lighthouse on the Oregon Coast, and you can climb all the way to the top. They do a living history presentation too. It's pretty interesting if you like that kind of thing.'

'All right, thanks.' Gina would have been drawn to the lighthouse like a moth to flame. Erin pulled the relevant brochure from the rack and set off.

The Yaquina Head Lighthouse was about four miles north of the hotel, at the end of a spit of land that flipped out into the ocean like a ruffle on a skirt. Erin parked and went into the visitor's center, which didn't greatly interest her but did provide an opportunity to sign up for a tour beginning in fifteen minutes. She spent the intervening time gazing out to sea and down to the beach below, which was not so much beach as low, rounded masses of rock with intervening tidepools. Gina had probably explored the tidepools, but one couldn't very well leave a breadcrumb in that environment that would endure for twenty years.

When the tour time came, Erin took her place in a line of people filing into the lighthouse itself. They were greeted at the door by a young man in an old-fashioned keeper's uniform of navy peacoat and peaked cap. His thick brown beard completed the authentic impression. 'Welcome to Yaquina Head,' he said to each party as they entered. 'I'm Keeper Wilson. Watch your step on the threshold and enter the room to your right, please.'

When they were all assembled, Keeper Wilson went into a spiel about the keeper's life and how the old oil-burning light was kept, staying in character and asking the audience to guess things like how many gallons of oil were contained in each of the barrels stacked against the wall. The audience wasn't terribly responsive, so Erin provided answers or guesses whenever she could. Keeper Wilson seemed grateful to have someone participate.

After the presentation, he led those who were willing and able up the iron staircase that circled the inside perimeter of the ninety-three-foot-tall tower. Halfway up the 114 steps, Erin wondered what on earth she'd let herself in for, but turning back was out of the question given all the people climbing behind her, so she persevered. And she had to admit the view from the top balcony that rimmed the lens room was worth the climb.

She could see for miles over land and sea. Something erupted from the water a few hundred yards out, and a young boy next to her yelled, 'Look, Dad! It's a whale! And there's another one!'

Erin squinted and could just make out a huge gray shape amid the spume. Her mother would have been thrilled. They'd seen whales at closer range in the Monterey Bay at home, but they never tired of the spectacle of the enormous, graceful beasts cavorting in the water, seemingly showing off for the humans' pleasure.

Erin had no reason to expect to find any specific breadcrumbs here, but nevertheless she could feel her mother's presence more strongly than ever as she laughed in delight at the whales' antics, then, when they tired and plunged underwater, turned inside to learn about the workings of the fascinatingly complex Fresnel lens. Gina was still with her, encouraging her, as she descended the stairs, which had somehow become steeper in the descent, threatening her with vertigo. Erin had to keep her focus forward and feel for each step with her foot in order to avoid succumbing. *Thanks, Mumsie*, she thought as she reached the bottom.

*That's my brave girl*, her mother's imagined voice replied.

Reluctant to leave this place lest the presence remain behind, Erin descended the steep walkway to the beach and explored the tidepools until her stomach reminded her it was well past time for lunch. She climbed back to the parking lot and stood by her car, sweeping her gaze across the panoramic view. 'I'm coming, Mumsie,' she whispered. 'I'll find you soon.'

The next morning, Saturday, Erin timed her breakfast to end exactly at ten o'clock and sped upstairs to the gift shop. Occupying a corner of the lobby rather than a separate room, the shop held an attractive if cluttered arrangement of mugs, blank books, notepads, and knickknacks in a mix of beachy and literary themes. But she had not come here to browse.

She found the checkout counter, but it was devoid of staffers. To the right, rearranging a rack of literary card games with her back to Erin, was a tiny woman with short, brilliant-orange hair, clad in a flowing dress that seemed to want to give equal time to every shade of green known to nature or chemistry.

'Geraldine?' Erin queried tentatively.

'Yes?' The tiny woman answered without turning, placing one last game in the rack. She stood back as if to admire her work, gave a brisk nod, and turned to face Erin. 'How can I help?'

'I'd like to ask you some questions, if I may. I'm told you have an excellent memory.'

Geraldine threw back her head and laughed. The deep lines on her face and neck confirmed what Erin was already sure of – her hair color couldn't be natural. Whether the hair itself was natural, Erin neither knew nor cared.

'Just call me Celeste,' Geraldine said. 'You know, Babar's wife? Memory like an elephant.'

Erin smiled. 'Those were some of my favorite stories growing up.'

Geraldine moved behind the counter and hopped onto a high stool. 'So. What would you like me to remember?'

'I have reason to believe my mother stayed here for a few days twenty years ago. I think she was going by the name Georgia

Galloway. Here's her picture.' Erin retrieved the precious photo from her notebook. 'Do you remember her at all?'

Geraldine took the photo and gave a little gasp. 'Oh my, yes. Georgia Galloway. I haven't thought of her in years, but that's her to the life.' She peered up at Erin. 'For that matter, *you're* her to the life. Or pretty nearly. Maybe a little taller. And a little – forgive me – more subdued?'

Erin blinked away a tear at Geraldine's insight. 'That's because I never saw my mother again after she left home to come here.'

Geraldine sucked in a sharp breath. 'I was afraid something might have happened to her. The way she spoke of you – she loved you so deeply, but she talked as if she never expected to see you again.' She shook her head. 'What a tragedy. What did happen to her? Do you know?'

'Not precisely. That's what I'm trying to find out. Did she by chance tell you anything about why she left home?'

'No, she wouldn't talk about that. I thought it must be something to do with her husband – but then why wouldn't she have taken you with her? I never could work that one out.'

Erin shook her head. 'I don't think she was very happy with my father, but I'm pretty sure he wasn't the reason she left. I think it may have had something to do with her work. She may have caught her boss doing something shady.'

'I see.' Geraldine nodded sagely. 'It sounds like you know more about that than I do, then. I'm sorry I couldn't be more help.'

'There is one more thing. Do you have any idea where she might have gone when she left here?'

The older woman scrunched up her eyes in thought. 'Now that's an interesting question. She didn't tell me her plans, but she did ask a lot of questions about other towns up the coast from here. I think she was looking for a quieter spot than Newport – and cheaper – where she could stay for a while.'

'Can you suggest what some of those towns might be?'

'I can do you one better.' She turned and pulled a folded map from a rack behind her. 'This shows the whole coast with information about every town that has any tourist draw whatsoever. Maybe you'll be able to figure out what would have appealed to her.'

Erin took the map eagerly and reached for her wallet. 'What do I owe you?'

Geraldine waved a dismissive hand. 'On the house. Anything I can do for Georgia's daughter. She was so sweet – she really touched my heart.' She paused as if remembering, then asked suddenly, 'You said she was *going by* the name Georgia Galloway. What was her real name?'

'Gina Washington. And I'm Erin.'

Geraldine stretched a tiny gnarled hand across the counter. 'Pleased to meet you, Erin Washington. And I wish you all the best with your search.'

# FIFTEEN

Erin took the map of the coast to her room and studied it. She could rule out some towns as being too big and busy, others because they had no beach access – she was sure that would have been a deal-breaker for Gina. She was left with a small selection but with no way to choose among them except eeny-meeny-miny-moe. Or she could drive up Highway 101 and stop when she began to feel her mother's presence.

She set the map aside and went back to her notebook, in which she'd recorded her findings and thoughts of the last two days, including the verses that had been highlighted in the Bible she'd found. The one from First Samuel gave her pause. It talked about people hiding 'in caves, and in thickets, and in rocks, and in high places, and in pits.' Ruling out any option that would require her mother to sleep rough, what clue could this list hold?

She turned to the map again, and the name Rockaway Beach jumped out at her. A small town of no great tourist pretensions about two hours up 101. 'In rocks' – Rockaway Beach. Tenuous to say the least, but it could be worth checking out. After all, it was the only clue she had.

She took out her computer and navigated first to Airbnb, then to a site that listed coastal rentals specifically. She could find no vacancies in Rockaway Beach for tonight – hardly surprising for a weekend in summer. But she did find one hotel room that was open for a few days beginning on Sunday. She could complete her reserved stay here and head north in the morning. Another delicious dinner and breakfast in the hotel's Table of Contents restaurant would be welcome fortification for whatever lay ahead.

Meanwhile, both Alex and Cat had been texting her several times a day asking for updates, and she had given them nothing. She called Alex's number first. When he answered, to her surprise she heard meowing and female laughter in the background.

'Where are you?' she blurted without stopping to think. He

might be on a date for all she knew. With some woman who had a cat. Miss Silver would be jealous if she found out.

'Your place,' he said, his voice light with amusement.

'What the heck is going on? Are you having a party there?'

'Just a little one. I came by to love on Maudie a bit, and your friend Cat – the human one – was here feeding her. We've all been getting to know each other.'

'You mean Maudie is playing you off against each other, trying to wheedle extra treats out of you.'

'Well, some of that, yeah. And also we humans are talking about you behind your back.'

Erin bristled in spite of herself. 'What are you saying about me?'

'Only good things, I promise. Total Erin lovefest going on over here. We know Maudie would be sure to report back to you if we said anything nasty.'

Erin chuckled at the thought of Miss Silver as spy. She'd have to rename her Cata Hari. 'I guess it's just as well you're together. Put me on speaker and I can give you both my progress report at once.'

'Will do. Barring interference from Maudie, of course.' A moment's pause, then, 'OK, you're on speaker. Proceed at will.'

'Hi, Erin!' Cat's voice called.

'Hi, Cat,' Erin responded, and Miss Silver chimed in with her own greeting. She evidently thought Erin had been talking to her – Erin did sometimes address her pet unceremoniously as 'Cat,' especially when she was annoyed.

When Miss Silver calmed down, Erin told them all about finding the name Georgia Galloway – the significance of which she had to explain – and the highlighted verses. Then she related her conversation with Geraldine and her decision to check out Rockaway Beach.

'That all sounds a little flimsy,' Cat said. 'Are you sure this is worth your while?'

'I'm not absolutely sure about anything, but what else am I going to do? This is the only thing resembling a lead I have at this point.'

'But how are you going to track Gina in Rockaway Beach? A place like that, full of transients all summer long – nobody's going to remember one woman who passed through twenty years ago. Especially if you have no name to give and no specific lodging to try.'

Erin sighed. 'I know. All I have is my intuition. Maybe it'll work like a very strong magnet.'

'Don't take too much time over a wild goose chase, OK?' Alex put in. 'There's bound to be more to discover here at home. I mean, if she actually – was killed – in Pacific Grove.' He hesitated over the bone-chilling words.

'Yeah, I know. But something's pulling me up there. I can't explain it.' Well, she could – Gina was pulling her. But she wasn't sure how credible that would be to her friends. 'Cat, isn't there anything you can do to help? With police resources?'

Cat blew out a breath. 'If I had a name – or a rental location – or *anything* specific, I could at least try. But as it is . . .'

Erin imagined her raising her hands in despair.

'I'll make it my mission to obtain something like that as soon as possible. Even if I have to visit every hotel, B and B, and vacation rental in town.'

'Shall I send you an extra pair of shoes?' Alex quipped. 'Sounds like you may be wearing out the ones you have.'

'Very funny. My shoes and I have plenty of stamina. We'll be fine.'

But Erin didn't feel as positive as she was trying to sound. She felt more like a young salmon about to make its first journey upstream.

'Take care of yourself, OK?' Alex said, his voice softening.

'I second that,' said Cat.

Alex and Cat seemed to be remarkably in agreement for two people who had just met. They must have bonded over Miss Silver. Erin felt just a teeny bit left out at the thought of the three of them enjoying themselves in her house without her.

'I will. Be good. That means you, Miss Silver,' Erin said sternly.

'Meow,' Miss Silver replied.

'And call us tomorrow,' Cat and Alex said in unison. Did that mean they were planning to continue their bonding through the following day? Erin wasn't at all sure how she felt about that.

* * *

On Sunday, she checked out after a late breakfast and drove up the coast to Rockaway Beach. It was a beautiful ride through varied terrain, as the road sometimes hugged the shoreline and sometimes veered inland to skirt a bay or outcropping. North of Lincoln City, the highway moved miles inland, passing through farmland and ranchland. The Tillamook area was particularly redolent of cows. But north of that town, the road moved back to the coastline and hugged it until she reached Rockaway. The scents in the air shifted to those of salt, sand, and fish.

She found her hotel without difficulty, since the business district of the town was concentrated within a few-block stretch of 101. But it was only one o'clock, and her check-in time was not till four. Her late breakfast still sustained her, so she made a snap decision to leave her car in the hotel parking lot and begin canvassing the local businesses right away.

Up and down the main street she went, stopping in every open shop, café, and hotel, saving the one where she'd be staying for last. In every place, she showed her mother's photo, asking if anyone remembered seeing her twenty years before. Not one person had anything to offer beyond polite disbelief.

At four o'clock, Erin checked into her hotel. The receptionist was college-aged, so there was no point in showing the photo to him. He wouldn't have the authority to search their records, and anyway, she was too tired to do the mental labor of trying to pull a likely alias out of a hat. She found her room, fell onto the bed, and slept for two hours.

When she woke, she was ravenous. She headed to a restaurant directly across the street, where on her earlier visit the man at the register had denied all knowledge of Gina. But they'd been in the middle of the lunch rush then, and she hadn't had the opportunity to question any of the other staff.

The dinner rush was picking up now. She'd noticed all the restaurants in town – all three or four of them – closed early, some as early as seven, so any tourist party in the know would claim their table as soon as possible.

Erin paused in the doorway. A plump middle-aged waitress glanced her way and motioned to her to choose a table, so she picked a small one near the window where she could watch the people going by. She had to wait ten minutes or so before the woman bustled up to her table with a menu. Erin looked up at her to smile her thanks.

The waitress froze, her jaw dropping and the blood draining from her face. '*Parker?*'

'Excuse me?' Erin replied.

The woman blinked rapidly and shook her head as if to clear it. 'I'm sorry. You reminded me of someone, so strong it took me back. But o' course you couldn't be her – that musta been, oh, goin' on twenty years ago. She'd be in her fifties by now.' The waitress smiled apologetically. 'Don't mind me, honey. Just an old woman's wishful thinking.' She turned to go.

'Wait,' Erin said, putting out an arm. 'What was the name you said?'

'Parker. Parker Forbes.' Parker had been Gina's maiden name. 'She worked in the hotel across the street, came in here sometimes for her meals. We got to be friends.'

Erin pulled the photo out of her notebook pocket. 'Is this her?'

The waitress took the photo and studied it, her face opening in amazement. 'Why, yes. Yes, it is. That's Parker, all right.' She compared Erin's face to the picture. 'Now that I look closer, I can see the difference. But you must be related, surely?'

'I'm her daughter.'

'Her daughter!' The waitress looked upward as if searching her memory. 'Erin, wasn't it? She talked about you all the time.'

'That's right. I'm Erin. But her name was Gina Washington, not Parker Forbes.'

'And I'm Crystal. Crystal Jackson.' They shook hands. 'You know, I'm not altogether surprised to hear she wasn't using her real name. Once in a while, I'd call her from across the room and she wouldn't answer, like she didn't recognize her name at all. Plus, she was real cagey about her background. Never would say where she came from nor nothin' like that. Only your name, like she couldn't help it cause she was always thinkin' about you.' Crystal looked furtively around and lowered her voice. 'She wasn't runnin' from the law, was she?'

'No. I think she was running from some other people who were running from the law.'

Crystal nodded. 'That sounds more like Parker. Integrity, that's what she had. Just oozed out of her.' Another patron called and she snapped to attention. 'I better get moving. But if you can stick around after the crowd's gone, I'd love to talk to you some more.'

'Sure thing. I'd like that, too.'

Erin put the photo away and tried to consult the menu, but her mind was buzzing. Parker Forbes. The Parker made sense, but Forbes? The only Forbeses Erin could think of were the financial magazine and the late artist from Carmel.

The artist. One more hint that something shady was going on in Cruikshank's galleries. But surely it was careless of her mother to have chosen that name for herself. Unless in some obscure way, perhaps unconsciously, she wanted to be found.

Erin turned her attention to the menu and chose a steak. She needed fortifying after her skipped lunch and afternoon of legwork. Crystal came back to take her order, then bustled off again with a conspiratorial smile.

A younger server brought her food and the red wine she'd asked for. Erin ate slowly, watching the tourists go by in their long shorts and loud shirts, with their ice-cream cones and bags of saltwater taffy, their children and beach toys and dogs. Normal families enjoying a vacation together, as her family had never done. Not with both parents in attendance.

Eventually, when she was finishing her cheesecake, the restaurant emptied out, and Crystal returned to plop her broad beam across from Erin. 'Whew!' she said, wiping a paper napkin across her brow. 'Busy one today. I'm glad to get a load off.' She stirred the cup of coffee she'd brought with her and took a sip. 'That hits the spot.'

Erin gave her a minute to catch her breath, then asked, 'Did you know my mother well?'

Crystal frowned into the air. 'Now, I don't know about *well*. She was a bit of a mystery woman, was Parker.' She cut her eyes back to Erin. 'I hope you don't mind me goin' on callin' her that – I'll always think of her as Parker, whatever her name really was.'

Erin smiled her acquiescence. 'Parker was her maiden name, so it wasn't completely fake.'

'Well, as I say, she was a bit of a mystery. But I liked her real well. She'd listen to me go on for hours about my family, my no-good husband, bellyachin' about this job, whatever. She didn't say much about herself, but she always seemed to have good advice to give. She was real thoughtful, ya know? Seemed way too smart to be workin' as a chambermaid. She coulda been runnin' that hotel, and doin' a damn sight better job than the owners were doin'. I told her so time and again.'

'I suppose she just did that to get by. She was in hiding, so she would have needed a job where she wasn't in the public eye.'

Crystal nodded. 'You got a point there. Though, o' course, I didn't think about her bein' on the run at the time. Unless it was just from some no-good man. Like mine.' She gave a wry grin.

'How long was she in town?' Erin asked.

'All summer. That is to say, she got here around the first of July, as I recall, but then she stayed on through Labor Day. Everything shuts down around here after that. All the summer jobs dry up, hotels close down, people go back where they came from. This here's one of the few spots that stays open all winter for the locals.'

'Do you have any idea where she went when she left here?'

'I think she had some idea of goin' back home, wherever home was. She missed you somethin' fierce. Said she had to see her baby girl no matter what it cost her. She said it just like that – no matter what it cost.'

Erin's heart welled up into her throat and pushed the tears into her eyes. She tried to blink them away, but they refused to go.

Crystal sat forward and pointed at her. 'Now, wait. I tell a lie. I do know where she went – at least for a little while. There's this spa up in Manzanita where my niece was working at the time. They needed a relief receptionist, just for a couple weeks while the one they had went on vacation. I believe she went up there.'

'A spa? That seems kind of public.'

'Well, they only take women there. If she was hiding from a man . . .'

'She would have been safe. Good point.' Erin smiled. 'Thanks so much, Crystal. You've been tremendously helpful.'

Crystal started to push herself up from her chair, then sat back down. 'But wait just a minute, Erin, honey – why all these questions? Do you mean to tell me your mother never did get home safe?'

Erin swallowed hard. 'No. She never did. She left home toward the end of June that year, and I never saw her again.'

# SIXTEEN

From her hotel room next morning, Erin Googled 'spa Manzanita OR' and came up with one option, helpfully named Manzanita Massage and Spa. They opened at ten, and Manzanita was about a twenty-minute drive away. She decided to get a real breakfast instead of the stale pastries, tired fruit, and over-boiled eggs that passed for that meal in most hotels.

Crystal's place of employment didn't open till lunchtime, but Erin followed a trail of what looked like locals to a little café with spots of black and white painted on its windows and a statue of a Holstein cow out front. If nothing else, they ought to serve good cheese, she thought, and went in.

It turned out they served good everything, including coffee. Erin dawdled over a marionberry waffle with scrambled eggs and bacon, cooked crispy just as she liked it. At nine thirty she paid her check, retrieved her car from the hotel, and drove to Manzanita, a bustling little beach town north of Nehalem Bay.

She found the spa tucked away in a small complex of service establishments in the main shopping area. It wasn't quite ten o'clock yet, but she tried the door and it opened. She found herself in a lobby where various self-care products were displayed for sale.

'We're not quite open yet,' a young woman said from beyond the door that led to the treatment area. 'Do you have an appointment?'

'No,' Erin replied. 'I was hoping to talk to the owner, or to anyone who's been here a long time. I'm trying to track down someone who used to work here.'

The young woman paused in the doorway. 'Hmm,' she said. 'The owner's not in today, but Grace has been here forever. Only you'll have to be quick – she has a massage client at ten.'

'Actually, I don't,' another, older voice chimed in from somewhere out of sight. 'She just cancelled.' The source of the voice came into view – a pleasant-looking gray-haired woman in a loose linen top and pants. She smiled at Erin and said, 'I'll be happy to help if I can. But wouldn't you like a massage while we talk? Otherwise I'll have to give the appointment to the next person who walks in the door.' Grace nodded toward the entrance.

Erin turned and saw two women approaching – one about her own age and the other in her fifties. They looked like mother and daughter. A wavelet of grief washed over her at the thought of yet one more experience she and her mother could never share.

She turned back to Grace. 'Yes, I'd like that.'

'Come on back. I have a two-hour slot available – would you care for a salt scrub first?'

Erin had no idea of the procedure or purpose of a salt scrub. But what the heck. 'Um – sure, I guess so.'

Once through the door into the inner sanctum, Grace pointed her toward a restroom. 'It's a good idea to use the restroom before we start, even if you don't think you need to. Otherwise you'll be hopping off the table halfway through.'

Grace was waiting when she emerged. 'Right in here.' She motioned toward a door at the end of the hallway.

Inside, Grace showed Erin where to put her clothes and explained that she had the choice to leave her underclothes on or take them off. 'You'll be covered with a towel either way,' she said. 'I want you to feel comfortable. But there is a chance of getting product on your underwear if you leave it on.' She left Erin to undress.

This entire experience was foreign to Erin. Other than the occasional medical checkup, she'd never had a stranger touch her in such an intimate manner. She had no idea whether it would be relaxing or terrifying. But she'd committed to it now. *In for a penny, in for a pound*, she thought, and stripped to the skin.

Grace returned with a discreet knock when Erin was lying on the table, on her back as instructed and covered neck to toe in a towel.

'Let's get started, and then you can ask me whatever you need to while I work.'

Erin thought she had never heard anyone speak in such soothing tones, yet without a shadow of condescension.

'Sit up, and we'll start with your back.'

She sat up, holding the towel to her chest, and Grace said, 'We'll need to get your hair out of the way first.' Erin's hair was already in a ponytail, so Grace doubled it over and secured it under the elastic.

Erin felt something mildly abrasive being spread with gentle, sweeping motions across her back. 'Now, who did you want to ask me about?'

'A woman who worked here as a temporary receptionist about twenty years ago. She was only here for a couple of weeks, as I understand, so I don't know whether you'd remember her. I believe she was going by the name Parker Forbes.'

The fluid motions halted momentarily, then resumed. 'I thought you reminded me of somebody! I remember Parker well, though I'm not sure the name alone would have triggered it. But you're the very image of her. Are you her daughter?'

'Yes, that's right.'

'Well, well, well. Whoever would have thought? What happened to Parker, anyway? All I knew when she left here was that she was going home to see you.'

Erin's hopes landed in her stomach with a thud. 'That's what I was hoping you could tell me. I never saw her again after she left home that June.'

Again the smoothing touch was withdrawn, but this time it was replaced by a warm, damp towel laid across Erin's back. 'I'm so sorry to hear that. I could tell Parker was in some kind of trouble, but she would never speak of it directly.'

Grace used the towel to wipe the abrasive solution off Erin's back, then helped her to lie down. 'Let's have this arm outside the towel.' She gently lifted Erin's right arm and began to apply the scrub. 'Do you suppose . . . I hate to say it . . . her trouble caught up with her?'

'Yes, I'm certain it did. But not before she got back to California. I think I know how, where, and when she died – what I don't know is who killed her and why.'

Grace took in a sharp breath and her hand closed momentarily over Erin's wrist, then released. 'Oh, I'm so sorry. You shocked me there. That's why I usually don't encourage unrelated conversation while I'm working – if I get emotional, it can affect my touch.' She resumed her gentle stroking. 'What a terrible thing for you to find out. But perhaps knowing she's dead is a little more bearable than being left wondering why she never came back.'

'I spent my whole adolescence wondering, until I finally accepted I wouldn't see her again. And yes, horrible as the thought of her being murdered is, on some level it's easier than thinking she didn't love me enough to come back.'

Grace finished her arm and wiped it with another warm towel. 'Oh, she loved you, dear. She was all eaten up with missing you and feeling guilty for having had to leave you behind. That much was obvious, even though she never explained why she had to do it.' Grace placed Erin's right arm back under the covering towel and moved to her left side. 'I felt so sorry for her, but of course there was nothing I could do. Except listen.'

'I'm sure she appreciated you listening.' Erin felt given the chance, she herself could talk to Grace for hours, about anything. She might as well have been a counselor-type therapist as well as a massage therapist.

Grace spread the scrub over her left arm, stroked it in, and toweled it off, then moved to her left leg before she spoke again. 'Now that I think about it, I do remember one thing she said before she left. I don't know if it's significant, but she said she missed the redwoods. Does that mean anything to you?'

'We used to walk in the redwood forest back home. She loved it there. She used to say the extra oxygen put off by the trees invigorated her.'

'I suppose that's what she meant, then. I think she said something about an avenue you could drive on?'

Erin's leg twitched, and Grace soothed it back into stillness. 'That's not near Santa Cruz. She was probably talking about the Avenue of the Giants, in a state park up north somewhere. North from Santa Cruz, that is – south from here.' One more item on the adventure list they had never had the opportunity to explore. Maybe Gina had planned to pass through there on the way home.

Grace finished the salt scrub in silence, then instructed Erin in the procedure for the massage. This began with replacing the towels she was lying on and under with clean sheets, a process Erin imagined must be akin to changing a hospital bed with the patient in it. Once she was on her front with her face in the cradle, they both lapsed into silence as Grace slathered her back with lotion and began the massage.

As Grace's practiced hands soothed and pressed the tension from her muscles, Erin fell gradually into a state of dreamy semi-consciousness. She felt not as if she were being treated or worked on, but as if she were being cared for by someone who loved her. She couldn't remember being touched in such a way since she was a child of perhaps six or seven, young enough for her mother to need to bathe her instead of her washing herself.

In a moment, Erin was overwhelmed with a deep sorrow and longing – longing for her mother, of course, but also for another sort of closeness that ought by rights to have succeeded naturally as the mother-daughter bond matured and receded into second place in her life. Erin felt her development as a woman had been truncated by her mother's disappearance, leaving no close friend, aunt, or grandmother to take her place in guiding her daughter through the dangerous rapids of puberty and adolescence. Erin was at once aged beyond her years by the tragedy and stuck forever at age twelve, on the brink of womanhood but never quite getting there, despite the inevitable maturation of her body.

By the time Grace asked her to turn onto her back again, the cloth covering the face cradle was soaked with her tears. Grace must have noticed but made no comment. Perhaps this kind of reaction was more common than Erin would have thought.

The massage moved on to her feet, legs, and hips, her arms, shoulders, and upper chest, her neck, face, and scalp. No part of her except her private zones was left uncared for. Erin's thoughts drifted toward her encounter with Finn. She knew that as a human being he was the last sort of person she should consider getting involved with. Cat had been right to warn her that if he got possession of her heart, he would certainly break it. But Erin couldn't help craving the kind of physical awakening she was sure he could masterfully provide.

When at last Grace withdrew her hands from Erin's body, telling her to take her time in getting up and dressed, she felt as if she had been through an emotional wringer and might never have the strength to stand. But eventually she summoned enough energy to sit up, put on her clothes, and slake her sudden thirst with the bottle of water Grace had left for her. She used the restroom again, then emerged into the corridor to see the older woman waiting for her.

'What do I owe you?' she said, suddenly becoming aware she had never asked the price of these services.

Grace smiled and put a hand on her arm. 'Consider it my gift – to you, and to your mother through you. We had to partially charge the client who cancelled, so the spa won't be the loser by it.'

'Thank you so much.' Erin gave the older woman an impulsive hug. 'And thank you for what you've told me about my mother. I think it will help me find out some more.'

'I'm so glad I could help. I'll hold you in my thoughts. And your mother as well.' Grace smiled her out the door.

Erin found a diner open in Nehalem for a quick lunch, then drove back to her hotel in Rockaway Beach. She took out her notebook and recorded her conversation with Grace, but the feelings she'd experienced during the massage could not be committed to paper. She couldn't understand them herself, let alone communicate them in words.

The Avenue of the Giants seemed like a slim lead, but a number of slim leads had panned out already in this search, so it was worth pursuing. Erin Googled it and found it was part of the Humboldt Redwoods State Park, located off Highway 101 about ten hours south of her current location and five hours north of home. She'd have to plan an overnight stay if she wanted to explore the vicinity. Presumably Gina would have done so as well.

The park itself offered no permanent lodgings, only camping. While her mother had certainly not been averse to camping, she hadn't taken any such gear from the house, and Erin thought it unlikely she would have bought a tent, sleeping bag, and all the assorted whatnots just for an overnight stay. There must be hotels in the area for the outdoor-sleeping-challenged.

Erin did a search of the nearby towns – the closest that offered accommodations seemed to be Garberville. Among the predictable chain representatives, a far more distinctive building caught her eye – the Benbow Historic Inn. The large Tudor-style building, perched on a forested hillside, looked like exactly the sort of characterful retreat Gina would have been looking for. It was pricey, but Erin hadn't run through all her insurance money yet.

The inn had several rooms open for the following night, so she reserved Clara's Suite – a beautifully appointed room with a stunning mountain view and a capacious clawfoot tub. She'd been missing the tub at Seafarer's Rest ever since she left there. If she had any money left when this was all over, she'd have to see if she could install something similar in her bathroom at home.

It was Monday – a workday – so she'd need to wait until evening to call Alex and Cat. She took advantage of the intervening hours for a walk along the beach.

The tide was low, the stretch of packed sand broad and easy to walk on. Erin relished the cool breeze on her face, even though the blowing sand stuck like barnacles to her recently lotioned skin. Every shell and sand crab, every seagull track and wavelet, and especially every mother and child playing happily in the sand and sea brought Gina vividly to mind. But now Erin felt not sorrow but a sense of comfort and communion, as if her mother were cradling her gently and commending her for her progress in her quest. She must be on the right track.

She ate an early dinner at Crystal's restaurant and thanked her again for her help. Then she returned to the hotel to call her allies. This time she dialed Cat's number, wondering whether she would hear Miss Silver and Alex in the background.

Miss Silver's plaintive cry came through the phone as Cat answered, but Erin heard no other human voice. 'Hi, Cat. Are you alone this time?'

'Yeah. Alex and I decided we should stagger our visits so your cat would get more total cuddle time.'

'Good thinking. And speaking of my cat – it's starting to get a little confusing calling the two of you by the same moniker. Any chance I could use your full name? Is it Catherine?'

Cat made a strangled noise. 'No. No chance. And it's not Catherine.'

Now Erin was intrigued. 'OK, if I promise not to use it, will you tell me what it is?'

Cat huffed. 'It's Catalina.' She gave it the proper Spanish pronunciation, with each consonant distinct.

'But that's a lovely name!'

A pregnant pause. 'I grew up in San Diego.'

This took a second to sink in. 'Ohh. I get it. What did the kids call you – Island?'

'Sometimes. Or Santa, since it's technically called Santa Catalina Island. The list of variations was long and excruciating.'

'OK, I promise never to call you Catalina. I guess I'll just have to stop calling Miss Silver "Cat." How is she, by the way?'

'Sleek and self-satisfied as only a Siamese can be. I'm getting kind of attached to her. I'm going to miss seeing her every day after you get back.' Erin laughed, then Cat asked, 'When are you getting back, by the way?'

'Soon, I think. I have a plan.' Erin told her what she'd learned from Crystal and Grace and what she'd deduced about the Benbow Inn. 'I'm going to head to that inn tomorrow. I reserved a room for two nights so I'd have a full day to investigate. Unless the trail leads me somewhere else, I should be home by Thursday night.'

Cat clucked her tongue. 'You have some kind o' luck, girl. First getting a cancellation at Sylvia Beach, then your *first night* in Rockaway running into somebody who knew your mother, then another cancellation at the spa? That would never happen to me. Or any cop. Not in a million years.'

Erin paused, then spoke barely above a whisper. 'It isn't luck, Cat. It's my mother. I'm convinced she's guiding me from beyond the grave.'

Cat's silence stretched out a little too long for comfort. 'If that's what you want to believe, I guess it's not my place to contradict you. But from where I'm standing, it looks like sheer, unadulterated luck.'

Erin sighed. Maybe Alex would be able to sway Cat's opinion if they continued to connect. 'Will you be seeing Alex at all? I'm not sure I'm up for repeating my report to him right now. I want to get an early start tomorrow.'

'I don't expect to see him, but I could call him and pass it on.'

'That would be great, thanks.' Alex might be disappointed not to hear from Erin personally, but it couldn't be helped. Erin needed to crash.

# SEVENTEEN

Although her GPS told her I-5 would be faster, Erin couldn't see driving inland, back down the highway she'd traversed only days ago, and then back out toward the coast. She took 101 instead, enjoying its ocean and cliff views and stopping in quaint little towns for breakfast and lunch. She drove through blink-and-you-miss-it Garberville about seven p.m. and continued a couple of miles to the Benbow Inn.

The inn stood on a hillside within the redwood forest like a sentinel – a welcoming one, with lights glimmering from the many bay windows on its long, four-story, partially half-timbered front. Erin checked into her room – Clara Benbow's suite, one of the rooms named for members of the inn's founding family – and thought she'd been transported to an English manor house. The spacious room, furnished with unique pieces in dark woods that proudly proclaimed their age, looked out over the forest through an expanse of windows. Personal touches such as old photos and books, a carafe of sherry, and an antique teapot completed the illusion of being a guest in a gracious home.

The bathroom was even grander than the room itself, with a clawfoot slipper tub in which Erin could stretch out her whole length, plus a huge, tiled shower. She was so looking forward to soaking in that tub that she paid little attention to her gourmet dinner on the hotel terrace, where she felt as if she were eating in the forest.

After a sybaritic bath, she went to bed early, but she slept fitfully in the unfamiliar bed. At some point during the night, she half woke to feel a presence at the side of the bed, leaning over her and whispering her name. Too sleepy to be frightened, she turned her head and looked but saw no one. Thinking perhaps it was her mother's ghost, she went back to sleep.

In the morning, Erin passed through the main lounge to the restaurant for breakfast. Now she took time to notice the antique furnishings, huge fireplace, tables with half-finished jigsaw puzzles, cabinet of antique tools, and the near-life-size stuffed grizzly bear parked in a chair by a door to the terrace. The sign he held proclaimed him to be Benson, hailing from England, where he had been made in 1876. He had watched over the Benbow since it was built in 1926. What stories that bear must have to tell! He could probably whisper to Erin something about her mother, if only she knew how to listen.

After breakfast, she went down to the front desk again. This time it was staffed by a middle-aged man in a navy suit who greeted her with a bright smile.

'Good morning! How are you enjoying your stay at the Benbow?'

'It's wonderful, thank you. That bathtub in Clara's Suite is to die for.'

He smiled proprietorially. 'Yes, our Founder's Suite bathtubs are some of our most popular features. Is there something I can do for you this morning?'

Erin hesitated, wondering what would be the best approach to take in this place, with this man, whose name tag read *Caspar Levant*. He had the air of someone with authority, so she went with the simple truth.

'I was hoping to get some information about someone who may have stayed here about twenty years ago.' She pulled out her photo and showed it to him. 'My mother. She disappeared when I was twelve, and I'm trying to trace her movements.'

Caspar took the photo and looked closely from the printed image to Erin. 'I can see the resemblance,' he said. 'But it's difficult for me to say whether I've seen this woman before. We get so many guests in and out, and twenty years is a long time.'

'But you have been here that long?'

'Oh, yes. I started during college vacations as a bellboy and worked my way up.' He stood straighter and adjusted his tie. 'I'm assistant manager now.'

'Impressive.' Erin gave him an admiring smile. Flattery would be the path to success in this case, she suspected. 'Would you have been here in September of 2001? Or would that have been during a school term for you?'

'Oh, by 2001 I was here full-time.' He smoothed his hair. 'You might not think it to look at me, but I am a bit over forty.'

She'd mentally placed him at forty-five plus. 'Really? I never would have known.' Another smile. 'Is there any chance you could check your guest register from that time?'

A small crease appeared between Caspar's brows. 'We wouldn't ordinarily divulge that information. But since she's your mother, and it has been twenty years . . .' He turned to his computer and tapped a few keys. 'What name should I be looking for?'

*Ay, there's the rub.* 'I'm not exactly sure. You see, she was sort of in hiding, and she used a variety of false names – usually something connected with the place she was staying.' Erin glanced behind the desk at a prominent photo of the large and illustrious Benbow family who had built the hotel. 'Perhaps the first name of one of the Benbow sisters? Combined with . . .' The redwood forest where they used to walk was in Henry Cowell State Park. 'Possibly Cowell? I can't say for sure, but it would be a place to start.'

Caspar eyed her skeptically. 'I don't know . . . This all sounds rather vague and insubstantial.'

Erin produced a yet more dazzling smile. 'You're a man of imagination, I'm sure. Don't you think this would be the perfect place for a woman in trouble to find respite for a while? The secluded location, the exclusive clientele . . . the luxury, the management's admirable discretion . . .?'

'Well, yes, there is a certain romance to the place. And it wouldn't be the first time this inn provided a refuge for those who needed privacy.' He lowered his voice and leaned toward her. 'We used to be a very popular retreat for Hollywood celebrities who wanted to escape the press. Not to mention presidents, first ladies, and foreign dignitaries.' He straightened again with a nod. 'Which sister do you like best? Clara, Helen, Evangeline, or Leta?'

She considered. Probably not Evangeline or Leta. 'Let's try Clara first. Since I'm staying in her room.'

He tapped and scrolled. 'In September 2001, I have a Clara Cartwright and . . . a Claire Bendigo?'

Erin shook her head. 'I don't think so. How about Helens?'

More tapping and scrolling. 'Let's see . . . Helen Waterson? . . . Helen Montgomery? No, I think she may be a Somebody . . . Aha. Here's a Helen Cowell.' He squinted at the screen. Probably too vain to use glasses, Erin thought – they might give away his age. 'September eighteenth to twentieth. In one of our historic queen rooms on the third floor.'

So this time she had not been guided to stay in the same room where her mother had stayed. Perhaps a repeat of that was too much to hope for. Of course, it was possible the breadcrumb Gina had left at this inn could be of a completely different nature – not a physical object at all. The room might be irrelevant.

She rewarded Caspar with her most adoring smile yet. 'Thank you so much. I can't tell you how helpful you've been. This will be reflected in my Tripadvisor review, I promise.' At his panicked look, she hastened to add, 'I won't mention what specifically you've done for me, of course. Just something like "exceptional attention to guests' individual needs."'

His relief was visible. 'It's all part of the service.'

Another guest approached needing Caspar's attention, so Erin sidled away. Just off the lobby was a closet-sized shop with a few necessities and snacks. Displayed on one shelf was a booklet titled *The Ghosts of the Benbow Historic Inn*. The word 'ghosts' brought back her experience during the night. Erin flipped through the booklet, which was a collection of accounts of spooky occurrences experienced by staff and guests, and noticed a couple of instances similar to her own midnight awakening. With a chill, she realized her invisible visitor might indeed have been a ghost – and possibly not her mother's.

But she was here to find clues, not to research the paranormal. Since the room Gina had stayed in seemed an unlikely prospect, Erin decided to explore outside the hotel. She glanced at the brochures displayed for local attractions, and her eye immediately fell on one for the Julia Morgan Redwood Grove estate. Her mother would certainly have been drawn to visit any place with a connection to Julia Morgan.

The estate was less than half a mile away, just across the South Fork Eel River from the inn, so Erin walked, crossing a stone bridge she had seen from the terrace the previous evening. The house itself, though beautiful and inviting, was not open to visitors at present, so she had to content herself with wandering around the extensive grounds, which included cultivated gardens and a long stretch of riverside in addition to the eponymous redwood grove. Erin admired the river and gardens, but she felt a whisper leading her toward the grove.

As she passed through the trees and approached a small clearing, she spotted a man standing before an easel, brush poised over the canvas. Given her mother's connection to the art world, she felt this was an opportunity not to be missed. She came close enough to get a glimpse of his painting and knew immediately that he was a professional, not a mere dabbler. His brushwork was masterful, and the way he'd caught the light filtering through the trees was arresting.

She moved in a wide circle around his position so she could approach from the side, where he would be able to see her in his peripheral vision but she would not be blocking his view.

He glimpsed her and turned in her direction with a frown. 'Come to gawp, have you? Tell me your brother-in-law paints in his spare time and he could do just as well?'

Erin stopped and pulled back a little. 'I'm sorry, I didn't mean to disturb you. Actually, I do know a little about art – enough to know that your work is exceptional.' Seeing his ruffled feathers smooth down a bit, she added, 'May I take a closer look?'

He stepped back and swooped his arm in an elaborate, if ironic, gesture of invitation.

She moved to face the painting square on. Yes, the light – she knew of only one other painter who treated light with so sure and delicate a touch.

'Your style reminds me a bit of Elliot Forbes,' she blurted. 'More modern, of course, but the way you treat the light is very similar. And this is a subject he might have chosen.'

Feeling the artist's eyes on her, Erin glanced over at him. He regarded her steadily but silently, giving her time to notice that whereas Finn was the stereotypical slovenly artist, this man presented a nearly opposite image. His smock was necessarily paint-stained but otherwise clean and neat. Below the smock he wore clean pressed chinos and leather moccasins with no socks. His hair was short and reddish under his broad sunhat, and his freckled cheeks were clean-shaven. She guessed him to be perhaps forty, no more.

'You are the second person who has ever said that to me,' he said at last. 'And now that I think about it, you rather resemble the first one. But that was years ago. Couldn't have been you.'

Erin's heart quickened. She pulled her notebook from her purse and the photo from the notebook. 'Was it her? She was my mother.'

The painter took the photo and studied it. 'Yes,' he said in a tone of marvel. 'I believe it was. Mind you, it's been a long time. But I have a good eye for bone structure, and hers was rare.' He handed the photo back. 'As is yours.'

She stowed the photo in its pocket. 'Did you converse with her at all, Mr . . .?'

He waved a hand. 'Evan. No one calls me Mister anything. And yes, I did. In fact, we had dinner together – at my request.' He regarded Erin thoughtfully. 'She was a remarkable woman, your mother. I tried to get her to stick around a while so I could paint her portrait, but she said she had business to attend to and needed to move on.'

Evan and Finn had one thing in common, at least.

'Did you talk about anything in particular at this dinner?'

He gave a one-sided smile. 'As a matter of fact, she quizzed me about my painting. Wanted to know whether I ever did flat-out imitations of Forbes or any other artist. I told her of course I did; I was a student at the time. I copied any decent painting I could get access to as a way of learning the craft. And when I finished one, I gessoed over it and copied someone else.'

'You must have been pretty good at copying Forbes for her to have noticed the similarity.'

Evan shrugged. 'He's always been one of my inspirations. Especially, as you so astutely noted, his treatment of light.'

Erin hovered, pretending to further examine the painting. She wanted more information from Evan but was unsure how to proceed. A suspicion was forming in her mind, but she could hardly come out and ask him, *Do you paint forgeries of Forbes paintings and sell them through Raymond Cruikshank?*

Instead she asked, 'Do you sell in Santa Cruz County at all? Or Monterey?' When he looked at her quizzically, she hastened to add, 'I live in that area. I'm wondering if any of the local galleries might have your work. I'd consider buying one – if I can afford it.'

An odd note came into his voice. 'I dealt with one gallery down there a long time ago. Briefly. It wasn't a good fit.'

Erin considered whether to press him further. Was his hesitation due to guilt, or could he have been one of the victims of Cruikshank's unfair business practices? Her mother had told her how some unscrupulous gallery owners would put up the price of a painting after agreeing with the artist for a flat fee, then pocket the surplus. By 'some unscrupulous gallery owners,' Erin now understood Cruikshank.

Evan surprised her by making the decision for her. 'Are you staying at the Benbow, by any chance?'

She blinked. 'Yes. You?'

He nodded. 'Have dinner with me.'

Erin hesitated, unsure of his motivation. But what could be the harm in dining with him in the public restaurant of the hotel where they both were staying? If she needed to escape or be rescued, help or an escape route would be close at hand. Besides, she had a strong feeling Evan was an important lead to pursue.

'All right. What time?'

'Seven. And now, if you'll excuse me, I need to get on. I can't waste this light.'

She turned to go, and he called after her. 'What's your name?'

'Erin,' she called back. He hadn't given her a surname. She'd hold on to hers for now.

# EIGHTEEN

Erin spent the afternoon like a regular tourist, driving the Avenue of the Giants and stopping to explore the woods here and there. She returned to the hotel at six thirty to dress for dinner. She'd packed hastily and economically for this trip, and dinner with a man in a fancy hotel had not been among her expectations. But she managed to put together a respectable-looking outfit from a black travel-knit skirt, a pair of black sandals, and a silky teal tee with a chiffon scarf draped around her shoulders and fastened with the cameo pin she'd inherited from Gina.

She arrived in the dining room promptly at seven and was asked for her reservation. She hoped Evan had made one, because she had not. 'I'm joining Mr . . .' Oh dear. She should have insisted on his last name after all. But then she spotted him in a far corner and pointed. 'Right over there.'

The host bowed and led her to the table, menu in hand. He pulled out the chair for her to sit across from Evan, who had stood at her approach.

She'd recognized him by the color of his hair, but in all other respects he could have been a different man. He was hatless, of course, and dressed in a dark grayish-brown suit with a pale yellow shirt and abstract print tie. He could have been a businessman, professional man, or even a politician. But when he smiled at her in greeting, his grin was far too natural and authentic for the last.

'I almost got into difficulty just now because I still don't know your last name.'

'Sorry about that. It's Gifford. And yours is Cowell?' His grin was triumphant. 'You see, I remembered your mother's name.'

'No, actually, it's Washington. And so was hers. Gina Washington. She was using a false name because she didn't want to be found.' She realized as she said this that she had decided to trust Evan. She couldn't be sure quite why.

His eyes widened. 'How intriguing. Found by whom? Not your father, I hope? I mean, I would hope it wasn't him she was running from.'

'No. And not the law, either. I haven't yet worked out exactly what was going on, but I know her life was in danger from someone on the wrong side of the law.'

'You haven't worked it out? You mean she never told you?'

Erin closed her eyes for a second. She was getting so weary of explaining this, time after time, to person after person. 'I never saw her again. She left home with no explanation a few months before you met her, and she never made it back.' She swallowed. 'I'm pretty sure whoever it was caught up with her and killed her.'

Evan gaped at her a moment, then sat back in his chair. 'I'm so sorry. How terrible for you. And, of course, for her.' He raked a hand through his hair, disheveling its wavy mass. 'She was one of the good ones. There was a light in her like I've rarely seen in anyone else. That's why I wanted to paint her – it wasn't just her unusual bone structure. I was longing to capture that light.'

'You wanted to capture it to preserve it. Someone else wanted to capture it to extinguish it.'

He shook his head as if unable to take this in. Then suddenly he sat forward. 'Listen, I was a little cagey earlier. I didn't want to speak out of turn. But when you asked about galleries in Santa Cruz – your mother told me she worked in a gallery. Did she work for Raymond Cruikshank, by any chance?'

Now it was Erin's turn to be startled. 'Yes, she did. Is he the one you had the bad experience with?'

Evan grimaced. 'I'll say. He took me for the rawest greenhorn ever to graduate from art school with a couple of decent canvases and the clothes on his back. The man's a weasel.'

'I know that. I've known it for some time. But I can't prove anything illegal against him.' Hope sparked inside her. 'Can you help?'

He slowly moved his head from side to side, gazing into the distance. 'Not to say prove.' He cut his eyes back to Erin. 'You were asking me about copying Forbes. You suspect forgery, don't you?'

'It would explain a few things, yes.'

'I don't have proof of anything, but I know a man who'd be capable of it.'

'Artistically or . . .' She groped for a word. 'Ethically?' Erin felt a sudden chill. She hoped passionately the man Evan was speaking of was not Seymour Finnegan.

'Both, I think. He's a cold bastard. Way too interested in cold, hard cash.'

Surely not the way anyone would describe Finn. To her, he was as fiery as an acetylene torch, and he didn't seem materialistic. Besides, he was successful in his own right; why would he want to take the risk of forging another artist's work?

But he hadn't been successful yet in 2001. He'd been young, just starting out, struggling to establish his career.

What if he'd seen that Gina was onto the scheme and had tried to seduce her in order to shut her up? Then when that didn't work . . .

No. Finn could not have killed Gina. Certainly not in cold blood, as her dream had shown it. She could never believe that of him.

It took only moments for her to think through this, but in that time a server materialized beside them. She realized she hadn't even looked at the menu. She picked it up and rattled off the first thing she saw – crab-and-spinach-stuffed mushrooms.

'And for your entrée?'

Oh, that was just an appetizer? She took a closer look and ordered the chicken piccata. 'But skip the stuffed mushrooms, please. That was a mistake.'

'And would you care for any wine?'

She shot a helpless look at Evan, who came to her rescue. 'We'll take a bottle of the Briceland Sauvignon Blanc Reserve.' He went on to order petrale sole for himself, the price of which made Erin blink. The server shimmered off.

Erin recovered her wits. 'You were about to tell me the name of this artist you suspect.'

He held up a hand. 'I didn't say I have any grounds to suspect him. I just think he's capable.'

She nodded. 'OK. I get that.'

'His name is Grigory Antonovich Mamelukov.'

She nearly sank into the floor in relief.

The Russian-style numbers on the Seafarer's Rest register swam into her mind. And Elise had said the man had an accent she couldn't place. Alex's mother's accent was so faint it wouldn't sound Russian to anyone who was only familiar with the cinema version. 'That's a bit of a mouthful,' she said.

'He's a bellyful, himself. But I'm not even sure if he's still around. He'd probably be in his eighties by now. I haven't seen anything with his name on it in years.'

'That could mean he's dead, or he's stopped painting. Or—'

'Or he's doing nothing but forgeries now.' Evan finished her sentence.

The server appeared with their wine and went through the full rigmarole of pouring a drop for Evan to sip and approve before filling their glasses. Erin took advantage of the enforced pause in conversation to consider her alternatives. The only one she could think of was to confront the painter directly. Not exactly an attractive option, but maybe if she took Cat along, with her badge . . . 'You wouldn't have any idea where to find this – Mamelukov, was it?'

'Sorry, no. But last I knew, he was somewhere in your neck of the woods. If you have any contacts in the art scene down there – besides Cruikshank, I mean . . .'

'I do have one.' Erin's heart did a double-take at the prospect of seeing Finn again. 'Do you happen to know Seymour Finnegan?'

Evan blinked. 'I know his work. Know him by reputation. Never met the man – I understand he doesn't get out much.'

'Yes, he is a bit of a recluse. But he agreed to meet with me because he knew my mother.' She hesitated, but she really needed an outside perspective. 'What do you know by reputation?'

Evan shrugged. 'That he has a temper. And an eye for the ladies.' He gave her a searching look that made her squirm internally. 'Stereotypical artist stuff – except he doesn't drink to excess.'

'No hint of anything . . . shady?'

'On the contrary. He's known for his integrity. He'll pull a painting from a show if he thinks another artist is being treated unfairly.'

The server sidled up to the table and laid down their entrées with a flourish. When she had sidled off again, Erin said, 'Finnegan had an opening at Cruikshank's Carmel gallery twenty years ago. And I saw one of his works there the other day. He must know how crooked Cruikshank is.'

'Twenty years ago, he probably didn't know. That would likely have been his first solo show – he'd have been so grateful he'd have overlooked anything untoward that didn't smack him in the face. As for the painting that's there now, it could be a resale. You said there was only one? If he were selling through Cruikshank, there would be a lot more.'

'Good point. I hadn't thought of that.'

'What style was the painting you saw?'

'Abstract. Bold brushstrokes, lots of color, liberal use of paint.'

'Yeah, that was one of his earlier phases. He does more representational now.'

Erin breathed easier. 'So you'd guess it would be safe to ask for his help?'

Evan scrutinized her face. 'Safe in the sense of he's unlikely to be involved in forgery, yes. Safe as in you personally being safe with him? I'd say that's another story.'

She tried to laugh that off, but Evan's seriousness made that difficult. 'Oh, he's already said he wants to paint me. But I'm not falling for it.'

He leaned forward and lightly brushed her hand, which sent an unexpected spark up her arm. 'Be careful, Erin. You have some of that same light your mother had, though yours is dimmed a bit. I'd hate to see some bastard like Finnegan snuff it out completely.'

Erin felt as if all her defenses had been stripped away and Evan was looking into her very soul. The feeling was both intimate and terrifying. At last he released her gaze, and she nearly shuddered with relief. She focused on her dinner, although at this point her appetite had fled.

The server shimmered into existence again next to their table. Erin laid her knife and fork across her plate to indicate she was finished. 'Could we tempt you to some dessert?' She flourished a menu card.

Evan took the card and skimmed it. 'I'll have the cheesecake. And coffee.' He passed the card to Erin. 'Anything catch your eye?'

Although she couldn't eat another bite of chicken, there was always room for chocolate. 'I'll have the flourless chocolate torte. And coffee as well.' She'd had more wine than she was used to, and she was feeling a little fuzzy. Not a good way to feel when combined with what Evan was beginning to do to her. She needed to stay in control.

'Will you be heading home tomorrow?' he asked.

'That's the plan. I only reserved for two nights, and I think I've found out what I needed to here.'

'Shame.' He contemplated her, and again she felt stripped to the bone. Then, unexpectedly, he grinned. 'I would have liked to paint you.'

'Not you too!' burst out of her. 'I mean . . . I'm flattered, but . . .'

'But you're planning to take up Finnegan's offer?' His voice went hard.

'No!' She was too flustered to think. 'I told him no already. I don't want anyone to paint me. At least not until this – whatever it is – is finished. For one thing, I can't take the time. And for another . . .'

She trailed off. She didn't know how to express her other reservation, but it was definitely there. Something about seeing herself through another person's eyes, perhaps. She wanted to figure out who she was before she allowed that to happen. Perhaps – to borrow Evan's own words – she wanted to discover how to let her light shine, undimmed by the tragedy of her past.

He pulled out his wallet and withdrew a business card, slightly bent around the edges. 'Will you call me if you ever change your mind?'

She hesitated, then took the card. 'Yes, all right. If.' Without knowing quite why, she dug a library business card of her own from her purse, scribbled her cell number on the back, and handed it to him.

He leaned forward, compelling her to look at him. 'And also call me if there's anything I can do to help with your investigation. I have a show coming up in your area next week, so I'll be nearby for a while. Your mother was a remarkable person. I'd like to see justice done for her sake – and for yours.'

* * *

Back in her room, replete with exquisite chocolate, Erin called Cat again, although fairness dictated it should have been Alex's turn to hear from her directly. Something made her reluctant to talk to Alex right now.

Cat answered with no feline accompaniment. Erin was calling later tonight – presumably Cat was at home, her feeding duties accomplished earlier in the evening.

'Any joy?' Cat asked after the preliminary greetings.

'Of a sort. I met an artist who knew my mother. He thinks the forgery angle is tenable, and he gave me a name of someone to talk to about it.' Erin made a face she knew Cat couldn't see. 'Only trouble is, the guy may be dead. Or in a nursing home or something. He'd be in his eighties now, and apparently he hasn't painted in some time. At least not under his own name.'

'You have a name? I could check him out. At least find out whether he's dead or alive, whether he has a record.'

'Please. Grigory Antonovich Mamelukov.'

Cat whistled. 'Can you spell that?'

Erin hadn't thought to ask, but she gave it her best shot based on the little she knew of Russian names and pronunciation from Alex.

'Got it. You coming home tomorrow, then?'

'That's the plan. Should be there by mid-afternoon.'

'Great. Call me when you get in. I'll have the skinny on this *tovarisch* by then.'

Erin laughed. 'No reason to think he's a communist, Cat. Rather the reverse, I'd say. Evan – the guy I met – said he's pretty fond of the capitalist dollar.'

'Oh, I get that. But it's the only Russian word I know, so I have to drop it in when I can.'

'Alex can teach you some more if you want. His mother's Russian – I think he's pretty fluent.' She paused. 'Have you run into each other at all since Sunday?'

'Yeah, I went by your place at lunch today since I knew I'd be working late. He was there, sucking up to Miss Silver as usual. He changed the litter box, by the way – I was going to, but it was already done.'

So Alex had mended his ways in that respect. Good. 'Would you mind calling him again to fill him in? I'm beat, and there's an amazing bathtub here calling my name.'

'Sure thing.'

She ended the call and started her bath. The hot water, softened with a heaping scoop of the lavender bath salts the hotel provided, surrounded Erin, caressing her skin. It was almost like having every bit of her massaged all at once. She slid down till her head was resting on the back of the tub and let herself drift into dreamland. There, Finn and Evan faced off in a redwood glade, painting each other's portraits with fierce, competitive strokes, while a creature with Cat's form and Miss Silver's fur and ears led a blindfolded Alex from tree to tree in the background. A shadow lurked within the trees, and Erin tried to call out a warning to the others – but the shadow pounced on her instead. Before she could scream, the dream dissolved.

# NINETEEN

Erin took Highway 101 as far as the Golden Gate Bridge, then, on the far side, peeled off to the right onto surface streets until she could pick up Highway 1, which ran along the coast. It was a slower route, but she wasn't up for the South Bay/Silicon Valley traffic on 101 or 280. Crawling along 19th Avenue through San Francisco was all the city she could handle.

She stopped for lunch in Half Moon Bay and pulled into her driveway around three o'clock. Miss Silver greeted her with a mixture of affection and reproach, both overshadowed by hunger. Erin filled her bowls before taking her bags to her room. She'd unpack later. First, she needed to check in with Cat.

'Hey, I'm glad you called. Give me a sec.' Erin heard doors opening and shutting in the background. 'Had to leave the bullpen so I could talk. I looked up Mamelukov. He's definitely still alive. No record of his own, but he has some pretty shady associates.'

'Did you get an address for him?'

'That's the tricky part. Apparently he's in a nursing home. With dementia.'

Erin wanted to scream. Her whole trip might just as well have been in vain. Mamelukov was the only solid lead she'd found, when all was said and done, and it looked like leading nowhere.

Cat spoke again. 'I think we need a council of war. You, me, and Alex – he might be useful with the Russian connection. Your place? Six thirty? I'll bring pizza.'

Erin sighed. 'Sure. Whatever.' It was too late to accomplish much this afternoon, anyway, even if she'd had a place to start. 'I'll call Alex.' She realized with a pang of guilt she hadn't spoken to him in four days.

'Hey, Alex, I'm home,' she said when he answered. 'Cat says we need a council of war at my place tonight. She'll bring pizza. Can you make it?'

'Oh, I think I might be able to rearrange my busy social

schedule to accommodate you.' His tone became a little forced. 'Good to finally hear from you in person.'

'Yeah, sorry about that. I needed Cat to check stuff for me in police records, and the whole business was so exhausting . . .'

'You didn't have the energy to talk to your oldest friend. Sure, I get it.'

Erin suspected he didn't get it in the way he meant – as in finding that to be an acceptable excuse – but on a deeper level, he probably did get that she sometimes found talking to him draining rather than refreshing. Especially now, with all the new and strange emotions swirling around inside her, connected with other men.

'We'll have a good catch-up tonight. I'm going to take a nap so I'll be fresh.'

Alex rang Erin's bell at six fifteen, having gotten off work at six. A transparent ploy to get a few minutes alone with her before Cat showed up with the flat boxes of sustenance.

Miss Silver wasn't having this one-on-one business, though. She inserted herself between Erin and Alex as soon as they both sat down on the couch.

'Oh, Maudie.' Alex sighed in feigned exasperation. 'What *am* I going to do with you?'

She meowed as if to say, *Adore me, of course*. He scratched her head as she put her face up to his.

Erin did not at all mind a true tête-à-tête being prevented. She had far too much to sort through. 'How's everything at the library?' she asked.

'Same old same old. Not so many student inquiries now that school's out, but otherwise normal.' He looked up from nuzzling Miss Silver. 'Everybody misses you, though. They're asking when you'll be back.'

Erin sighed and ran a hand over her ponytail. 'That depends a great deal on what we figure out tonight. It looks like we may have hit a dead end.'

The bell rang again, and Erin got up to admit Cat, whose arms were loaded with pizza, a computer bag hanging off one arm. 'Let me help,' Erin said, taking the pizza and heading for the dining room. 'We'll have more room here than in the kitchen.'

She fetched plates and napkins from the built-in hutch and set them out. Alex joined them, Miss Silver making her displeasure at being abandoned known. She took one disdainful sniff of the pizza and then retired to her favorite sleeping spot on the couch.

When they'd all appeased their initial hunger, Alex wiped his mouth and said, 'So, what's the posish?'

Cat raised one eyebrow. 'Posish?'

Erin waved one hand. 'Don't mind him, he's just doing his Bertie Wooster imitation. Proceed, O enlightened one. Share your arcane knowledge with us benighted mortals.'

Cat looked even more bewildered, but shook her head and opened her computer. 'I can't access police records from my personal laptop, of course, so I copied over the relevant details. Which, I might add, is strictly against the rules.' She looked pointedly from one of them to the other.

'Right. You never told us that,' said Erin.

Cat gave a brisk nod. 'As I told Erin earlier, the artist whose name she was given as a possible forger is in a nursing home with dementia. So on the one hand, we might not be able to get any sense out of him at all. But on the other hand—'

'His guard might be down, and he might let something slip accidentally that he never would have admitted when he was in his right mind.' Alex smiled triumphantly at his own deduction.

'Right.' Cat shot him a sidelong look that might have held either admiration of his perspicacity or annoyance at his preempting her conclusion. 'Anyway, this Mamelukov appears to have connections to the Russian mafia.'

The color drained from Alex's face. 'Oh, shit. You don't want to mess with those guys. I hate to speak ill of my own countrymen, as it were, but they're the most ruthless set of bastards since Ivan the Terrible's *oprichniki*.' He focused on Erin. 'Promise me you won't pursue this. Leave it to the police. I don't want to see you end up sharing your mother's grave.'

Erin was taken aback. She'd known all along that this quest she'd embarked on could entail personal danger, but so far she hadn't encountered anyone who evoked in her that level of fear.

'Surely you're exaggerating, Alex. Whatever happened to my mother, it was twenty years ago. The man who killed her could even be dead by now. And the forgery scheme probably ended with Mamelukov's decline. What could they have to fear from me that would lead to such an extreme reaction?'

Cat fixed her with a somber gaze. 'He's right, Erin. No statute of limitations on murder – especially when the body's never been found. If we find it, or find enough of any kind of evidence to reopen the case, anybody who might have been involved in a conspiracy to kill your mother would still be looking at a life sentence. They'd consider that plenty reason enough to bump you off, if you were the only witness.'

Erin looked from Cat to Alex, a worm of fear growing in her belly. 'But I won't be the only witness. We're all in this together. Right? All for one and one for all?'

'Of course.' Alex laid a reassuring hand on her arm. 'I'm sure as hell not letting you go into this vipers' den alone.' He sent a glance of entreaty toward Cat. 'Nor will Cat. Right?'

'Hey, danger is my job. Once we have a case, I'll have the whole authority of the force behind me. It'll be pointless to get rid of me. But until then . . .' She cleared her throat. 'Until then, we all need to be very careful. And not do anything alone.'

They all digested that for a moment. 'So what's our next step?' Erin asked.

'I called someone I know in the art squad up in San Francisco and got the scoop. We need to verify that forgery is, or was, even happening. Mamelukov's one possible source, but we need physical proof – ideally, a forged painting that we can trace back to a specific chain. From artist to middleman – that's where the mafia come in – to gallery owners and/or private collectors. If Cruikshank is involved, you can bet he's only one of many. They have to spread the forgeries around, avoid saturating any one particular market.'

'Like with counterfeit currency,' Alex put in.

'Exactly. Now, Erin, was there one particular artist you thought Cruikshank might have a forged painting by? I mean, not by, because it's forged, but . . .'

'I know what you mean. Elliot Forbes.'

Cat looked bemused. 'Is he somebody?'

'Only the most famous artist ever to come out of the central California coast.'

'Right. So somehow we need to get our hands on that supposed

Forbes and get it examined by our expert on the art squad. How could we do that?'

'Can't you get a warrant?'

Cat grimaced. 'Not without having an official case open. And that would take Carver's OK.'

'We could hardly buy it. Cruikshank told me it wasn't for sale, but if it were – and I'm sure it would be, to the right person for the right price – it would cost in the hundreds of thousands. Where could we get that kind of money?'

Alex drummed a pencil against the table. 'If someone really wanted to buy a painting like that, wouldn't they insist on getting it authenticated first?'

Erin huffed. 'I'm sure Cruikshank has a certificate of authentication from some tame expert on his payroll. Or the mafia's.'

'But couldn't a buyer get their own second opinion? I know I'd want to if I were putting out that kind of dough.'

'I guess it would look pretty suspicious if he refused. He'd never let the painting out of his gallery, though.'

Cat set down her glass with a decisive clink. 'OK, here's the plan. Alex will pose as the potential buyer.' Alex opened his mouth to protest, but Cat said, 'You look the part. I don't. And obviously it can't be Erin because he knows her.'

Alex shut his mouth again.

'I'll get the woman from the San Francisco Police Department to come down and be your independent expert. Meanwhile, Erin and I will go and see what we can get out of Mamelukov. Sound like a plan?'

Alex shot Erin a glance full of trepidation. 'Yeah, all right. But it'll have to be Saturday. I'm working tomorrow.'

'Saturday it is.'

The plan left Erin with all of Friday to devote to something other than the investigation, since she had no further leads to pursue. In accordance with her initial purpose for this time off work – what had been her purpose before the dream – she spent the morning going through her father's things, arranging to have the hospital bed removed, and sorting his personal belongings into piles for trash, thrift store, and a few things – mainly books – to keep.

But all the time, her mind was on her mother. She was beginning to feel as if she'd never really known her – though the truth was, she'd known her as well as any child knows her mother. The adult side of Gina, the private side, the side that had burdens she did not want her daughter to share – that was what Erin was learning about now. And it was crucial for her to gain a better understanding of her mother as a woman, or learning the truth of her fate would be a job only half done.

The obvious place to start was in her mother's studio on the north side of the second floor of the house. Neither Erin nor her father had ever had the heart to dismantle Gina's private space. Erin had tidied it a bit during the first week her mother was gone, so it would be nice for her when she returned – cleaning the brushes, making sure the paints were capped, and straightening the sketches and canvases without examining their contents. But other than that, the room was untouched.

She approached it now with hesitation. Not because she expected to find anything disturbing or even revelatory, but because the room had always been a kind of holy ground – a place where art was made, a place her mother would come when she needed quiet and solitude. Erin was allowed in, but only with special permission; and often when she knocked, the answer would be 'Not now, sweetheart. Mumsie needs to be alone.'

But Mumsie had been alone for twenty years. Surely she would welcome her daughter's company now. Erin turned the knob, which creaked a rusty protest under her hand, and stepped inside.

Everything was just as she remembered it: the shallow shelves of paper along one wall; the drawers of paints and brushes, neatly aligned; the racks of canvases, both painted and empty; the easel in the center on its drop cloth – but all was covered with a thick layer of dust. Erin picked up a stray bandanna, shook the dust from it, and tied it over her nose and mouth. She would clean in here soon, but not now.

She made a slow circuit of the room, pausing to pick up a familiar object here and there – a little model of the Pigeon Point Lighthouse, souvenir of one of their adventures; a book of Monet's paintings, which as a child she had loved to pore through while sitting on her own special stool in the corner; a stack of small canvases Erin herself had created with non-toxic paints when she was small; a half-eaten box of fossilized chocolates from Mackenzies that Father had given Mumsie for her birthday a couple of weeks before she left.

She flipped through the painted canvases. They ranged over a variety of subjects, from landscapes, seascapes, and cityscapes to portraits of Erin at a variety of ages, documenting her little-girl fantasies of being a fairy, a princess, a ballerina. As she grew older, she was often posed with a book in her hand, sometimes echoing the composition of famous paintings with similar subjects. Erin thought any of these works could easily have held their own against most of the pictures on offer in Cruikshank's galleries; yet Gina had chosen to hide them all away.

At the back of the racks, she came upon some smaller canvases that she initially thought must be the work of another artist. At first they looked like abstracts, painted in swirling bursts of intense color that conveyed a sense of anguish and despair. But when she looked more closely, she realized that at the center of every picture was a surreal figure of a woman – sometimes contorted in agony, sometimes curled in a fetal position, sometimes wringing the bars of a cage, but always, always conveying rebellion against an unwelcome fate.

Erin felt as if she'd been skewered. Could her mother really have been so unhappy and hidden it so well?

She pulled out one of the surreal pictures and one of herself reading, intending to prop them side by side on the easel. But the easel was occupied by a large canvas draped in a cloth.

Now she remembered. The painting Gina had been working on before she left was one she'd never allowed Erin to see. When she was engaged on what Erin had now begun to consider her public work, although she never showed it in public – the outdoor scenes and portraits – Gina had been happy to have her daughter watch her work. But in this case she would only say, 'It's too awful. I can't bear for anyone to see.' Erin had swallowed her curiosity, accepting that her mother had her reasons.

But now she set down the other canvases and moved toward the easel, expecting perhaps another of the surreal women – possibly the most anguished of them all. She lifted the dust cloth slowly, almost afraid of what she might see. But she never expected the painting that now confronted her.

It was no woman, but a naked male torso sketched in with careless lines that faded out at the waist. And above it, glaring out at her, was the face of Seymour Finnegan.

Gina had painted the younger Finn in a few bold strokes resembling those of his own early style, defining the hollows of his face with swathes of purple, olive green, and midnight blue. His wild hair dissolved into a dark, featureless background in which many colors merged into a rich black.

But with his eyes she had taken special care. Gina had used a fine brush to delineate their exact contours and capture the precise, unique grayish-greenish blue of the irises inside their indigo rim. The eyes stared with living intensity from under heavy overhanging brows. The message those eyes had conveyed to Gina, Erin couldn't guess, but to her they seemed to say, 'Get out of here, woman! Can't you see I want to be alone?'

But the face as a whole belied that message. Instead it exuded the same magnetic sensuality with which the living man had turned Erin's world on its head.

His presence here, in her mother's room, was too much for Erin. Her stomach revolted. Like the young Sandy in *The Prime of Miss Jean Brodie* discovering her teacher's face looking out of the portrait Teddy Lloyd was supposedly painting of Sandy herself, Erin turned and fled.

# TWENTY

The nursing home where Grigory Mamelukov was serving the life sentence of his dementia was unlike a prison in any physical way. He'd made enough money during his active career to buy himself a place in the poshest retirement center in Santa Cruz County, where each nurse served only two or three patients and each patient was surrounded by familiar furnishings and possessions brought in from his or her own home.

When Cat, flashing her badge at the front desk, asked to see Mamelukov, the head nurse at first demurred, saying Mr Mamelukov did not receive visitors and was not lucid enough to converse with them if he did. But Cat persisted, and eventually her badge won the day.

The head nurse called Mamelukov's own nurse, who escorted them to his apartment – a spacious, airy suite of rooms with a balcony overlooking a flower garden in full bloom. A thin strip of blue ocean was visible in the distance. 'I should live like this,' Cat muttered under her breath. 'The criminals get the ocean view, and the cops get the cockroaches.'

Cockroaches were not a big problem in this part of the country, but Erin knew what Cat meant. Her own salary at the county library would never pay for a retirement like this. It was always the civil servants who had to scrape the bottom of the barrel of life while the self-serving climbers, law-abiding or otherwise, skimmed the cream off the top. That was probably a mixed metaphor, but at this moment she didn't care.

Erin looked around for the suite's resident and finally spotted a shriveled form slumped in a wheelchair, parked well away from the railing in the corner of the balcony. 'I'm afraid this isn't one of his good days,' the nurse apologized. 'He's hardly spoken at all today.' She approached the wheelchair and said in a loud, artificially cheerful voice, 'Look, Mr Mamelukov! You have visitors! Isn't that nice?' She pushed the chair out from the corner and brought it into the room, parking it to face the sofa where Cat and Erin sat.

Erin looked at the figure before her with its vacant eyes, slack jaw, and line of drool snaking down the chin, and despaired. She cleared her throat, unsure how to begin. Again, she could hardly lead off with the bald question, 'Are you an art forger?' She looked around the room, hoping to see something that could spark a neutral lead-in to the conversation.

Meanwhile, Cat plunged ahead. 'Mr Mamelukov? I'm Cat Herrera, and this is my friend Erin Washington.' Erin noted she'd opted to skip her own title of Detective. No doubt a wise move. 'I understand you're an artist.'

The eyes sharpened their focus for a millisecond, and Erin took the advantage. 'I see you have a Forbes on your wall,' she said, pointing to a small beachscape in a high corner under the vaulted ceiling.

The artist's eyes shifted upward, but the painting was behind him, and no doubt his neck was too stiff with age and arthritis to turn that far. One corner of his mouth sneaked upward, and a glint came into his eye, as of a child who has successfully put one over on his parent.

'Could we see it up close?' Erin asked. The old man in the wheelchair didn't say no.

'Do you have a stepladder?' Cat asked the nurse, and she scurried to fetch one. Erin mounted the steps and lifted the frame from its hook, then descended holding the Forbes in her hand.

Only it wasn't a Forbes at all. It certainly looked like one – the light and the brushwork were perfect, exactly those of the master. And in the bottom left corner, the famously looped signature 'E. Forbes' crossed the sand at the base of a clump of three Monterey pine trees. But threaded into the bark of the pines, as in a sophisticated version of a child's 'find the hidden words' cartoon, were the barely discernible letters 'G A M.'

Erin brought the painting back to the couch and silently pointed out the letters to Cat. Cat nodded and mimed the clicking of a camera shutter. Erin took the painting back to the stepladder, took several shots of the whole thing plus half a dozen closeups of the initials and signature, and then restored the frame to its place on the wall.

Cat watched her, then at Erin's nod, said to their unwilling host, 'I can see you're not in the mood to talk today, Mr Mamelukov. We won't bother you anymore.' She stood and walked to the door.

Erin fell in after her, looking back to see the old man's eyes following them out. Their expression was unreadable, but even assuming he understood what had just transpired, she thought he was more likely gloating than alarmed. What could the law do to him that nature had not done already? His surroundings might be luxurious, but his body and mind had become a prison from which he could only escape through death.

In the parking lot, Cat said, 'Did you get it?'

Erin nodded. 'Clear as day. Be pretty hard to Photoshop, too, I would think. We've got our evidence.'

'But he never sold this one, so it isn't technically forgery – just copying for personal use. You don't suppose he hid his initials in all his forgeries, do you? Thumbing his nose at people he thought too ignorant to figure it out?'

'Unlikely. There was always the chance one of the forgeries would be evaluated by a real expert – one who wasn't in somebody's pocket. I don't think he'd take the risk. No, this was probably just his private joke.' Erin's mouth quirked. 'I have to admit, it's a pretty good one.'

'But if this is the only example of it, the joke's on us. We have something highly suggestive – proof he was capable of convincing forgery – but still no proof he actually painted such things for sale.'

Erin swore under her breath. 'This is a hell of a job you've got, Cat. How do you ever bring a single criminal to book? Every time we think we have something, it slips through our fingers.'

'Oh, you'd be surprised,' Cat replied. 'These people are smart – that's what makes them slippery. The average criminal is a moron who leaves tracks a mile wide for us to follow. You know those Darwin awards you read about, where some idiot has obligingly removed himself from the gene pool by his own stupidity? That's what most crimes are like. As if the forger had taken a red marker and written in six-inch letters across the whole painting, "THIS IS A FAKE." Then we would just say "thank you very much" and haul him in.'

Erin gave a hollow laugh. 'Let's just hope our Mr Alexander Larson, the wealthy but not very savvy collector from Minnesota, is having better luck.'

Erin and Cat met Alex and the expert from SFPD for lunch at the Whole Enchilada in Moss Landing, roughly halfway between Santa Cruz and Carmel. Cat introduced Erin to Victoria Yoshima, whose chic gray sheath and sleekly styled black hair made Erin wish she'd given more thought to her own appearance. She was wearing a typical work outfit of generic black slacks and nondescript top, with her hair in its usual ponytail.

Once they'd ordered and dispensed with the niceties, Cat led off the real conversation. 'How'd it go, you two?'

Alex, looking quite the gent in an off-white linen jacket over navy slacks, blew out a long breath. 'I think I was fairly convincing. At least, Cruikshank acted like he bought my story. We pretended to be a couple' – he shot a laughing look at Victoria, who simply nodded – 'and told him we were interested in something collectible. I hinted money was no object. It wasn't long before he pulled the supposed Forbes out of the window.' He handed the baton to Victoria with a look.

'I waited until he was distracted with another customer to pull out my loupe and examine the painting. Of course, I can't be definitive without testing the canvas, paint, and so forth in the lab. On the surface, the execution is indistinguishable from Forbes's. But I did notice one telling detail.'

Victoria produced her phone and pulled up a photo of the painting, then set the phone on the table facing Cat and Erin. 'You see that rock formation off to the right? With the edge that looks a bit like a face looking toward the center of the picture?'

They both nodded.

'In a real Forbes that hangs in the de Young museum, that exact rock formation is visible – but it's on the left, and it looks toward the center as well. This painting is a mirror image. It wasn't done from nature.'

Cat and Erin exchanged excited glances. 'You mean we've got him?'

'I mean you have probable cause to impound the painting as evidence and let me give it a thorough going-over in the lab.'

Cat pumped a fist and rose slightly in her chair, as if barely containing herself from jumping up and doing a victory dance right there in the restaurant. 'Yes! I can't wait to see Carver's face when I tell him. I've uncovered an art forgery ring right under his nose. Promotion, here I come!'

Victoria watched her with what looked like a mixture of patient affection and regret. In a gentle voice, she uttered the single word, 'Jurisdiction?'

Cat fell to earth with a thud. 'Oh, shit. I'll have to liaise with Carmel. And that means going through Carver.' She buried her face in her hands. 'He'll take the whole thing away from me faster than you can say *glory-hound*. If only this were happening a week from now – he's literally seven days from retirement.' She sent a look of entreaty around the table. 'I don't suppose we could sit on this for a few days?'

'I have to go back to work next week,' Erin said. She was torn between the impulse to pounce on Cruikshank and his associates as quickly as possible and a small voice in the back of her mind that told her Carver might not be an ally – not even with compelling evidence to convince him there was a legitimate case to pursue. If she and her friends had been able to get to this point twenty years after the fact, surely Carver could have discovered some sort of lead back when Gina first disappeared. If, that is, he had truly wanted to.

Cat turned to her with a face full of sympathy. 'I know this is really important to you, but now that we have some actual evidence, the police can take over. You don't need to be personally involved – and it would be a lot safer for you not to be.'

'You have evidence of the current forgery. But there's still no solid proof it has anything to do with my mother's death. I suspect that she suspected what we suspect was happening – that's as far as it goes.'

'Oh.' Cat deflated. 'That's true.' Then she brightened again. 'But we can still work on the murder angle without involving other departments, at least for now. Gina went missing in Santa Cruz, she worked for Cruikshank in Santa Cruz – whatever connections she made in her mind, she made there. The probability of a forgery ring just confirms we're on the right track.'

'But to nail an individual for her murder, we'll have to find all the people involved in this ring,' Alex reminded her. 'Or those who were involved twenty years ago. Short of squeezing a full confession of conspiracy with names of associates out of Cruikshank, how do you propose to do that?'

'We do have some idea who's involved in the Russian mob in this area,' Cat replied. 'Who Mamelukov's associates were, for a start. Assuming they're not all as old and decrepit as he is.'

'And you think they're going to tell you anything if you can't even bring a charge of conspiracy to sell forged art?' Victoria put in. 'I may not be a beat cop, but even I know that's a non-starter.'

Cat sank down until her head was resting on the back of the booth. 'You're right, of course. What was I thinking? We're hosed.'

Erin had been listening to this exchange with a growing conviction. She had to solve the mystery, not only of her mother's death, but of her life. And to do that, she would have to confront her own personal demon in the flesh.

'There is still one other avenue open to us. I can snoop around in the art world.'

'Not Finnegan?' Cat sat up straight. 'No, Erin. It's not worth that.'

Alex looked from one of them to the other. 'Not worth what? You said Finnegan knew your mother, right? Sounds like he could be helpful.'

Erin quelled Cat with a look. 'Yes. He could be helpful. He's a bit of a loose cannon – that's all Cat's concerned about. But he's certainly worth another conversation.'

And that conversation could only be inaugurated by Erin agreeing to sit for him. A process that she knew, even if she never removed a stitch of clothing, would lead to her baring her soul.

# TWENTY-ONE

Cat drove Erin home from the restaurant. 'You will be careful, won't you?' she pleaded. 'Don't let this guy get under your skin.'

*Too late for that*, Erin thought but didn't say. 'I'll be careful.'

At home, she retrieved Finn's card from her wallet and forced her shaking fingers to tap in his number. As expected, he didn't pick up, so she left a message: 'This is Erin Washington. I've decided I will sit for you after all. I'm free the rest of the weekend, but I have to go back to work on Monday, so if you can fit me in today or tomorrow, that would be ideal.'

She was about to hang up when Finn's gruff voice cut in: 'Now. Come now. I'll be ready in an hour.'

That left her a few minutes to brush her hair out, decide he'd probably prefer her without makeup, and change into a red blouse that had garnered her more compliments than anything else in her wardrobe. Putting on the confidence she needed to go through with this mad plan was not so easy.

On impulse, she went into Gina's studio and wrapped up one of the smaller surreal paintings to take with her. She needed another perspective on them, and Finn was the only person she knew who might possibly have understood the side of Gina that was revealed there.

Finn answered his door almost before she had time to knock. She tried not to show how his magnetism overwhelmed her at first sight, but she could feel a flush creeping up her neck. He looked her over, right there in the doorway, and nodded. The painter was clearly foremost this afternoon and not the man.

'You've changed,' he stated flatly.

Erin blinked in surprise. 'I let my hair down.'

Brisk head-shake. 'No. Something in your eyes.'

Could her experiences over the last week have affected her so profoundly as to be visible to the casual observer? But then, Finn was far from a casual observer.

One corner of his mouth curled. 'You may be starting to wake up. This could be better than I thought.'

He pointed to a corner occupied by a coatrack. 'Put your stuff over there.' She hung her purse and leaned the painting against the rack, wishing for a more appropriate place to leave it.

He led her to a stool in the middle of the studio. Behind it was a soft blue-gray drape.

'The blouse is good. I see you got a bit of your mother's aesthetic sense, at least.' Finn helped her onto the stool and adjusted her hair and the draped neck of her top. Then he grabbed a camera and took about a thousand photos from every possible angle.

Erin couldn't conceal her surprise. 'You're going to paint from a photograph?'

'Nope. Just for reference,' he said between clicks. At last, he set the camera down and picked up a sketchpad and charcoal. With these, he dashed off sketch after sketch, until Erin's back was starting to ache from sitting on the backless stool.

Finally he moved to the easel, where a large fresh canvas stood waiting, and took out a soft pencil. 'Could I have a break first?' Erin asked timidly. 'My back hurts already, and I'm thirsty.'

Finn set his pencil down. 'Sorry, got carried away. Sit over there.' He pointed to the decrepit couch, then vanished into another room and came back with a cold bottle of water. 'Five minutes do you?'

'I hope so.' Erin drank deeply, then realized she might not get a restroom break for a while and slowed to sipping.

Finn paced in front of the easel while she rested, then checked his watch. 'Ready?'

Erin nodded and assumed the position. He adjusted her again, then retreated behind the easel, not speaking, his eyes moving rapidly between her and his drawing. After a few minutes, he nodded to himself and took up a palette, which he loaded with paints. Erin was already sore again, but at this point she didn't dare disturb his flow. He painted until she entered a state of altered consciousness in which all the individual parts of her body that had started to ache merged into a symphony of pain.

At last, what seemed like hours after they'd begun, he laid his palette down and dropped his brushes into a can. 'That's it for today,' he said. 'The light's going. You can get down.'

Erin eased herself off the stool and stretched, willing blood back into her legs, then moved to the couch and fell onto it. She gulped the rest of the water, which had gone lukewarm. Finn continued to stare at the canvas.

'Am I allowed to look?' she asked.

'Not till it's done,' he said. 'You won't be able to judge till then. Anyway, whether you love it or hate it, I don't want to know.'

He stared a little longer, then glanced at her as if surprised to see her still there. 'You can go. Come back tomorrow at noon.'

Erin blinked at this summary dismissal. 'I was hoping to talk to you some more. About my mother.'

'Oh.' He took off his paint-spattered shirt, revealing a black T-shirt underneath, and ran his hands over his wild hair as if effecting a transformation from painter to man. 'I'll need a drink.'

Erin was slightly alarmed at this, but she remembered Evan telling her Finn did not drink to excess. And indeed, when he returned from the kitchen, he was holding two more bottles of water.

He handed her one and pulled up a wooden chair to sit opposite her. 'What do you want to know?'

Where to begin? 'A couple of things. One is about her personally and the other about her disappearance.'

She retrieved the painting from the corner where she'd left it and unwrapped it. 'I found a bunch of paintings like this in her studio. I'd never seen them before. They're totally unlike anything she ever let me look at. I thought you might be able to tell me . . . well, something about what they mean. What led her to paint this way.'

Finn took the painting from her as if it were a holy relic and placed it on a second easel that stood against one wall. He stepped back and gazed at it, frowning. 'You say there were a bunch of these?'

Erin went to stand beside him and nodded, though he wasn't looking at her. 'Different sizes, different backgrounds, different positions, but all with a figure of a woman. Always looking tortured.'

He gazed a while longer, then turned to her with glistening eyes. 'These are probably her best work. She put her soul into them. But you knew that, right? You didn't really need me to tell you.'

Erin swallowed. 'I . . . I guess I knew the woman in the pictures had to be herself. Obviously she wasn't the happy person I thought she was. But the depth of anguish there . . . I was hoping you could tell me something about what caused it.'

His mouth curled in a sardonic imitation of a grin. 'I wish I could say it was me. That she was so tormented about wanting me but feeling the need to keep her marriage together. But the truth is, she was already tied in knots when I met her. She was an artist – she felt the pain of the universe, as all true artists do. But she had no outlet for that pain, except these pictures.'

He fixed Erin with an accusatory eye. 'She was a passionate woman trapped in a loveless marriage by a kid. A kid she loved too much to hurt.'

Erin felt his glare like a spear piercing her heart. '*I* made her that unhappy?'

His face softened, and he turned to face her fully. 'You gave her the only happiness she knew. Gina was a woman created to love, and she loved you without limit. But she needed to love and be loved by a man as well.' He took her by the shoulders and sent his soul-baring gaze into her eyes. 'As do you.'

Erin's mouth went dry and she quaked under his touch, transfixed by his gaze. She knew her moment had come, and she was powerless to do anything to avoid it. She prayed to the God she did not believe in not to let her be destroyed by what was to come.

Finn leaned in and touched his mouth to hers. His kiss was gentle at first, but when she responded, he deepened it and wrapped his arms around her, almost crushing her. She lost herself in his embrace. Nothing existed except the electricity of his mouth on hers, the taste of stale coffee on his breath, the scratch of his stubble against her lip, the heady smell he carried of paint and turpentine mixed with manly sweat. She had no mind, no heart even, but only a body, whose senses and powers were all trained now to one object. She was at once terrified and grateful to lose control at last.

Then suddenly he released her and took a full pace back, his chest heaving.

She stared at him in consternation, her insides roiling. How could he stir her up only to abandon her? Where was all that newfound energy to go?

He gave her an apologetic half-smile. 'But much as I might like to, I'm not the one to do it. You're a beautiful woman, Erin Washington, and you'll make some man a hell of a lover once you learn how to trust. But when I look at you – when I kissed you – all I can see is your mother.' His eyes misted. 'You deserve better than her leftovers.'

He turned and began to wrap the painting back in the brown paper she'd brought it in. 'Besides, I'd be no good for you. I'm fine for a fling but not for a constancy. You need someone you can rely on. You've been abandoned once – you can't face having that happen again.'

Erin stared at his rough-cut profile as he was intent on his task. How could this man – on the surface so insensitive to others' feelings – see so deeply into her heart? Because he was right – another abandonment would kill her. That was why she'd never sought a relationship. Paul Simon's 'I Am a Rock' was her theme song.

Finn tied the string around the wrapped painting and handed it to her. 'Still, you're going to have to take the risk sometime. Or else you'll be wasted. You'll shrivel up inside until your soul is the size of a pea, and you'll be no good to this world or anyone in it.' He smiled fully this time. 'And that would be a crying shame – because you are Gina Washington's daughter, and you have a hell of a lot to give.'

After what had passed between them, Erin found it impossible to segue into a discussion of what Finn might know about a forgery ring. That would have to wait till the following day. She could only hope her wild new feelings would have calmed down by then.

She avoided calling Cat or Alex to report on the afternoon, since she'd accomplished nothing of value for the investigation and certainly had no intention of telling either of them what had actually happened. Cat texted her, but she responded simply,

*Nothing to report. Going back tomorrow. Don't worry*. She knew Alex always went to church on Saturday night and Sunday morning, so he wouldn't be pestering her for updates.

The subject of Alex himself cost her some thought, however. Finn had said she should find someone reliable, and Alex was nothing if not reliable. And if she was honest with herself, she had to admit he had given subtle signs that he cared for her more than as a friend. What was less clear to her was whether she could ever feel that way about him. He'd certainly never sparked an iota of the physical response that Finn had evoked so effortlessly.

Was that the way it worked? Would she have to choose between passion with a risk – almost a guarantee – of heartbreak, and a stable relationship completely lacking in excitement? Presumably the latter was the choice her mother had made – and lived to regret. Could it be worse to be trapped for life without love than to know that fire for only a short time?

But Finn had made it clear that a brief affair with him was not an option. Surely it would be madness to go looking for such feelings elsewhere.

She was left where she'd begun – with no one to whom she could give her heart. But perhaps that was just as well. She didn't need that kind of distraction while she still had the mystery of her mother's disappearance to solve.

Erin left early on Sunday morning for Finn's studio, partly to allow for slow weekend beach traffic and partly because she couldn't bear her own four walls any longer. She arrived a few minutes before noon, and he answered the door in a threadbare bathrobe – apparently with nothing underneath – with a steaming mug of coffee in his hand. She swallowed down the urge to untie the belt of his robe.

'Don't you know never to come early to a sitting, woman?' he said, but there was a teasing note beneath the gruffness. 'I suppose you'd better come in. Coffee?'

'Please.'

She followed him into a kitchen that nearly made her retch. Every spare inch of its cramped surfaces was covered with dirty dishes and near-empty takeout containers. But the cup he handed her was clean and the coffee delicious.

'I've been thinking some more about that painting you showed me,' he said. 'Apart from its emotional significance for you, it was a remarkable piece of art. Would you be willing to let me see the rest of them?'

Erin blinked. She'd never considered the possibility that Finn would see her mother's work as worthy of his notice from a purely artistic point of view. 'I don't know. Don't you think if she'd wanted you to see them, she would have shown them to you back then?'

He sipped his coffee while shaking his head, a maneuver that made Erin nervous, but he neither choked nor spilled. 'Not necessarily. She had no faith in herself as a painter. She was always telling me she only dabbled, she wasn't a real artist like me or others that showed in Cruikshank's. So she might have held back more out of a lack of confidence than a reluctance to share something personal.'

'But you think the one I showed you was worthwhile?'

'Absolutely. She'd clearly found her own style – not derivative of anyone I know. And like I said last night, she let her heart bleed onto the canvas. That's the first prerequisite of decent art.'

Erin bit her lip. Transporting all those canvases would be problematic. But was she ready to allow Finn into her home? Into Gina's studio? Then she told herself, *Don't be silly. He's already penetrated your soul, and your mother's. Your physical space is nothing compared to that.*

'All right. I guess. You could come over some evening after work.'

He shook his head, dumping his mug in the crowded sink. 'I'll surprise you.'

'I don't like surprises.' Especially not from someone as dangerous to her equanimity as Finn.

'I know.' He shot her a wicked grin. 'Consider it part of your education.'

'My education?'

'You know what I mean.' And strangely, she did, though she couldn't put it into words. 'Finish your coffee and get ready to pose. I'll go get dressed.'

Again she sat on the stool until she could no longer feel her legs. At last he allowed her a break. 'More coffee?'

'Water, please.'

He disappeared into the kitchen and emerged with a steaming mug for himself and a bottle of water, which he tossed to her as she sat on the couch. She poured half of it down her throat before saying, 'I never got around to the second thing I wanted to ask you about yesterday.'

'Oh, yeah. We got a little sidetracked, didn't we?' He grinned as if unconscious that he had turned her world on its head the day before. 'OK, shoot.'

'I have reason to suspect Cruikshank may be involved in selling forged paintings – and has been for some time. I think my mother may have found out about it, and that's what got her killed.'

Finn sputtered into his coffee. Erin went on. 'We found one artist who may have been doing the forgeries twenty years ago, but he's senile now and couldn't tell us anything if he wanted to. Have you ever gotten any whiff of anything like that going on?'

Finn coughed and wiped his mouth on his sleeve. 'You mean now, or back then?'

'Either. Both.'

'Back then, no. The only suspicious thing I ever saw was the way Gina behaved at my opening. If she was onto something, though, that would make sense. But now . . .' He took a long sip. 'I guess I have wondered about that Forbes Cruikshank has in his front window. Where the hell would he get something like that?'

'Exactly. We had an expert look at it – not formally, just there in the gallery – and she thinks it's fake. But we need to find out where Cruikshank got it. Most likely, not directly from the forger – we think there's a middleman involved. Or middlemen.'

Finn scratched his stubble. 'Who's this *we* you keep talking about?'

'My friends who are helping me look into this. One's a work colleague and the other's a cop. But she's doing this on her own time, so she can't access all the usual police resources. Plus Carmel is out of her jurisdiction.'

'Right.' Finn looked a little baffled. 'I don't know anything about middlemen. But I can think of one painter who might be capable of forging a Forbes. Maybe other artists too, I don't know. But I've seen her knock off Forbes, and she's damn good.'

'Is she local?'

Finn nodded. 'Name of Mariana Pescarelli. Her studio's just a few blocks from here. I could take you over there when we're done.'

'She's a friend of yours?'

'I wouldn't say that. More of an ex. But we're on reasonably friendly terms. Now.'

'And yet you think she could be a forger?'

'I think she's capable of anything.' He grinned. 'That's what made her exciting – for a while. Until she threw a can of turpentine at my head.' He rubbed a spot on his scalp and winced.

Erin shook her head. Artists. Would she ever understand them? Would she ever cease to be drawn to them?

# TWENTY-TWO

When the sitting was finished for the day, Erin was exhausted and starving. But if she wanted to meet Mariana Pescarelli, it was now or never. She drew on her reserves of strength to walk with Finn a couple of blocks south on Seaside and up a narrow cross street to a tiny cabin perched at the top of a hill.

'That's her studio?' Erin said as they looked up at the cabin from the street. 'She doesn't live there, does she?'

'Nah, she has an actual house somewhere else. Pretty fancy house for an artist, come to think of it.' He led the way up the steep drive. A red Ferrari was parked at the top. Pretty fancy car for an artist, too.

'What excuse are you going to give for introducing me?'

He shot her a look. 'You're interested in her paintings, of course. Why else?'

'Got it. And what does she paint – beyond possibly forged Forbeses, that is?'

He gave her a wicked grin. 'You'll see.'

He knocked loudly on the rough wooden door. Erin could hear a coloratura soprano singing impossibly high notes in Italian in the background. The aria concluded and the music was switched off before a non-recorded voice called, 'Come in!'

Finn pushed open the door. 'Mariana? It's Finn. With a friend who wants to see your pictures.'

Erin followed him into a volcano of color. Every inch of wall space was covered with paintings that exploded in violent tones of red, orange, purple, and gold. She couldn't begin to guess at their subject matter for the moment; her senses were completely overwhelmed.

Out of the volcano stepped a voluptuous figure clad in similar colors but with plenty of skin on view, all topped by a waterfall of thick, wavy black hair. 'Finn, *caro mio*! I have not seen you for eons!' She came up to him and planted a long, sloppy kiss on his mouth, rubbing her ample assets against his chest.

Finn took her by the shoulders and set her back a pace. 'Good to see you too, Mariana. This is Erin Washington. She's . . . a family friend.' He gave Erin a suggestion of a wink.

Mariana turned to her and immediately transformed into a professional. She held out a paint-spattered hand. 'Ms Washington. Delighted to make your acquaintance. You are an art lover, yes? You want to see my paintings?' She gave Erin the once-over and glanced doubtfully at Finn, as if to say, *Are you sure this little girl is ready for my art?*

Erin shook her hand and said, 'Yes, please.' But she wasn't at all sure herself that she was ready for it. Now that her eyes had had a minute to recover from the initial assault of color, she had begun to distinguish the subjects of the paintings. They were highly stylized, but as far as she could tell, they were all essentially pornographic, depicting either lovers *in flagrante* or abstracted extreme closeups of body parts. Erin devoutly wished that if she had to view such pictures, she could do it without Finn at her side.

She forced herself to say, 'You certainly have a fascinating approach, Ms Pescarelli.'

Mariana smirked. 'I think these are not what you would hang over your sofa in your bourgeois living room, no?'

'Perhaps not.' She gave a perfunctory smile. 'But then I don't go in much for bourgeois living rooms.'

Mariana raised an eyebrow, digesting this remark, then proceeded to take Erin on a tour of her displayed art, describing each picture in lurid, excruciating detail. Behind her back, Erin attempted to telegraph to Finn, *How could a woman who paints like this do a convincing imitation of Forbes?*

He returned a look that said, *You'd be surprised.*

When she could bear no more, Erin said, 'These are all quite fascinating, but I'm curious – just academically, as it were – whether you ever paint different subjects . . . or in a different style?'

Mariana ceased her explication abruptly, her mouth turning down in disgust. 'You mean you want to see what I hang in the galleries for the tourists? You can go to Raymonds for that. Why come here?'

'I'll do that the first chance I get, but they're closed now. Don't you have anything here you could show me?' Erin put on her best smile, but she knew it was Finn's smoldering smirk that Mariana responded to.

'Oh, very well. If you must.' She turned to a rack like the one in Gina's studio, where canvases were lined up with their stretchers toward the room, and drew one out. 'Is this drab enough for you?'

It was a seascape of the Carmel coastline, expertly if spiritlessly painted in a vaguely Impressionist style. The brushwork was quite different from Forbes's, but there was something about the light coming through the waves that looked familiar. At the very least, this picture was proof that Mariana could change her style and subject matter at will.

'It's lovely,' Erin said. 'Much more what I had in mind. But I'm sure you have an exclusive agreement with Raymonds, don't you? I'll stop by there next weekend when they're open.'

Mariana rolled her eyes and slid the painting back into the rack, then sidled up to Finn. 'You will have a glass of wine with me, *caro mio*, will you not? So this interruption will not be entirely wasted?' She shot a disgusted glance at Erin, to whom the invitation clearly did not extend.

Finn removed her hands from his chest. 'Sorry, love. Not this time. I have to be somewhere. But we'll get together soon.' He bypassed her puckered lips and planted a peck on her forehead. 'We'd better go, Erin, or we'll miss our reservation.'

Erin scurried after him, feeling fortunate to make her escape before Mariana's furious glare burned a hole in her back.

When they had reached the street in safety, she said to Finn, 'What reservation? Are you taking me to dinner?'

'That was a ruse.' He barked a laugh. 'Though I bet you have plenty of reservations! But speaking of dinner, I'm starved. Come on, I'll take you to my favorite dive. We won't need reservations there.'

Once again, the restaurant was only a few blocks away, so they walked. The evening was balmy with a cool breeze off the ocean – a refreshment Erin badly needed after the overheated atmosphere of Mariana's studio.

Strangely enough, she was beginning to feel almost comfortable with Finn. The previous day's kiss and subsequent renunciation had cleared the air between them. Although her blood still rose at his nearness, she no longer felt in danger of losing her reason in his company.

The restaurant Finn took her to was a little Mexican place on a side street, clearly a spot favored by locals rather than tourists. Erin glanced at the simple decor and the straightforward menu and decided Cat would probably approve.

'Order me a chile relleno and a plain margarita, would you? I need the ladies' room,' she said to Finn and headed toward a sign in one corner. Inside what proved to be the sole restroom in the place, she called Cat.

'Hey, long time no hear from! What's the scoop?'

'I found someone who might be our forger. It's a long shot, but Finn says he's seen her do a pretty impressive Forbes. And based on our brief interaction, I'm betting she doesn't have much in the way of principles.'

'Sounds promising. Not sure how to pursue it, though. Thinking someone capable of a crime doesn't exactly constitute probable cause for a search warrant. And I don't dare stick my nose into someone else's jurisdiction to question her.'

Erin couldn't believe what she was about to say was coming out of her own law-abiding mouth. 'She doesn't live in her studio. I was thinking we could break in.'

Cat whistled. 'That's as much as my job is worth, Erin. If we got caught, that is.'

She should have thought of that. 'Never mind. I wasn't thinking. I don't want to get you in trouble. I'll go by myself.'

'Now that would really be stupid.' A pause in which Erin could almost hear the gears turning in Cat's brain. 'How sure are you about this painter?'

'I'm not *sure* of anything, but I have a pretty strong feeling about her. And I've been going on not much more than feelings all along.'

Cat heaved a great sigh. 'When do you want to do it? We have to be as sure as possible of not being interrupted.'

'I was thinking tonight. She won't keep painting past dark. I'm having dinner with Finn here in Carmel – if you drive down,

I can meet you. I'll wait in my car a discreet distance from her studio and make sure she's gone.'

Cat chuckled. 'We're going to make a cop of you yet. Or maybe a criminal. OK, give me the address.'

Erin told her how to find Mariana's studio, then ended the call in response to an impatient knock on the restroom door. 'Just a second!' she called, flushing the toilet for verisimilitude.

She rejoined Finn at their table – presumably with a mischievous light in her eye, because he looked her over with a raised eyebrow. 'What's got you looking like the cat that got the cream? I never found the toilet here that interesting, myself.'

'Never you mind,' she said. She suspected Finn might be quite willing to enter into her plan for the evening, but she didn't want to get him in trouble unnecessarily if anything went wrong.

They had a pleasant dinner, chatting about neutral subjects like old friends. Finn told anecdotes about his acquaintances in the art world that had Erin nearly choking on her food. She in turn shared a few colorful stories about library patrons and their unusual research requests.

Erin found herself talking and laughing more easily than she could remember doing in years, and it wasn't only because of the margarita. From time to time, she glimpsed something in Finn's eyes as he looked at her that she hadn't seen there before.

As they were finishing their meal, he said out of the blue, 'I'm going to need another sitting.'

Erin blinked. 'I assumed you would.'

He waved a hand. 'You don't get it. When we quit this afternoon, I thought I had enough to finish on my own. But now I'm seeing something different in you. I have to catch it.' He frowned. 'If I can.'

A deep thrill ran through her. Not a thrill of attraction this time – rather, the first stirrings of a suspicion that she might be starting to come into her own.

# TWENTY-THREE

Erin said goodnight to Finn at her car and drove off as if heading home, then doubled back to park down the street from Mariana's studio. No light showed from the cabin, and the Ferrari was gone from the driveway. She settled back to wait for Cat. After a few minutes, the margarita took hold and she dozed, only to be awakened by a tap at her window.

Cat stood back to let her out. 'Fine stakeout officer you'd make,' she teased. 'Falling asleep on the job.'

Erin yawned. 'She was already gone when I got here. Nothing to watch.'

'Assuming she didn't come back for something and spot you. Which house is it?'

'There.' Erin pointed. 'That tiny cabin at the top of the hill.'

Cat eyed the long, exposed driveway and winced. 'It would have to be a full moon. Let's hope the neighbors are oblivious.'

They climbed the steep drive as quietly as they could without seeming furtive. At the top, Cat motioned Erin to wait while she pasted her back against the cabin wall and inched toward a window. She took a pinpoint flashlight from one pocket of her cargo vest and shined it cautiously inside.

'Nobody home,' she said in a loud whisper. 'Come on.'

Cat tried the window first, but it appeared to be locked. Then she approached the front door and clapped a hand over her mouth to stifle a burst of laughter. 'This lock's a dinosaur,' she whispered. She pulled a roll of tools from an inside pocket and selected two long, thin implements that resembled something a dental hygienist might use. She inserted one of them into the lock and held it steady while she poked around with the other. Soon Erin heard a satisfying click.

'We're in.' Cat pushed the door open. 'Not too security conscious, is she?'

'I guess not. But honestly, if you could see these paintings properly – I doubt they command very high prices.'

'I thought you said she was good?'

'She's skilled, yes. But in her own work she has a – shall we say, a distinctive style. And choice of subject matter.'

Cat shrugged. 'Whatever you say. Where do we start?'

'We'll need more light. If we close the blinds and turn the lights on, that will look less suspicious than a moving flashlight beam, won't it? On the off-chance anyone's looking.'

'Right.' Cat moved to pull down the blinds on the two front windows while Erin found the light switches.

Cat blinked in the sudden light, then, as her eyes adjusted, she whistled. 'I see what you mean. From what you've told me, this stuff is nothing like Forbes, is it?'

'Couldn't be more different. But she's a versatile painter. Come and look at these.' Erin began pulling paintings from the rack and lining them up for inspection.

Cat gazed at the innocuous Carmel seascapes and landscapes in bafflement. 'The same artist did these and those?' She gestured to the obscenities hanging on the walls.

Erin nodded. 'Hard to believe, isn't it? And none of them are what I would call worthy of her obvious talent. For different reasons.' She pulled out the last of the 'tourist' paintings, then slid them all back in their places. These were not what she was looking for.

She turned to survey the small room. A door at the back caught her eye, but it proved to lead only to a tiny cupboard into which were crammed a toilet, sink, espresso machine, and assorted supplies. She closed the door and turned back into the room. Then her eye fell on a set of shallow drawers like those her mother kept her papers and sketches in. Her thumbs began to tingle.

She reached the drawers in two strides and pulled out the bottom one. It was full of used sketchbooks. Erin flipped through them and saw only what the artist's displayed paintings would lead her to expect. The next drawer held larger loose sketches of the same ilk, the one above that unused sketchbooks and paper. More of the same until she came to the top drawer, which was locked.

'Need some more of your magic here, Cat,' she said. She stood aside and let Cat's tools do their work.

Erin pulled out the drawer to see another pile of sketches, all turned face down. She pulled them out, one by one.

Carmel seascapes, possible precursors to the tourist pictures in the rack. But the sketches did not convey any particular painting style. The subjects could as easily be those chosen by Forbes.

Then she found it: a sketch identical in subject to the supposed Forbes that hung in the Raymonds window. This one was far more detailed than the others – more so even than the Impressionist style of the finished tourist paintings. And in the bottom right corner was penciled the signature 'E. Forbes.'

'Gotcha,' she whispered, and pulled out her phone to take a picture. 'This is it, Cat. Any chance we can get away with taking it as evidence?'

'No chance,' came a voice from the doorway. The voice wasn't Cat's.

All senses on high alert, Erin turned slowly to face the door. There stood Mariana Pescarelli, eyes flaming, holding a tiny gold pistol aimed at Erin's heart.

Cat stood off to one side, her hands raised. Erin didn't need to be told to follow suit. She told herself this was really happening, the gun was most likely loaded, her life was in danger – but something in her didn't believe it. Being held at gunpoint was something that happened on TV, not in real life – at least not to people like her. Her disbelief held total panic at bay.

'Your phone,' Mariana said, coming close and holding out her free hand. Erin placed her phone in it.

'Please . . .' she began. But Mariana cut her off.

'Don't worry, little girl. I won't smash your precious phone. I'm just going to make sure you don't leave here with any pictures of my work.' She gave a sardonic smile. 'I must protect my intellectual property rights. You understand.'

'You don't respect other artists' rights,' Erin blurted. 'Elliot Forbes, for example.'

Mariana shrugged. 'He is dead. Like so many great painters.' She glanced up from the phone with a cold light in her dark eyes. 'Like so many busybodies might be if they don't watch their step.'

Cat spoke up for the first time. 'I'm a police officer,' she said in a loud, commanding voice that was a bit too shaky to be convincing. 'I pushed the panic button on my phone when I saw you coming. Backup is on the way.'

Mariana gave Cat a sidelong look, sizing her up. 'I do not believe you,' she said calmly. 'You may be a police officer, but you have no backup coming. And clearly you have no warrant, or you would not have broken in. You would have knocked on the door when I was here to open it.'

Erin's mind raced. There were two of them to one of Mariana, and Cat at least was undoubtedly stronger than their captor. If they were in the movies, they would have pulled some clever move to disarm her by now. But Erin's mind was empty of such strategies, and Cat didn't look full of ideas, either. Erin's only hope lay in Mariana's words about her leaving there with pictures. She couldn't do that if she were dead.

Mariana finished with Erin's phone and handed it back to her. 'Now take that sketch you were looking at and throw it on the floor.'

Erin did as requested, memorizing the sketch as far as she could in a couple of seconds. Too bad she couldn't download her mental picture for anyone else to see.

With her sandaled foot, Mariana pushed the sketch away from the two of them on the painted concrete floor. Then, with the gun still trained on Erin, she took a book of matches from her pocket, tore one off and struck it with a practiced one-hand move, and dropped it on top of the sketch. The thick paper took a moment to catch fire, then the flames spread out from the center until all Erin's precious evidence was consumed.

Mariana looked from Erin to Cat and made a quick gesture with her gun in the direction of the door. 'Now get out.'

Their eyes glued to the gunwoman, Erin and Cat sidled toward the door and slid out of it. Then they turned and ran down the driveway and back to Erin's car. They both scrambled in, and Erin locked the doors.

Cat leaned her head back on the headrest and groaned. 'I didn't exactly cover myself with glory back there.'

'We're all still alive,' Erin reassured her. 'That's the most important thing, right?'

'I suppose. But I was trained to handle situations like that. I should have been able to either talk her down or disarm and arrest her. But I just froze. I couldn't remember one single thing I'd been taught. And now we're back where we were, without a shred of evidence.'

'At least we have a name to give the Carmel police, though, right?'

Cat shot her a skeptical look in the moonlight. 'And tell them what? That I, a serving police officer, broke into the premises of a civilian with no probable cause, no warrant, and outside my jurisdiction to boot? Bye-bye, career.'

Erin sighed and dropped her head back as well. They'd risked their lives for nothing. No proof, anyway. What good was knowledge of criminality if you couldn't prove it?

'Now that painter's onto us, there's no way we can sit on this for a week,' Cat said. 'She'll put the wind up everybody involved, and they'll all go to ground. I'm just going to have to swallow my pride and turn this thing over to Carver in the morning. There's nothing else for it.'

'But turn what over? We still have nothing concrete.'

'We have Victoria's expert opinion. That should count for something even without a full analysis. And you could tell the Carmel police you saw the sketch when you were there earlier with Finn. Couldn't you?' Cat entreated her. 'I hate to ask you to lie, but it would almost be true, right? And it could save my bacon.' She snorted. 'Me being a pig and all.'

Erin nodded. She didn't like lying, but she had gotten Cat into this – she owed her that much. 'Yes. I could do that.' Her reservations about Carver had not diminished, but she couldn't see another way forward; Cat was perfectly right about the consequences of delay. 'So shall I meet you at the station tomorrow morning?'

'Nine o'clock. That'll give me time to lay the groundwork.' Cat reached over and squeezed Erin's hand. 'Thanks. I owe you one.'

'No, you don't. I got you into this, remember? Whatever comes of it, I owe you. And I won't forget it.'

Erin arrived at the police station promptly at nine the next morning with a heart full of foreboding. She couldn't remember much about her dreams – something about being lost in a redwood forest and the trees turning into men with guns – but they had left her with a strong feeling that she had taken a wrong turn somewhere and was getting, if anything, further from finding out the truth about her mother's death.

Cat was waiting in the lobby to meet her. 'Carver's expecting us,' she said. Erin wondered whether warning him had been wise, but perhaps it was the only way to be sure he'd be disengaged. Erin was due at work at ten, so she couldn't afford to wait around.

They climbed the stairs to the bullpen. Cat knocked on the door of Carver's office, then opened it without waiting for him to answer. He hastily ended a phone call as they entered.

'Erin.' He extended a hand over the desk to shake hers. 'Good to see you again. What can I do for you this time?'

Erin glanced at Cat, who nodded to her to proceed. 'We've found some evidence that Raymond Cruikshank's galleries are involved in selling forged paintings. I believe that was going on twenty years ago, and I think my mother found out about it. I think that had something to do with her disappearance – and her death.'

Carver swallowed visibly. He made a business of leaning back in his chair and casually linking his hands behind his head. 'That's quite a leap from what you brought me a couple weeks ago. How did you get there?'

Erin waved a hand as if brushing away a fly. 'The steps aren't important. What matters is that we had an expert look at a supposed Elliot Forbes painting in Cruikshank's Carmel gallery. She's as sure as she can be without formally examining it in her lab that it's a fake. And I've talked to a couple of artists who knew my mother – who saw her after she left home – and they both believe she was investigating something shady going on with her boss. It just makes sense that the two things are connected.'

Carver leaned forward and folded his hands on the desk. 'But you have no hard evidence of any of this?'

Cat broke in. 'Only the forged painting currently hanging in Raymonds-by-the-Sea. But that's enough to base an investigation on, isn't it? I'm thinking we liaise with the Carmel police, get a warrant to seize the painting, have it formally confirmed as a forgery, then use the fraud charge as leverage to get Cruikshank to talk about the situation around Gina's disappearance.'

Carver held up a restraining palm. 'Whoa there, Nelly. I'm with you as far as "liaise with the Carmel police." After that, the forgery business is their baby, not ours. And anyway, what makes you think Cruikshank is in on the deal? Couldn't he be deceived about this one picture himself?'

Erin shook her head. 'No way. One, he's too knowledgeable about Forbes and the market to be easily taken in, and two, he was extremely cagey when I asked him about the painting. Claimed it was from his own collection and not for sale. But when our expert went in and claimed to be thinking of buying it, he was more than ready to sell.'

Carver drummed his fingers on the desk, his eyes darting around the room as if searching for some excuse not to proceed. 'All right. I'll pass on the information about the possible forgery to Carmel, and they can decide how they want to proceed. But I don't see that there's anything to go on with this supposed connection to Gina's disappearance. If fraud is happening, what are the chances the same people were even involved twenty years ago? They could all be dead by now.'

Cat and Erin exchanged glances. Erin telegraphed caution, but Cat pushed on. 'We think the actual forger *is* someone different. In fact, we think we know who both of them are – the one who was doing it twenty years ago and the one who's doing it now.'

Carver gave a tiny jerk, then controlled himself. 'Do enlighten me, Detective. It sounds like you've been doing quite a bit of unauthorized investigation into this non-case.'

'Only on my own time, sir,' she said hastily. 'I haven't committed any police resources without permission.'

He narrowed his eyes. 'Tell me.'

Erin cut in. 'I got the names of a couple of artists who were thought to be capable of doing a convincing Forbes and visited them. One turned out to be senile and incapacitated in a nursing home, but he had a painting on his wall that looked every bit like a Forbes, except the artist had worked his own initials subtly into the design. We're pretty sure he was the one doing it twenty years ago. And the other one, we – I visited just yesterday, pretending to be a potential customer. She had a sketch that was identical in subject and style to the Forbes in the Raymonds window. It's pretty clear she's the one doing it now.'

'And she just showed you this sketch, did she?' Carver's voice dripped sarcasm.

'Well, no – not exactly. I sort of . . . found it. Poking about when she wasn't looking. The man who took me there was an ex-lover of hers, and she was preoccupied with him.'

'And did you get a photo of this sketch? Or any other physical evidence?'

Erin shot a glance at Cat. 'I'm afraid not. I was about to photograph it when the artist looked my way. I had to get the sketch out of sight quickly.' Erin prayed she wasn't giving herself away with these lies. She'd heard every liar had a 'tell,' a characteristic gesture that revealed when he or she was bending the truth, but since she wasn't an habitual liar, she had no idea what hers might be.

'I see.' Carver pierced her with his eyes. It was all she could do not to flinch.

He turned to Cat. 'Put all this in a report, with names, of course, and I'll send it along to Carmel. This is all clearly out of our jurisdiction.' He sat back with a self-satisfied smile. 'Nothing I need to get involved in during my last week on the job.'

'Yessir.' Cat stood, and Erin followed suit. They'd accomplished exactly what she expected from this interview – nothing.

Cat walked her back to the lobby. 'I'm sorry, Erin. It looks like we're still nowhere on this. And I'm not sure what else I can do.'

'I'm fresh out of ideas myself.' Erin listened a moment to the voice in the back of her mind that she was sure came from her mother. 'I think I've gotten off track somehow pursuing this forgery thing. Even if it is involved – which I still think it is – I'm not convinced it will lead us to the truth about my mother's death. I need to take some time to think it all through again.' She faced Cat at the station's front door. 'And in the meantime, I need to get to work.'

# TWENTY-FOUR

Erin had barely settled in at her workstation when Alex ambushed her. At least he came with coffee in hand.

'So, you've been incommunicado all weekend. You must have been sleuthing. Did you get anywhere?'

Erin accepted the coffee gratefully, noting he'd gotten the quantity of cream just right, and took a sip before answering. 'Hang on there, Watson, give me a minute to get my bearings.'

His face brightened. 'Oh, so I'm Watson, am I? I thought that honor belonged to Cat.'

'Cat is Lestrade, obviously, since she's a cop. Although she's a lot smarter than Lestrade. I'd give her Frank Abbott status as far as fictional police associates of private detectives are concerned.' She took another sip of coffee, then shook her head. 'But honestly, I don't feel much like Sherlock right now. Though it's hard to see what even he could have accomplished with a case that's twenty years cold. Deductive reasoning doesn't get you very far without evidence to reason from.'

Alex's face fell. 'So you didn't learn anything from your art contacts?'

'I didn't say that. Actually, I think Cat and I have found the current forger.'

'But that's fantastic! Do tell!' He leaned his elbows on the counter opposite her, as rapt an audience as anyone could wish for. If only she had a story worth his attention.

'I talked to Finn – Seymour Finnegan' – Erin hoped she wasn't blushing – 'and he told me about a woman he thought would be capable of doing a convincing Forbes. Mariana Pescarelli. He took me to her studio. That told me nothing except that she's skilled and versatile – she does one kind of thing for her own artistic satisfaction, I suppose, and a completely different kind of thing to sell in Cruikshank's galleries. But I had a feeling she was worth pursuing, so I got Cat to go back with me after the artist had left.'

Alex's eyes went round. 'You broke in? And you called Cat and not me?' His brows drew in. 'Sherlock would have called Watson. Never Lestrade, unless it was to make an arrest.'

Oh dear. Now she'd hurt his feelings. 'I wanted a police presence in case anything unexpected happened. And the more people you have involved in something like that, the worse it can go wrong.' She winced. 'And it did. Go wrong.'

'You mean you got caught?' Alex leaned all the way over the counter and gripped the edge on her side so that his panicked face was inches from hers.

She nodded. 'I found a sketch that had to be for the forged Forbes in Raymonds-by-the-Sea. But as soon as I'd snapped a photo of it, Pescarelli came back.' Erin didn't want to mention the gun unless she had to. Alex would go – well, ballistic. 'She deleted the photo from my phone and burned the sketch. So we have a very strong supposition but no evidence.'

'And Cat just let her get away with that? Why didn't she flash her badge and confiscate the sketch?'

'She was out of her jurisdiction, as well as being way out of line, breaking in there without a warrant. She didn't have a legal leg to stand on. And Pescarelli was very . . . forceful.' She grimaced in spite of herself.

Immediately Alex was all concern. 'You're not hurt, are you? Or Cat?'

'No, no, nothing like that. She's a strong personality, is all.'

Alex sighed. 'So having a police presence ultimately didn't do you any good.'

'Well, Cat did pick the lock and get us in. If Pescarelli hadn't happened to come back, she'd never have known we'd been there. Whereas if you'd smashed a window or broken down the door or something . . .'

'Yeah, I can see how badly that could have gone.' He drummed his fingers on the desk. 'So we're no further ahead than we were before.'

'Not much. Cat and I met with her boss, Carver, this morning, and he's going to turn what little we have on the forgery over to the Carmel police. But we have absolutely nothing solid to link any of this to my mother's disappearance. So I'm going to go back to focusing on that.'

'But how? What else do you have to go on?'

'Pretty nearly damn-all. I just have to hope she'll lead me to a clue.'

Erin got through the workday somehow, though she could hardly concentrate on anything other than her quest. Alex covered for her as much as he could, and she hoped anyone else who noticed would chalk it up to the transition from being on leave to working again.

She refused Alex's dinner invitation on the grounds of exhaustion, which was not entirely fabricated. But mainly she wanted to be alone to go over her investigation to date in detail and hopefully spot something of significance she'd missed along the way.

At home, she fed the insistent Miss Silver and cuddled her for a while to make up for having ignored her over the weekend. Then she fixed herself a quick salad and took it along with her case notebook up to Gina's studio. She felt closer to her mother there than anywhere else in the house.

Having made sure the unfinished portrait of Finn was covered, Erin perched on a stool and laid her notebook open on a tilted drawing desk. As she ate, she read through her notes, then updated them with everything that had happened over the weekend. Everything relevant to the investigation, that is. Some of what had passed between her and Finn would remain forever locked in her memory – the memory of her flesh as well as her brain. She certainly wouldn't write about it here in the studio, where she felt the presence of her mother's spirit as if Gina were leaning over her shoulder, reading everything she wrote.

As she read, she was struck by an apparent gap in the dates, so she drew up a timeline of what she had discovered about her mother's movements after leaving home.

| | |
|---|---|
| June 19 | first overnight stay at Tor House Lodge |
| June 21 | left home, drove to Newport, OR |
| June 21–24 | stayed at Sylvia Beach Hotel, met Geraldine |
| June 24–Sept. 4 | stayed and worked at Rockaway Beach Hotel, met Crystal |
| Sept. 5 | began work at Manzanita Massage & Spa, met Grace |

| | |
|---|---|
| Sept. 18 | left Oregon to drive homeward |
| Sept. 18–20 | stayed at Benbow Inn, met Evan |
| Sept. 27–30 | stayed at Tor House Lodge |
| Sept. 29 | attended Finn's opening |
| Sept. 30–Oct. 5 | stayed at Asilomar |
| Oct. 5 | stayed half a night at Seafarer's Rest |

She was right – there was a gap of an entire week between Gina's leaving Benbow Inn and checking in at Tor House Lodge for the second time.

Gina's friends in Oregon had said she was longing for home. The Benbow Inn in Garberville had been about two-thirds of the way, only five or six hours from home. Surely she wouldn't have taken an entire week to inch her way through the last third of the trip. She would have driven straight from Garberville to Santa Cruz.

And done what? She certainly hadn't come *home* home, to this house. If she knew she was in danger, would she even have stayed in Santa Cruz proper? Surely she would have chosen someplace close but more out of the way – up in the San Lorenzo Valley, perhaps. That would fit in with the redwoods theme Grace from the spa had mentioned.

Erin screwed up her eyes and tried to remember what lodging places she knew of in the San Lorenzo Valley back in 2001. Nowadays, the area abounded with private rooms and cottages advertised on Airbnb, but back then a visitor's options would have been limited mostly to motels and perhaps the odd actual B&B.

She could remember nothing of the sort in Felton, where their favorite walks in Henry Cowell Park were located. Traveling mentally north on Highway 9, the main artery that wound along the narrow, steep-walled valley following the route of the San Lorenzo River, she thought she could recall one motel south of Ben Lomond and another in Ben Lomond proper, neither of them in any way unusual or appealing. But in the next town north – yes, there was Brookdale Lodge, a quirky place full of history and, reputedly, ghosts that Gina had hoped to explore one day. Surely if she had stayed in the San Lorenzo Valley, Brookdale Lodge would have been her choice.

Erin vaguely recalled hearing about some disaster at the lodge a while back, so she looked it up on the internet to see if it was still in business. The fire that wiped out half the hotel's rooms had occurred in 2007. The owner had been jailed for insurance fraud, and the lodge had sat empty for several years. But it had been bought and renovated and was now open for business again.

Erin's heart sank. With a new owner and with such a gap since the tenure of the previous one – not to mention his having departed in disgrace – the chances of finding records or living memories going back to 2001 were slim indeed. But she could hear her mother's voice whispering that it would be worth a try.

Perhaps an indirect approach would be best. She might be conspicuous dining alone, but Alex could easily be persuaded to take her to dinner in the Brook Room, the lodge's unique restaurant dating back to the 1920s, named for the creek that flowed through the middle of the dining room. Or perhaps she could join one of the paranormal tours that exploited the lodge's history of tragedy and its reputation for being home to various spooky manifestations as well as at least one ghost. The ghosts, as permanent residents, would know whether Gina had been there – but would they tell?

The next paranormal tour turned out to be a couple of weeks away, so Erin approached Alex the following day about joining her for dinner in the Brook Room for research purposes. At first he brightened at the invitation, but then a shadow crossed his face.

'Isn't that the place where all those bad things have happened?'

'Yeah, it has quite a history. Supposed to be haunted, too.'

Alex shivered. 'I don't know, Erin. Putting ourselves deliberately in the way of evil doesn't sound like the best idea.'

'Evil? Isn't that a bit strong?'

'Not from what I've heard. I mean, I'm sure a lot of the ghost sightings and whatnot are inventions, but it sounds like there's something real at the bottom of it. I think the place is cursed.'

She frowned in disgust. 'I thought you were above all that superstitious stuff.'

'It isn't superstition to believe in demonic activity. Demons are as real as guardian angels – and very dangerous.'

'So are the people who killed my mother. And we might be able to do something about them, given the right information. Demons are beyond us.' She smirked at him. 'Unless you carry an exorcism kit in your pocket.'

He shook his head. 'I'm serious, Erin. I'm begging you – please don't go there. What could you learn, anyway? The lodge has burned down and changed hands since your mother was there – if she was there. And it's so out of the way. We know it wasn't the last stop on her journey, so what's the point?'

Erin sighed. She didn't know if Alex could ever understand the guidance provided by her mother's voice. 'I have a really strong feeling that she was there, and that I could learn something by going there myself. If you don't want to come, fine. I'll go alone. Or get Cat to go with me.'

Alex squared his shoulders. 'No. If you're determined to go, I'll go with you. And I'll wear my biggest cross. A cop would be no use against the kind of forces we might meet at Brookdale Lodge. At least I can pray for angelic protection if things go seriously wrong.'

Erin would never have admitted it aloud, but deep down she felt a tiny bit reassured by this. After all, if spiritual forces did not exist at all in the world, how could she account for her certain knowledge that her mother was guiding her in her quest?

She called the lodge and made a reservation for seven thirty that evening to give herself and Alex time to go home and change before driving the forty minutes to Brookdale. No point in dilly-dallying now that their minds were made up.

# TWENTY-FIVE

The summer evening was still light, though dimmed by the redwoods lining the road, as they drove up Highway 9.

'It's so beautiful here,' Alex said. 'I should really come up here more often. When you have the beach so close by, it's easy to forget about other types of natural beauty.'

'My mother and I used to come up here all the time,' Erin said. 'We'd walk in Henry Cowell Park or sometimes drive all the way up to Big Basin. You get a really different feeling in the forest as opposed to the beach. Sort of close and protected. And quiet. I miss it. I've never been able to bring myself to come back on my own.'

Alex took one hand off the wheel and reached over to squeeze hers. 'We'll do it together,' he said. 'Make new memories.'

She gave him a small smile, but she couldn't help wondering if he had a certain kind of memory creation in mind – in which case it might not go as well as he hoped. Still, it would be good to walk in the woods again.

The town of Brookdale was little more than a bend in the road. It boasted a few houses and a post office, but by far the dominant feature was the lodge. The sprawling complex consisted of the original low, multi-gabled Tudor-style buildings that contained the hotel lobby, a lounge, and the Brook Room, plus a couple of generic motel-style two-story wings housing guest rooms and a fifties-style diner. A huge mural of James Dean adorned the street-facing end of the nearest wing.

'The place has character, you have to give it that,' Alex said as they got out of the car.

'I think you mean it *is* a character,' Erin rejoined. 'Let's hope there's at least one human character around who goes back to the old days.'

They entered the lobby and approached the host, a well-groomed man in his fifties, at the table just inside the Brook

Room door. 'We have a reservation for seven thirty under Washington. We're a bit early,' Gina said.

The host consulted an iPad. 'Ah yes, I see. I'm afraid your table isn't quite ready yet. Perhaps you'd like to wait in the lounge? It'll be about fifteen minutes.'

Erin nodded. The more of the lodge she could explore, the better. 'Thanks, we'll do that.'

They found a table, and Erin ordered a sidecar to honor the 1920s history of the place. Alex asked for sparkling water. 'I'm driving,' he said in response to her raised eyebrow. 'And I want to keep a clear head in case . . .'

'In case we get attacked by demons. I know.' Erin still wasn't ready to take Alex's caution seriously.

'Please don't joke about it,' he said in a low voice. 'I've armed myself with prayer and a cross, and I've even got a tiny vial of holy water in my pocket. I believe with all my heart that Christ is stronger than any demon. But that doesn't mean I want to put it to the test.'

His earnestness subdued her. Anyway, if pressed, she would have to admit that her flippancy was only a cover for her own trepidation. Maybe it was the effect of all the ghost stories working on her imagination, but she could feel something in the atmosphere of this place that gave her pause.

As she had that thought, a sudden coldness enveloped her, chilling her spirit more than her body before passing on as if it had never been. She stared wide-eyed at Alex. 'Did you feel that? That was no ordinary draft.'

He stared back at her and nodded, his Adam's apple bobbing. 'See what I mean?'

Erin hurried to finish her drink as if that would hurry their table getting ready. Her illogical ploy seemed to work, though, because it was only moments before the host came in to fetch them. As they followed him back through the lobby, Erin's eye fell on a painting she hadn't noticed before, hanging on the front wall. The two-by-three-foot canvas depicted a forest scene with light filtering through redwood treetops and glinting off the foaming water of a stream that tripped over rocks in its downhill race – possibly the very stream that ran through the Brook Room, pictured higher in its course above the restaurant.

The subject was common enough for this area, but something about the style of the painting arrested her. 'You go ahead,' she said to Alex as the host hovered impatiently. 'I'll be there in a minute.'

She came up close to the painting and examined the brushwork. It reminded her strongly of the paintings she'd found in her mother's studio – not the intense, surreal ones, but the landscapes. Gina had never brought her painting gear when they came to the forest together, but she had remarked on being inspired by the majesty of the ancient trees; she could easily have come here alone while Erin was in school.

Erin checked the lower right corner of the painting and could just make out the signature, which was painted in a brown that almost hid itself amid the detritus of the forest floor: *G. Parker*. Gina had used her maiden name. Given what she had begun to learn and suspect about her parents' marriage, Erin was not surprised.

Her thumbs were throbbing now. This was it – proof her mother had been here, and the reason Erin had been led to follow her.

She hurried after Alex down the stairs that led into the Brook Room and stopped the host with a hand on his arm. 'Excuse me,' she said. 'Do you know anything about that painting in the lobby?'

He frowned slightly. 'Not really. Only that it was here when the new owner took over. He assumed it was part of the lodge's history and kept it hanging in the same spot.'

'I have reason to believe that painting is only about twenty years old. It was painted by my mother.'

'Really? I'm sure Mr Patel would be interested to hear that.' Erin couldn't be sure whether he was serious – and if so, what Mr Patel's interest would mean. Knowing the painting did not go back to the lodge's early days, would he decide to get rid of it?

'Is there anyone working here now who was here under the previous management?' she asked.

The host pursed his lips and looked skyward. 'I believe Mrs Chambers may have been here then. She's the night manager of the hotel. If you'd like to speak to her, I can ask her to come to your table.' He gestured toward an empty table a short way off. Clearly he was eager to get Erin and Alex settled so he could get back to his desk.

'Would you? That would be so very kind.' Erin favored him with her best smile and saw him soften slightly.

Once they were seated, she had leisure to look around at the remarkable setting for their meal. The long dining room was built in several terraces that rose up the hillside, divided into two curving longitudinal sections bordered by railings and greenery. Down the middle of the room, over its natural rocky bed, flowed a small creek. The year had been a dry one, so the creek was now little more than a trickle; but in wet years it had been known to overflow its banks and flood the restaurant.

At the far end of the room, a bridge connected the two sides of the dining room, and beyond that, the back wall rose two stories to the vaulted ceiling, with a group of gothic-arched windows looking out over the green hillside beyond. All around the room ran a narrow wood-railed gallery that gave access to doors leading who-knew-where.

'I have to say, this place is impressive,' Alex said. 'If it weren't for the haunted bit, I could really enjoy being here.'

'It is lovely, isn't it? My mother must have been thrilled to be here.'

Alex leaned forward and looked into her eyes. 'Erin, I hate to say this, but . . . well, the fact that they have a painting she did doesn't necessarily mean she herself was actually here. Does it? I mean, the then-owner could have bought it from her somewhere else and brought it here.'

Erin shook her head. 'I can see why you say that, and with any other artist, it might be true. But my mother didn't sell her work. Not as a rule. In all the time she was at home, she never exhibited or sold a single piece. And when I looked through the paintings in her studio, I didn't see anything with a similar subject. My guess is, by the time she got here she was running out of money, so she offered to do a custom piece for the lodge on commission. It looks like she was here for a week – that would have been enough time. She could work fast when she wanted to.'

'Hmm. It could've happened that way, I guess, but there are other possibilities. She could have taken the painting with her when she left home. Or she could have snuck back into the house when you and your father were out and grabbed it.'

That last supposition stung Erin to the core. 'No. She would never have come to the house without seeing me. It would have been too painful. And as for taking the painting with her – why would she? It's not likely she knew when she left that she'd end up staying here, so even if she had taken a painting or two to sell in an emergency, why pick one so particularly suited to this lodge? It doesn't make sense.'

Alex sighed. 'No, I suppose you're right.'

A middle-aged woman in a dark suit approached their table, and Erin had a flash of guilt, thinking this was their server and she hadn't even glanced at the menu. But then the woman spoke.

'Hello, I'm Mrs Chambers. I understand you wanted to speak to me?'

'Oh, yes, thank you for taking the time to come in. I'm Erin Washington, and this is my friend Alex Braithwaite. I wanted to ask you what you might remember about the painting in the lobby. The artist was my mother.'

Mrs Chambers' face opened in delight. 'Georgina Parker was your mother? How extraordinary! I'm delighted to meet you, my dear. May I sit down?' She laid a hand on the back of the third chair at their table.

'Please. So you knew her? My mother? She was staying here when she painted it?'

Mrs Chambers nodded. 'She was here for about a week, back in – oh, maybe 2000 or so. The previous owner was looking for something unique to hang in the lobby, so she offered to do him a picture of part of the grounds.' She lowered her voice and leaned in. 'That spot is actually supposed to be where little Sarah Logan drowned back in 1892, not long after the lodge was built. She was the founder's daughter, you know, and she's our most famous ghost. The owner wanted Georgina to paint her into the picture somehow – just a suggestion, you know, an eerie light or something – but she couldn't bring herself to do it. "I have enough tragedy in my own life," she said. "I don't want to paint someone else's."'

Mrs Chambers sat back in her chair. 'But why are you asking me about all this? Didn't she tell you herself?'

Erin swallowed. 'My mother disappeared from home in June

of 2001. I never saw her again. I believe it was in September of that year that she stayed here.'

'Oh, you poor thing. I'm so sorry. And you don't have any idea what happened to her?'

'I'm starting to piece it together.' She gathered her courage. 'It sounds like you were friendly with her. Did she confide in you at all? Say anything about why she was here or where she was going when she left?'

Mrs Chambers screwed up her eyes and stared into the distance. 'Not directly, I don't think. She seemed a little nervy – starting at shadows, that kind of thing. But then a lot of people get like that here if they're especially sensitive to the paranormal. And I think she may have dropped a hint or two. I do remember sensing there was something not right at home, something she was afraid of or running away from.' She grimaced. 'I'm afraid I kind of assumed it was her husband.'

'That's logical, but I don't believe it was him. She didn't mention a daughter – me – at all?'

'Not that I remember. But there was one odd thing – she always left the lodge at seven thirty sharp every morning and came back about an hour, hour and a half later. And she always looked like she'd been crying. But she never told me why.'

Erin exchanged a long look with Alex. 'Did your school day start at eight?' he asked her.

'Eight fifteen. She could have been driving to my school and watching to see me arrive.' Tears started to Erin's eyes. 'And I never knew. Never suspected. If I'd only had my eyes open, I could have seen her again.' The thought ripped her in two.

Alex laid a gentle hand over hers. 'She must have had a reason not to approach you. She must have worried she'd be putting you in danger if someone was watching her.'

Erin pulled herself together with an effort. 'You're right, of course. Whatever made her leave home would have stopped her from making direct contact with me.' She turned to Mrs Chambers. 'Is there anything else you can tell me?'

The older woman gave her a sad smile. 'Only that she was a lovely person and a very talented artist. I wish I could have known her better.' She patted Erin's other hand. 'But then, you already knew that.'

'Yes. That I knew.' She managed a teary smile. 'Thank you, Mrs Chambers. Thank you very much.'

'You're very welcome, dear. And now I must get back to work.' She pushed herself to her feet and bustled off.

Alex sighed. 'So we're not really any farther forward.'

'Not in terms of knowing what or who she was running from, no. But at least I can fill in the gap in my timeline. And I can kind of imagine what she might have been thinking.'

'How so?'

'Her Oregon friends said she was longing for home, for me. I think that longing drew her back to the area, and watching me at school every day brought it to a head. She must have felt the need to find out for certain whether the threat that drove her away was still a threat – or if it might be possible for her to come home. That's what took her back to Carmel. She wanted to resolve the situation once and for all.'

She looked up into Alex's eyes. 'And that's what I need to do. Resolve this. Whatever it takes.'

# TWENTY-SIX

Alex went broody during their meal. Erin was too preoccupied to converse about ordinary things, so they dined mostly in silence. From a purely culinary point of view, the meal was wasted on them.

On the drive home, Alex finally spoke. 'What do you have in mind when you talk about "resolving" this?'

Erin blew out a long breath. 'Honestly? I'm not sure. We've run into so many dead ends. The only thing I can think of is to confront Cruikshank directly.'

Alex jerked, and the car swerved momentarily into the opposite lane of the narrow, winding road. 'Erin, you can't do that! He could be dangerous. For all you know, he could have been the one who killed your mother.'

'He doesn't fit the description of the man who collected her things from Seafarer's Rest. The innkeeper described that guy as exotic – nobody would say that about Cruikshank. And he wouldn't write his numbers like a Russian.'

'True, I guess, but he's obviously connected to someone who would. Plus, you don't know for certain the murderer was the same one who collected her things – they could have been working together. You confront him and you'll be in as much danger as your mother was – maybe not right on the spot, but ultimately.' He took his right hand off the steering wheel and squeezed hers. 'I don't want you having to run away.'

Erin gently removed her hand. 'The thing is, I'd be willing to bet Mariana Pescarelli let him know immediately that I'm on his trail. Chances are the danger is already live.'

'Lord, have mercy.' He groaned. 'Well, I'm not letting you do this alone. I'm going with you.'

She shot him a look that she knew he couldn't see in the dark car. 'Do you seriously think we can both get time off on the same day? The reference desk would be empty.'

'I don't care. I'll take off whether they let me or not. Damn the consequences. I am *not* letting you walk into that den of vipers on your own.'

'Then I'll take Cat. We don't want to blow your cover as a potential art buyer yet, anyway. It could still come in useful.'

'How? Aren't the Carmel police onto the forgery thing by now?'

'I wouldn't count on it. The way Carver was behaving, I wouldn't be surprised if he sent Cat's report straight to email jail.'

'Then surely the first step is to check up on that? If you're wrong and the Carmel police are on it, they're a lot better placed to put pressure on Cruikshank than you are.'

'Yeah, but they won't know anything about the murder angle.'

'Then you can tell them. Cat's hands may be tied by interdepartmental protocol, but yours aren't.' He shot her a glance full of entreaty. 'Please, Erin. Go to the police. Don't put yourself in harm's way.'

*Again*, she added silently. Truth be told, she had no desire to find herself at the business end of a gun for a second time. The person holding it would probably have no compunction in pulling the trigger.

'All right. I'll go to the police first. But if they won't act . . .'

'Promise me you won't go off on your own without consulting me or Cat. That's all I ask.'

'I promise.'

It was getting late when Alex dropped her off, but Erin guessed it wouldn't be too late for Cat. With an insistent Miss Silver standing on her lap and nuzzling her face, Erin called Cat's number.

'Hey, I've been meaning to check in with you,' Cat answered. 'Any developments? There's nothing on my end.'

'You did turn in your report?'

'Yup. Yesterday. I don't think Carver's followed up on it, though.'

'I had a feeling he wouldn't. I've been following a different sort of lead.' Erin told her about the Brookdale adventure.

'But . . . does that help us at all?' Cat said when she'd finished.

'Not directly, but like I told Alex, I think my mother left

Brookdale Lodge determined to bring the situation to a head. And that's what I intend to do. Unless you have a better idea, I'm going to the Carmel police tomorrow and find out whether they got your report and whether they intend to act.'

Cat paused a moment before she said, 'I don't have a better idea. I'd like to go with you, but under the circs, I don't think I should. You OK on your own?'

Silly question. Until the last couple of weeks, Erin had always been on her own. 'Sure. I'll let you know how it goes.'

The next morning, Erin phoned in sick. Not sick, exactly, but she explained to her sympathetic supervisor that she'd discovered after a couple days of work she wasn't emotionally ready to be back and needed to take the rest of the week off. Whatever happened with her trip to Carmel, Erin suspected it would not be resolved in a single day.

She was filling Miss Silver's food and water bowls when the cat pricked up her ears and looked toward the front door. It would take something unusual to distract her from her meal. A second later Erin heard a knock. Her own senses on the alert, she looked through the peephole before opening the door and was flabbergasted to see the back of a head of short, wavy red hair. The head turned to reveal the face of Evan Gifford.

Erin unlocked the door and pulled it open. 'Evan! What on earth are you doing here? And for that matter, how did you find me? I only gave you my cell number, not my address.'

'Old school – I looked in the phone book. There were only half a dozen Washingtons, so I was prepared to try them all. But I got lucky on the second one.' His grin was disarming in its childlike satisfaction.

The phone book. Of course. Her father had insisted on maintaining a landline, and she hadn't yet gotten around to having it disconnected.

Evan went on. 'As for your first question, I have a show coming up in Carmel – not Cruikshank's, another gallery – and I thought I'd drop in and see how your investigation is coming along.'

Now that he mentioned it, Erin vaguely remembered him mentioning his upcoming show. 'It's good to see you. Come in.'

Miss Silver left her unfinished meal to check out the visitor. She approached as far as Erin's leg and meowed up at Evan.

'Well, hello, there,' he said, bending to offer her his hand to sniff. She nuzzled it, and he gave her head a scratch. 'Aren't you a beauty!' Miss Silver stood and put her front paws on his knee, so he picked her up. 'And friendly, too. What's your name?'

'That's Miss Silver,' Erin said. 'She's highly susceptible to flattery.' Which was true, but Erin knew the cat was also a good judge of character. She was relieved to have her own prior snap judgment of Evan's trustworthiness confirmed. 'Would you like some coffee?'

'Please. I had some brown liquid at the hotel, but I wouldn't exactly call it coffee.'

'Anything in it?'

'Just cream, please.' The same way Erin took it herself.

She left him in the living room, made two cups in her single-cup machine, and took one out to him. Miss Silver stopped prowling around his lap and settled down so he could take the mug. She must be very favorably impressed to be so cooperative.

Evan sipped from his mug in one hand and petted the cat with the other. 'Mmm, that's better. Thanks.' He looked around the room. 'Nice place you've got here. Was this your family home?'

Erin nodded. 'My librarian's salary would never run to a house like this in this county. I'm lucky to have it.'

'You live alone? You and Miss Silver, that is?' The cat lifted her face at hearing her name, and Evan touched his nose to hers.

'Yes. My father died a few weeks ago.'

He opened his mouth, presumably to offer condolences, but she held up a palm to forestall him.

'He'd been ill for a long time, and frankly we were never close. In the end, it was more a relief than anything.' She sipped her own coffee. 'Lately, though, I've been feeling as if my mother were back here with me. Especially when I'm in her studio.'

Evan sat forward abruptly, causing Miss Silver to glare at him. 'Is there any remote chance you'd allow me to see her studio?' he said. 'She spoke disparagingly of her own work, but I've always had a feeling she might have been a better painter than she gave herself credit for.'

'She was. I didn't realize it myself – as a child I wasn't able to judge, and we kept her studio closed, untouched, as long as my father was alive. But I went in there the other day and discovered a whole new side to her.'

Evan sat back. 'In that case, I withdraw my request. This is clearly a private and sensitive area for you. I won't intrude.'

Erin gazed at him in wonder. Of all her acquaintance, she didn't know anyone who would have understood her feelings so instantly and completely. Even Alex, though he was always considerate, had never been that perceptive.

She made a snap decision. 'I think I'd like you to see her work. I'd value your opinion.' Finn's judgment had been colored by his own feelings for Gina; Erin wanted a more objective view.

They stood, and Miss Silver, indignant at losing her seat on Evan's lap, went back to her interrupted meal. Erin led him upstairs to the door that she still hesitated to open, feeling like a trespasser. But she steeled herself and turned the knob.

Evan came in like an archeologist approaching a new site, primed with excitement for any great finds he might uncover. As he looked around at the 'public' paintings that were out on view, Erin watched the light dim from his eyes.

'She was certainly competent,' he said carefully.

'You're looking at the work she let me see as a child – what I used to think was the only kind of thing she did. But look at these.' Erin pulled the surreal paintings from the racks and propped them up along the counter.

Evan's face changed immediately, as if he'd just dug up a Roman coin in his California backyard. He swooped on one of the paintings and picked it up by the stretchers to look more closely.

'Now, these are extraordinary.' He glanced at Erin. 'Do you mean to say you didn't know these existed until recently?'

She nodded. 'Until last week. When I came in here for the first time in twenty years.'

He set the painting down and turned to her. 'That must have been quite a shock to you. Not discovering how talented she was, I mean, but seeing this' – he gestured toward one of the tortured figures – 'this glimpse into her soul.'

Erin was annoyed to feel tears starting to her eyes. 'Yes. It was. I already had an inkling that she wasn't as happy as I'd thought she was, because . . .' She hesitated, then decided there was no point in holding anything back. She strode to the easel and threw back the dust cover. 'Because of this.'

Evan came up to within a couple of paces of the easel and studied the painting with growing astonishment. 'Is that . . .?'

'Seymour Finnegan. Yes.'

He glanced at her and swallowed. 'Were they . . .?'

'Having an affair? Not exactly. I think he was in love with her, and possibly she with him, but he told me she refused to sleep with him because she wouldn't risk her marriage. Not for my father's sake, but for mine.'

They were standing side by side, regarding the painting, and now she felt his arm around her shoulder as if it were the most natural thing in the world. 'You have been through the wringer, haven't you?' he said gently.

'You don't know the half of it.' And the other half – her own experience with Finn – was something she was not yet prepared to share.

They stood for a moment in silent communion, then Evan said, 'Have you thought what you'll do with all these?' He swept his free arm around the room to include all the paintings, public and private – except the unfinished one of Finn.

'Not really. It's all so new.'

Evan nodded. 'When it's had time to sink in – and when your investigation is finished – you might think about having a show of her work. As a sort of memorial.'

'You mean – all of it? Together?'

His arm tightened slightly on her shoulder. 'All of it. The landscapes and portraits may not be inspired, but they're decent and workmanlike and would probably sell, if that's what you want. But these others . . . they're the work of a budding genius. If she'd lived to realize her potential, she could have made her mark on the art world in a big way. I think you owe it to the world to let them be seen.'

Erin leaned into him, feeling suddenly a need for support. 'I'll think about it. Seriously.'

A plaintive meow outside the closed door broke the spell. Evan blinked as if waking from a dream. 'Speaking of your investigation, would you like to update me on that?'

'Definitely. Let's go back downstairs.'

Evan picked up Miss Silver again and they returned to the living room. 'More coffee?' Erin asked, picking up the half-full mugs they'd left behind. Their contents were cold now.

'Please.' This time he followed her. She was glad she'd cleaned house so that her Craftsman-style kitchen showed to its best advantage.

He leaned against the wall, scratching Miss Silver behind the ears, as Erin busied herself with the coffee. 'You must have remodeled this kitchen at some point,' he said. 'You've done a great job integrating newer appliances and whatnot with Craftsman woodwork.'

'I can't take the credit. It's all my mother's design. I do love it, though.'

'You plan to stay in this house indefinitely, then?'

She shrugged. 'I have no reason to go anywhere else. And as I said before, I'm lucky to have it.'

He nodded, but not necessarily in agreement. 'Sometimes we have to leave a place before we can really appreciate it.'

'I feel like I've been on a journey of exploration the last few weeks. I haven't seen this house in a new light, necessarily, but I'm certainly seeing my parents differently.' She paused, stirring cream into the two mugs. 'And myself.'

'I sensed that,' he said, setting Miss Silver down and taking the mug she offered him. 'I can see a change in you even since we met last week.'

She felt the blood rise in her neck. Surely he couldn't read her mind to know what had happened with Finn. 'What kind of change?'

'Mmm . . . Hard to put words to it. I could paint it, though.' He gave her an impish grin. 'If you'd let me.'

She pulled out a chair and sat at the table. He followed suit. If she was really going to let Evan into her investigation, she would have to tell at least most of the truth.

'I have a confession to make. I've already sat for Finn. Finnegan.' Seeing his expression of pained surprise, she hastened to add, 'But only in aid of the investigation. I needed an excuse to talk to him again. He was the only link to the Carmel art world that I could trust.'

He sat back and crossed his arms over his chest. 'You'd better start from the beginning.'

So she did. She told him about Mamelukov, the Russian mafia connection, the stealth operation to evaluate the supposed Forbes. She skated quickly over the weekend with Finn, avoiding Evan's gaze, but told him everything about breaking into Mariana Pescarelli's studio – including the gun. His eyes widened at that, but he didn't comment. She summarized the interview with Carver, then gave only a quick précis of the Brookdale visit, since it hadn't contributed much useful information. Evan listened intently to every word.

Finally, Erin said, 'Cat doesn't trust that Carver passed on her report to the Carmel police, so I was about to head down there to check up on it when you arrived.'

He drained his mug and set it down decisively. 'Let's go, then. No time to waste.'

She started. 'You're coming with me?'

'Of course. You have me hooked into this story now – you're not getting rid of me until it's over.'

Something inside Erin relaxed at these words – something that had been wound tight for the last twenty years.

# TWENTY-SEVEN

The Carmel police station was in the downtown area but turned out to be so unassuming a building that Erin's hopes fell on seeing it. She parked in the small lot and said to Evan, 'This looks like a department that deals with parking tickets and vagrancy. Maybe the odd lost dog. Do you suppose they've even heard of art fraud?'

Evan regarded the building with pouched lips. 'Art is a big business in this town. You never know – it's worth a try.'

'I suppose. Anyway, we're here, and it's too long a drive to make for nothing.'

Inside, they were greeted by a young receptionist in a colorful dress who might have been found in any mid-sized office building. 'Welcome to Carmel,' she said brightly. 'How can I help you today?'

Erin shot a told-you-so glance at Evan. 'We're here to report a crime.'

The young woman reached toward a metal file organizer full of forms. 'Traffic, property, or personal injury?'

'None of those, exactly. It's a suspected case of art fraud.'

The receptionist's hand stopped in midair as she gaped at them. 'I don't think we have a form for that.' She stood. 'Excuse me for just one minute.'

Erin leaned one elbow on the counter and raised an eyebrow at Evan. He shrugged.

A couple of minutes later, the receptionist returned, followed by a middle-aged female officer whose uniform looked to be due for a size upgrade. 'Good morning,' she said. 'I'm Officer Vernon. I understand you want to report a suspected case of art fraud?' Her tone might have implied skepticism or merely astonishment.

'That's correct. I'm Erin Washington. This is my friend Evan Gifford.'

'Come this way.' Officer Vernon led them out of the lobby and into an open room with several desks. She sat behind one and motioned them to two visitor chairs in front of it.

The officer leaned forward with her elbows on the desk. 'What exactly are we talking about here?'

'There's a painting for sale in a Carmel gallery that I have reason to believe is a forgery. Furthermore, I believe I know who painted it. And I'm quite sure the gallery owner is involved.'

Officer Vernon raised an eyebrow. 'And you're an expert, are you?'

Erin swallowed. 'No, but I've had an expert check it out informally, and she's as certain as she can be without a full lab examination that it's a fake.'

The officer picked up a pen and pulled a notepad in front of her. 'I'll take the details, but I have to tell you, we're not equipped to deal with this kind of thing locally. If we conclude there's a case, we'll refer it to the CBI's White Collar Investigation Teams. If there's any kind of systematic fraud going on, no doubt it would extend beyond our jurisdiction anyway.'

'I see.' And suddenly Erin did see. It made some sense that Cat, as a newbie detective, would be unfamiliar with this protocol, but for Carver it made no sense at all. He must have known, and could surely have called in the California Bureau of Investigation himself without going through the Carmel police – if, that is, he had seriously wanted to further the investigation.

She collected herself enough to give Officer Vernon the name of Raymonds-by-the-Sea and Raymond Cruikshank as the owner, along with a description of the suspect Forbes. Then she told her about seeing a sketch of the painting in Mariana Pescarelli's studio – without, of course, mentioning that she and Cat had broken in to find it.

'I'm afraid the sketch has been destroyed, though. Along with the photo I took of it. Destroyed by the artist herself – which is surely a pretty good indication of her guilt in the matter.'

'I see. Well, all this does seem like a case the CBI will want to look into. Let me have your contact info. I'm sure they'll want to talk to you.'

Evan, who had sat silent through all of this, handed over a business card. 'I'm only here for moral support,' he said. 'I don't have any firsthand knowledge of the situation, only what Erin has told me. But I am an artist and know some of the people involved, so if they want to talk to me, I'm available.'

Erin wrote her home address, cell number, and email address on a notepad. She didn't want to use a business card and risk getting the library involved.

She hesitated before asking her final question. 'If there were a murder connected with this fraud operation – an old one, going back twenty years – would that be a matter for the CBI as well?'

Officer Vernon's eyes went wide. 'A murder? Here in Carmel?' Apparently that wasn't something that happened every year.

'I think it actually took place in Pacific Grove. I can't be certain – the body was never found, so I can't even prove the murder occurred. But I believe the person or persons responsible were connected with a forgery ring that operated in Carmel.'

The officer blew out a long breath. 'That would be a case for the CBI, yes. Assuming they're convinced a genuine case exists. They'll definitely want to talk to you about that.'

'Can I leave that with you, or should I contact them directly?'

'I'll include it with this report. What was the alleged victim's name? And when do you think the murder occurred?'

'Gina Washington. October of 2001.'

Officer Vernon repeated the name slowly as she wrote it down. 'Gina Washington.' She looked up sharply. 'Relation of yours?'

'My mother.' Erin swallowed and went on. 'Her disappearance was investigated by the Santa Cruz police – that's where we lived – but they never found any trace of her.'

The officer gave a low whistle. 'Right. Thanks for coming in. I'll pass this on, and I guarantee the CBI will be in touch. Probably in the next few days.' She looked Erin full in the face. 'And I'm sorry for your loss.'

'Well, that was interesting,' Evan said as they walked back to Erin's car. 'Did you have anything else on your agenda for today?'

Erin shook her head, preoccupied and only half listening.

'Then what say we explore Carmel a bit? I haven't spent much time here. I'd be interested to see the galleries. And I'd also like some lunch.'

Right. Lunch. 'Sure. We can't leave the car here, though.'

They moved the car to a public lot and set out on foot. The first restaurant they came to was a French bistro. 'This looks good,' Evan said, skimming the menu posted in the window. Erin took a glance at the prices and gaped, but Evan said, 'My treat,' took her elbow, and guided her inside.

When they were seated, Erin ran her eyes down the menu, which was full of French names and flowery English descriptions, and settled on the first familiar dish she came to – quiche Lorraine. But when she gave her order to the server, Evan said, 'Come now, surely you can be more adventurous than that.'

Erin closed her menu and sat back. 'Fine, you order for me. I don't have the brain space to wade through all this.'

He smirked at her and said to the server, 'We'll both have the *magret de canard*. With a half bottle of the Miraval.'

When the server had bowed herself off, Erin said, 'What have you let me in for?'

'Roast duck. You'll love it, I promise.'

'If I can even taste it.'

He leaned forward over the table. 'All right, now tell me what's bothering you. You've obviously been chewing over something ever since we left the police station.'

'It's Carver. The Santa Cruz detective. Why didn't he hand the case over to the CBI? Even twenty years ago, that would have made sense, once he'd established my mother was no longer in Santa Cruz. But the other day, when I told him about the forgery connection, the CBI should have been his first thought. He must have known the Carmel police wouldn't be equipped to handle it. Instead, he made Cat write a report that he knew was never going farther than his inbox.'

Evan pondered, stroking his chin. The gesture distracted Erin.

'You look like you're stroking the beard you don't have,' she said.

He grinned sheepishly. 'It's the hair. I tried growing a beard, but it made me look like Van Gogh. I didn't want people to think I was cultivating that resemblance on purpose.' He clasped his hands on the table instead. 'Didn't you say Carver was close to retirement? Maybe he just doesn't want to open a can of worms that will keep crawling around him after he leaves.'

Erin grimaced at the image. 'But why, though? There's no reason for him to be involved in an investigation into art fraud that's outside his patch. The only way the CBI would need his input is if they decided to look into my mother's disappearance, and that wasn't part of the package Cat and I presented to him. It doesn't add up, Evan. Carver is fishy. I've suspected it for a while, and now I'm certain.'

'But couldn't he just be trying to avoid stirring up the past? His failure to find your mother must have been a blot on his career. Naturally he wouldn't want that brought to the forefront of everyone's mind just as he's leaving.'

She shook her head. 'That's still not a reason not to pass on the forgery case to the CBI.'

Evan sat back. 'OK. I've been playing devil's advocate, but in fact I agree with you. He messed up. The only question is why.'

'The usual reason, don't you think? He's on the take.'

'That's one possibility. Another is that he's been intimidated. The Russian mafia are not people you want to mess around with. If he got too close last time, they could have threatened him or his family – just as they presumably threatened your mother.'

'True. That would be slightly more forgivable.' Erin took up her fork and traced its tines along her folded napkin. 'But there is one more possibility that's crossed my mind. Though I hate to even think it.' She looked up at Evan. 'He could have actually been involved in my mother's death.'

Evan gave a low whistle. 'He doesn't match that innkeeper's description of the man who picked up her things, does he?'

'No, but we don't know for sure that was the same man who killed her. And anyway, he wouldn't have to be the actual murderer to be involved. He could have tracked her down and betrayed her location to the bad guys.'

'True.' He drummed his fingers on the tablecloth. 'So what's our next move? Report your suspicions to the CBI and let them deal with it?'

'That might be the sensible thing to do. But this is personal. If he's crooked in any way, that means he's been lying to me for the last twenty years. I want to confront him face to face.'

Evan's fair, freckled face drained of color. 'Shouldn't you get some hard evidence of his involvement before you do that?'

'Ideally, but how? I have no hard evidence of anything except the forgery. And that's only hard-*ish*. There's nothing at all to connect it to my mother's death except my own gut feeling.'

The server hovered near, and Evan sat back to give her space to set down their plates. 'Let's talk about something else while we enjoy our food.'

Erin grudgingly agreed, if only because they seemed to have reached a dead end. The roast duck did indeed look worthy of her full attention.

After a few ecstatic bites, she asked him, 'Are you like a super-successful artist that I should have heard of before I met you? How do you afford this lifestyle? The Benbow Inn, and now this.'

He gave a rueful smile. 'Not super-successful, no. As I'm sure you're aware, very few artists achieve that status in their lifetime. The fact is my father was a super-successful businessman. I never had any interest in following him into business, and he died before he could force me to, so he involuntarily ended up funding my painting career instead. I sell enough to not-quite-starve in a garret, but garrets aren't really my style. I'm afraid I'm rather spoiled as far as creature comforts are concerned.'

He made an apologetic grimace. Despite her own semi-Spartan existence, Erin found that fault remarkably easy to forgive – especially as she was currently benefitting from it. She returned his grimace with a sympathetic smile.

Evan went on. 'I use enough of my inheritance to live comfortably, travel when I feel like it, and keep myself in paint and canvas. With the rest, I try to do a little good in the world.'

'Like what, for instance?'

'Oh, like helping struggling young artists, for one. I contribute to a few scholarships and grants. And programs to get serious art instruction back into the schools.'

Erin set down her fork, tearing up. 'My mother would have loved that.'

Evan looked down, a blush creeping up his cheeks. 'My alma mater has been pressing me to give a formal name to the scholarship I recently started funding there. I don't want it to end up as the Gifford scholarship by default.' He looked up at her. 'With your permission, I'd like to name it after your mother.'

Without thinking about what she was doing, Erin reached across the table and pressed his hand. The wave of tingling warmth that shot through her at the skin-to-skin contact took her completely by surprise.

'That's the most wonderful idea I've heard in a long, long time.'

He turned his hand over to lightly clasp hers. 'I hoped you'd like it.'

They looked into each other's eyes for a moment, the bond between them growing by the second, until Erin began to fear she'd never be able to break free. She pulled back her hand and concentrated on cutting her duck with knife and fork, although it was tender enough that was hardly necessary.

When she'd collected herself, she asked in a voice that strove for normality but didn't quite get there, 'What is your alma mater?'

'A little place called Cornish College of the Arts. In Seattle.'

'Is that where you grew up?'

'No. San Francisco. There are lots of fine art schools in the Bay Area, but I wanted to get a little distance from my family.' He also returned to eating, a tiny smile playing around his mouth. 'Didn't you go away to school?'

'No. UC Santa Cruz. My father needed me close by.'

'Ah.' A world of understanding resounded in that monosyllable. How did he do that? 'So it was just the two of you? After your mother disappeared?'

'Yes. He was hardly ever around before that, but he took early retirement from the airline after she was gone. Supposedly to take care of me.' She didn't mean to say the rest, but it spilled out. 'But I ended up taking care of him. He was kind of a wreck.'

'Drinking?'

'Not constantly, but yes. Among other things.'

'So you basically had no adolescence. You grew up, bang, at age twelve.'

She nodded, daring another glance at him. She'd never said all this to anyone, not even Alex. But Evan sat calmly taking it in with a depth of compassion and acceptance in his eyes that she hadn't known since – well, since her mother disappeared. Her throat swelled till she couldn't swallow. She took a sip of wine, hoping to relax it again.

'And you've never been much of anywhere? Until recently, that is.' A grin recalled their initial meeting in Garberville.

'My mother and I traveled when I was a child. She was from

England, and we went back there to see her family several times. And some other places as well, once I was old enough not to be a nuisance. But between . . . losing her and last week, I don't think I've been more than a couple hours from home.' As she spoke the words, it struck her how pitiful that sounded.

'We'll have to do something about that,' Evan said, exactly as if they were an established couple making plans together. Erin opened her mouth to object, but the words died on her lips. She found the prospect of traveling with Evan more appealing than anything she'd contemplated in a long time.

'Where is home for you now?' she asked. 'Or do you travel all the time?'

He chuckled. 'Everybody needs a place to come home to. I have a house in Point Reyes.' Erin vaguely knew where that was – on a rural peninsula to the northwest of San Francisco. 'It's secluded enough that I can hole up and paint for weeks undisturbed, but close enough to the city that I can pop down whenever I need to.' He gave her a smile more intimate than any she'd seen yet. 'That's where I'd like to paint you – in my own studio. When you're ready.'

*When*, not *if*. It might be presumptuous on his part, but Erin knew he was right. The day would come, and soon. Her fear of being seen had become irrelevant – he was already seeing her, not in a way that stripped her bare to the harsh winds of judgment, but in a way that enfolded her as if in a bath of sunlight. She had no desire to hide herself from his gaze.

# TWENTY-EIGHT

After lunch, they strolled down Ocean Avenue and the streets that opened off it, visiting every open gallery they came to. Erin watched with interest the way Evan approached the pieces they saw. Whereas she herself would pass slowly by each picture until she came to one that appealed to her, then stop and look for a minute, Evan would evaluate an entire group of paintings by a given artist with one glance, then either linger to examine each one in the group or pass quickly on to the next artist's offerings. Those he passed by vastly outnumbered those he lingered for.

The group of paintings that held him the longest Erin immediately recognized as Finn's. She joined him as he stood contemplating them.

'He's got something,' Evan said after a long silence. 'But I'm not sure I'd want to see his portrait of you. I suspect his vision would be quite different from mine.'

'I haven't seen it myself,' she replied. 'He wouldn't let me look before it was finished, and it wasn't finished when I left.'

'Quite right, too. Never let a subject look until it's done. And unless it's a commission, sometimes not even then.'

'So you don't think a model has any sort of ownership in a painting unless they're paying for it?'

He shook his head decisively. 'Once a model agrees to sit, his or her likeness ceases to be the model's property. It becomes a part of a work of art that exists in its own right. The art is about the painter's interpretation of the subject as much as the subject itself.'

Erin was startled. Her own comfort level with sitting for Evan ratcheted down a few clicks. 'Doesn't that rather objectify the model?'

'Not in the hands of a real painter.' He turned to face her, his eyes registering his comprehension of her alarm. 'It's a synergy. The painting can't exist without the model, but the artist brings out something in the model that couldn't be seen before. So the painting is a new creation – not just as a work of art, but almost as a new living being.' He took her hand, as if to emphasize the humanity in his words. 'I suppose it's kind of like having a child – the model and the artist are like parents, each giving something of themselves to create a new person in the world. A person that ultimately has to have its own independent life.'

Evan turned back to the painting he'd been contemplating, which happened to be a portrait. But Erin couldn't take her eyes off Evan's profile. Getting to know him was like watching a flower unfold, each petal flaring out to reveal an unsuspected depth of further petals within.

Their hands remained linked as Evan finished his perusal of Finn's work and moved on to another artist. All through that gallery and on to the next, neither of them moved to disengage. That simple contact was more powerful than Finn's passionate kiss had been. The kiss was a flame that threatened more to consume than to warm. This was – synergy. A merging of two parts to become a whole greater than either could ever be alone.

Inevitably they came to Raymonds-by-the-Sea. Erin stopped outside the window. The suspect Forbes was no longer on display. Had it been sold, or had Pescarelli alerted Cruikshank to Erin's suspicions, leading him to hide it away or even destroy it? She was desperate to know, partly so she could properly inform the CBI investigators when they contacted her, but also because that painting had become a sort of symbol for her of all the perfidy involved in her mother's disappearance and death.

'You go in without me,' she said in a low voice to Evan. 'If Cruikshank sees me, he'll be on his guard. Say you've heard he has a Forbes for sale and ask to see it.'

Evan raised his eyebrows. 'Seeing me may put him on his guard too, given the way we parted last time we met.'

'Do you think he'll remember you from all those years ago? You can't be the only young artist he tried to cheat.'

Evan grimaced. 'People tend to remember me. It's the curse of having red hair. Or occasionally the blessing.'

'Well, at least he wouldn't connect you with accusations of forgery. Couldn't you pretend to be just any old potential buyer?'

'I can try.' Before she knew what was happening, he bent

down and gave her a quick kiss. Then he grinned at her. 'For luck.'

Grinning foolishly herself, Erin hovered at one side of the window where she could see into the gallery but, she hoped, not be seen clearly from inside. She tried to focus on Evan's upcoming confrontation with Cruikshank, but silly little imps of joy kept hopping up inside her. A part of her wanted to open the door and call out to Evan to forget the whole thing, leave the investigation to the CBI, and whisk her off to someplace magical. It hardly mattered where – anyplace would be magical with him at her side.

But another part of her spoke firmly to this carefree newcomer, reminding her that she could never be fully at peace until she had uncovered the truth and laid her mother's ghost to rest. And besides, what was she thinking to even consider giving her heart away to a virtual stranger? Even after years of building friendship and trust with Alex, something had always held her back from taking the next step. But here was Evan, swooping in and bowling her over like some swashbuckling pirate king, and despite the suspicious grumblings of her traumatized brain, she had not the slightest desire to resist.

Her eyes fastened on Evan as he moved through the gallery, strategically stopping to gaze at some of the more expensive paintings. What a luxury to be able to watch him, absorb every detail of him, while he was unaware of her scrutiny. The vibrant red hair on the back of his neck curled cockily in defiance of the close-cropped discipline imposed on it. The set of his shoulders was easy without being lazy or cowed, and he moved with the assurance of one for whom the world was a friend and ally to be embraced in fellowship rather than a suspicious stranger or, as might have been expected from one of his wealth, a servant to be used for his every whim.

Before long, she spotted Cruikshank a short way off, talking with a man whose face she couldn't see – a tall man in a dark suit whose black hair was lightly threaded with gray. Cruikshank spotted Evan and shimmered to his side, an oily smile plastered to his features, undisturbed by any flicker of recognition.

As they talked, Erin could see the gallery owner full face and Evan at most in profile, but it wasn't difficult to follow their conversation. She could tell when Evan mentioned the Forbes because Cruikshank's smile wavered, then reformed itself into an expression of regret.

So he had been warned and, with a wave of his illusionist's wand, caused the forged painting to disappear. The only question was how. Had he been spooked enough to destroy it, and with it the possibility of a substantial profit? Had he transferred it to one of the other galleries he had a stake in, perhaps out of state? Or had he simply hidden it away, intending to bring it out again when the unhealthy interest in it had died down?

Cruikshank made a gesture as if inviting Evan to consider some other offering, but Evan shook his head and turned to go. Cruikshank glanced past him toward the window, and his face hardened. Erin ducked out of sight, but she was sure it was too late. Despite her attempt at concealment, he had seen her, and she had glimpsed a flash of pure hatred in his eyes.

She was shivering when Evan came out to her. 'Erin, what's wrong?' He took her by the shoulders and looked into her eyes. 'You look like you've seen a ghost.'

'Worse than a ghost. Maybe a demon. He saw me, Evan. He knows.'

Evan folded her into his arms, and the steady warmth of him gradually calmed her. Fate had rarely been kind to her in the past, but she would not allow this newfound happiness to be snatched from her – or she from it – before it even had a chance to blossom.

'I think you're right,' Evan said after a minute. 'He told me the Forbes had been sold, but he was obviously nervous. There's a muscle in his left eyebrow that twitches when he's lying – I noticed it when I dealt with him before. It was twitching like crazy the whole time.'

'So what do we do?' She pulled back enough to meet his eyes.

He shrugged. 'One more piece of information to give the CBI. I don't see what else we can do.'

She heaved a sigh. 'I suppose you're right. When I started all this, I wanted to be in on the kill, as it were. But now I'm starting to think I'm out of my depth. Let the authorities deal with it.' She smiled into his eyes. 'I have a feeling I'm going to have better things to do.'

His face lit up. He pulled her into a narrow space between the Raymonds building and the one next to it and kissed her properly. A kiss full of promise, in which their souls mingled as well as their lips. A kiss more sustaining than the richest food.

Finn's words about learning to trust came back to her, as well as her own despair of finding a love that could be both passionate and reliable. Who knew it had been just around the corner all the time?

When they'd drunk their fill of each other for the moment – Erin knew she could never have enough of him in a larger sense – he released her, and her knees buckled under her. They'd been walking and window-shopping for several hours, and her strength was exhausted.

'How about coffee?' Evan said as he steadied her by the elbow. He'd read her mind again. Before today, coming from anyone else, she would have found that intrusive, but now it was part and parcel of the warm blanket of sunshine with which he enfolded her. She was seen. She was known. She was loved.

'Perfect,' she said, smiling at him.

They emerged onto the sidewalk again, and Evan pointed across the street to an outdoor café where couples and threes sat at small iron tables sipping from china cups. 'That place looks promising,' he said.

They crossed the road and found a table. When a server appeared, Evan asked for a large white-chocolate mocha – Erin's own typical order. 'Same for me, please,' she said to the server, then to Evan as the server departed, 'I'm not copying you. That's what I always have.'

He gave her a slow smile and reached for her hand. 'Why am I not surprised?'

She held his gaze until her happiness overwhelmed her, then dropped her eyes to their joined hands. Slowly she stroked his fingertips with her thumb. All these unaccustomed actions were coming so naturally to her.

'Evan,' she said softly, relishing the feel of his name on her tongue. 'What's happening to us?'

He matched her tone. 'No great mystery, is there? We're falling in love.' He paused, stroking her fingers in return. 'Not that love isn't the greatest mystery of all.'

She looked up at him, her heart in her throat. 'I suppose you've done all this before.' An attractive man like Evan couldn't have reached forty without some kind of romance in his life.

'Once or twice. But it's never felt quite like this.'

Erin felt a wave of irrational resentment against those one or two women who had gotten to Evan before her. She had to remind herself that the first of them, at least, had probably gotten to him while Erin herself was still too young to be in the running.

A movement behind Evan caught her eye. She shifted her gaze from him for a second but saw only a man in a dark suit alone at a table, holding a newspaper in front of his face. Perhaps the movement had been him raising the paper. She shook off the niggle of alarm that nagged at the back of her brain and focused on Evan again.

'Where do we go from here?' she asked him. She was in an undiscovered country and felt the need of a map.

'Wherever you like. I don't want to rush you into anything.' He lifted her hand and kissed a knuckle. 'I'm guessing this is all rather new to you.'

She nodded. 'I had a crush on a guy in high school, but it never came to anything. Since then, I've been . . .' She searched for words to describe the half-waking state in which she'd lived most of the last twenty years, but gave up at last. Evan probably knew without being told.

'On hold?' he supplied.

'Yes.' He did understand. 'On hold.'

'I can stay in Santa Cruz indefinitely,' he said. 'If that's what you want. Or I can go away if you need some time to think about things.'

'Stay,' she said quickly. 'Please. I do need some time, but not to think. I've done too much thinking in my life. I need time to resolve this thing with my mother. Or see it resolved, at any rate. After that . . .' A world of possibilities opened before her – a world in which her house, her job at the library, her everyday round of activities played no part. In which timid, risk-averse, emotionally closed-off Erin remained behind as well, allowing the true Erin – the joyful, emboldened, life- and love-embracing Erin – to break free.

The server came back with their coffee. They drank it and

agreed they'd had enough galleries for one afternoon; it was time to head back to Santa Cruz. They strolled at a leisurely pace to the parking lot where they'd left Erin's car.

As she unlocked it from a few paces away, she turned and swept her eyes around for a last look at downtown Carmel before she had to focus on driving. Out of the corner of her eye, she caught a glimpse of a dark sleeve disappearing into a doorway. The niggle of alarm she'd felt earlier grew into a siren.

She stopped Evan with a hand on his arm. 'Evan,' she whispered, 'I think we're being followed.'

On alert, he scanned the parking lot. 'I don't see anyone. Is he gone?'

'He ducked into a doorway. I think it was the same man Cruikshank was talking to in the gallery – tall, dark suit, dark hair. Did you notice him?'

Evan frowned. 'I did see Cruikshank talking to someone. I'm afraid I didn't pay much attention.'

'He was in the café, too. At least, there was a man in a dark suit, and that's not exactly the preferred attire in Carmel on a summer afternoon.' Evan was wearing chinos and a pale yellow polo shirt, which blended in perfectly with the other tourists.

'True. Should I go flush him out? Confront him?'

'No. I have a feeling he could be dangerous. Let's get out of here.'

Erin drove as quickly as she dared through the town toward the freeway. Evan kept his eye on the mirrors. 'There's a black sedan close behind us,' he said. 'I can't tell if they're *following* or just following, if you know what I mean.' There was only one main route out of town, so another car going in the same direction was not inherently suspect.

They pulled onto the freeway, and the black car sped up and passed them. 'So much for him,' Evan said. 'Just in a hurry.'

Erin took a deep breath. 'Thank God. Maybe I imagined the whole thing.'

'I doubt that. In cases like this, it's a good idea to trust one's instincts.'

She shot him a glance. 'Have you been in a situation like this before?'

'Not exactly. But I've been in danger. We have animal instincts we usually ignore that kick in to warn us when something's not right.'

'What kind of danger?' She wanted to know everything about him.

'Once I was painting in the woods, up in the Garberville area, when a wildfire started nearby. I couldn't hear it, see it, or smell it, but something told me to get out of there. I was the last car through before they closed the road.'

She shivered at the thought that she could have lost him before she'd even found him. 'Maybe you saw animals running from the fire?'

'That could be it. Or I may have sensed a change in the wind. Who knows? The point is, you scented danger just now, and I believe that means danger exists. Any idea who Dark Suit could have been?'

He did it, too – labeling people with some obvious characteristic when he didn't know their names. 'He fits the description the innkeeper at Seafarer's Rest gave of the man who picked up my mother's things. Only older. I didn't see his face, but there's a bit of gray in his hair.'

'And that guy back then was probably Russian, right? Based on the way he wrote his numbers?'

'Right. And given the forgery connection, I assume Russian mafia.'

Evan whistled. 'In that case, I'm glad I didn't confront him. I hope this doesn't disappoint you, but I'm not a natural hero. I'll always do my best to protect you, but I won't go looking for trouble. I prefer to stay alive.'

'I prefer you alive, too. Believe me, I am perfectly happy to leave those guys to the CBI. We are way out of our depth messing with them.'

# TWENTY-NINE

Erin was nervous about going home. Dark Suit might not have followed them to Santa Cruz, but Cruikshank knew her address. And on a more mundane level, given Evan's gourmet tastes, she didn't feel up to cooking for him, but she certainly didn't want to be left alone. Intuiting all this, as usual, Evan suggested dinner at Shadowbrook.

'But that's the priciest place in town!' Erin couldn't help exclaiming. 'And no way could we get in without a reservation.'

'On a Wednesday night at' – he checked his watch – 'five thirty? I don't think it'll be a problem. Anyway, they know me there.'

Erin shook her head in bewilderment. How had she ended up with a man who was known at Shadowbrook?

He had to direct her there, since she knew it only by reputation. The host greeted Evan like an old friend and showed them to a corner table shielded by extravagant greenery.

'So you've really never been here?' he asked as they tucked into their baked brie appetizer.

She shook her head, savoring the contrast of the creamy cheese with the bite of the jalapeño jelly. 'My parents used to come here once in a while. Anniversaries or whatever. I was not invited.'

'And quite right, too. Who brings their twelve-year-old along to an anniversary dinner? You would have ruined the romantic atmosphere.'

Erin sighed. 'I'm not sure how romantic it was even without me. You've seen my mother's paintings. They're not the work of a happy woman.'

'True.' Evan gazed at her thoughtfully. 'You don't have much reason to expect happiness, do you? Or to trust it when it comes.'

Something twisted inside her. She'd been reveling in her newfound feelings, not allowing her deep-seated fears to overwhelm them. But she couldn't deny the thorny seedlings she could already sense poking their nasty heads out through the lush green grass of her joy, waiting to spear the feet of unwary wanderers.

'No. I don't.' She reached for his hand. 'But I want to. I want this to be real. To be—' What she wanted to say was far too presumptuous for a relationship that was only a few hours old.

Evan said it for her. 'To be lasting. Even permanent.' He lifted her hand to his lips. 'It sounds crazy, but I want that, too.' He kissed the base of her ring finger, like a promise. 'It feels as if we've been together always but didn't realize it. I don't believe in reincarnation, but if I did, I'd say we'd been lovers in a previous life.'

Erin was too choked up to reply that was exactly how she felt. She said it with her eyes instead.

'I sensed it back in Garberville,' he went on. 'Did you?'

She cast her mind back. When they dined together at the Benbow Inn, she'd been focused on getting information from him rather than getting to know him. But there had definitely been something – some frisson, some premonition of what was to come. She'd fled from it before it could engulf her.

'I think I was beginning to. Though I didn't recognize it at the time.'

He peered disconcertingly into her soul. 'I wonder . . . Something must have happened between then and now. To make you take notice.'

She felt the blood rising to her cheeks and broke away from his gaze.

'Something happened with Finnegan, didn't it?' His tone was gentle, but his grip on her hand tightened slightly.

She couldn't be less than honest with Evan. Not now. 'I was . . . attracted to him.' Past tense. In another life. Another universe. 'And he kissed me. Once. At the time, it was overwhelming, but it was nothing like . . . He stirred my blood. But he didn't touch my heart.'

The muscles in Evan's jaw tensed, but he spoke in the same calm tone. 'What did he say to you?'

'That I needed a man.' She essayed a laugh. 'Why do men always assume all a woman's problems can be solved by sex? But funnily enough, he said the man shouldn't be him, because he would only break my heart. And I knew he was right.'

Evan searched her eyes. 'No regrets?'

'No regrets. It was pure pheromones, my reaction to him. And maybe the headiness of stepping outside my ordinary world. Nothing more.' She kissed his hand in her turn. 'If I never see him again, that will be just fine with me.'

'Not even to see your portrait?' he said with a teasing smile.

'Well . . . I guess I am curious about that. Though I'm not at all sure I'll like what I see.'

He was silent a moment, his eyes on their joined hands as they lay on the table. 'I suppose I should be grateful to Finnegan. It seems he cleared a path for me, in a way.'

She chewed over this idea. 'I guess he did. He led me to think about love, which I'd hardly dared to do before. At that point I more or less concluded I'd never find a man who would stir my heart but not break it.' She smiled at him. 'And then you showed up at my door.'

He smiled back. 'I'm known for my excellent timing. But I couldn't have stayed away another day. You were drawing me without knowing it.'

'Not me. But something was drawing us both.' Erin had a momentary vision of her mother's face, smiling in blessing. 'Or someone.'

Perhaps the true purpose of her whole journey of the last few weeks did not, after all, lie in discovering the truth of what had happened to her mother. Perhaps it had more to do with discovering herself.

They chatted happily through dinner, having infinite words to say to each other and finite time in which to say them. When at last they left the restaurant, the cool evening air recalled Erin to the world in which Dark Suit and the CBI would soon be facing off, with herself and her comrades caught in the middle. And Cat and Alex didn't even know what had been going on.

'Much as I hate to break up our tête-à-tête, I do feel I should update Cat and Alex on the situation,' she said to Evan. 'Do you mind if I call them to come to the house?'

'Of course not,' he said. 'I know you want to get through this before . . .'

He trailed off, but she knew what he meant and appreciated

his forbearance. 'Yes. I do. When the time comes, I want to be thinking of nothing but you.'

He pulled her into a long embrace before she unlocked the car. 'Just a little promise of things to come,' he whispered in her ear as he released her. Those things couldn't come too soon for Erin.

She handed him her keys. 'You drive while I make the calls.' *And while I pull myself together*, she thought. With her heart racing and every nerve engaged, she wasn't sure she'd be able to drive safely.

Cat and Alex both pressed her for details right then on the phone, but she put them off. 'I'll explain everything when we're together,' she said. 'I don't want to go over it all twice.' To Cat she added, 'And I have a surprise for you.' She couldn't bring herself to warn Alex that the hopes she suspected he cherished in regard to her were about to be dashed forever.

Cat's Jeep was already coming down the street when Evan pulled Erin's car into her driveway. Alex was not far behind. Erin was glad the twilight concealed his expression when he saw Evan climb out of her car.

Erin and Evan waited in the driveway for the others to join them. 'Cat Herrera, Alex Braithwaite, I'd like you to meet Evan Gifford. Evan's the painter I met in Garberville who put me on to Mamelukov. He's come down to help with the investigation.' That was all she'd say for now. The rest would no doubt become obvious soon enough. Erin was sure her and Evan's feelings for each other must create a visible aura around the two of them even if they never touched.

Alex darted a glance between Evan and Erin before extending his hand to Evan. 'Good to meet you,' he said, his tone sounding a little forced. 'We need all the help we can get.'

Cat greeted Evan with one eyebrow raised toward Erin. Erin willed herself not to blush but feared she was unsuccessful.

'Let's get inside,' she said, scanning the street for unfamiliar cars or lurking figures. So far so good.

Miss Silver greeted them all at the door and prowled among their collected legs in an excess of joy. So many potential sycophants to choose from! To Erin's relief, familiarity won the day and Miss Silver put her paws up on Alex's knee, asking to be picked up. If Alex couldn't have Erin's love, at least he could have her cat's.

Erin handed Evan a bottle of wine to open while she pulled four glasses from the built-in hutch in the dining area. When they were all settled – Erin and Evan not too close together on the loveseat, Cat and Alex in facing armchairs – Erin related their visit to the Carmel police and the immediate referral to the CBI.

Cat smacked her palm against her forehead. 'Idiot! Why didn't I think of that? Of *course* it would be a matter for the CBI. That's in, like, Police Procedure 101.' She shook her head as if to shake her brain into working order.

'I'm sure if it had been a normal case, you would have thought of it,' Erin said. 'But we were all so focused on trying to find some kind of hard evidence while working around Carver being obstructive.'

'But the CBI would have been the perfect way to work around him!'

'Wouldn't he have had to be the one to call them in, though?' Erin asked. 'As the senior officer?'

Cat stared at her, open-mouthed. 'Yeah, now that you mention it, he would. And why the hell didn't he? I mean, when you first came in, he thought there was no case at all. But when he had me write up that report for the Carmel police – that should have gone straight to the CBI. A veteran like Carver has absolutely no excuse for ignoring protocol like that.'

Erin exchanged glances with Evan. 'That's what we thought.' She hesitated before asking, 'Have you ever had any reason to doubt Carver's integrity?'

'Not really. Of course I haven't been working with him very long.' She peered into the distance. 'Come to think of it, though, there have been times I wondered why he didn't pursue something that looked like a good lead to me. I guess I just chalked it up to the natural laziness of an officer nearing retirement.'

Alex looked up from adoring Miss Silver to speak for the first time since the discussion began. 'I've never met the guy, but couldn't this be natural laziness, too? Not wanting to start something he won't be around to see through?'

Erin and Cat both shook their heads. 'I don't think so,' Erin said. 'I've been getting a weird vibe from him since our first meeting. I think he's involved in this somehow. That's why I hope the CBI gets in touch ASAP. Preferably around eight o'clock tomorrow morning.'

She was about to tell the others about their visit to the gallery and being followed by Dark Suit when a knock came at the door. Miss Silver was instantly on the alert, ears back and tail twitching. A low growl issued from her throat.

Erin's own animal instincts kicked in as well. This was no ordinary friendly visitor.

She started to rise, but Evan put his hand on her arm. 'Let me handle this.'

She shook her head. 'If it's someone I know, you won't recognize them.' Though everyone who was likely to visit her at that hour was already in the room.

He acknowledged that by dropping his hand. 'I'm going with you, then.'

Erin walked to the door as if moving into battle. She peered through the peephole and saw the balding head of Detective Carver. He appeared to be alone.

'It's Carver,' she mouthed to the others.

'Let him in,' said Cat. 'He's not going to shoot us, and I for one want an explanation.'

Erin nodded, steeling herself. For twenty years, she'd seen this man as a sheep, or maybe an ineffective sheepdog. But now she was about to peel back his phony fleece to reveal a wolf.

Or maybe he'd do that all on his own.

Evan hovered behind her to her right, where the newcomer wouldn't see him immediately, as she opened the door.

'Detective Carver. What a surprise.' She kept her tone neutral, neither welcoming nor suspicious. Let him take it how he would.

'Erin,' he said with his usual sad smile. She wondered how she ever could have trusted it. 'May I come in?'

'Of course. I have some friends here who'd like to meet you. And one you already know.'

Carver came a few steps inside, caught sight of Cat, and stopped dead. 'Herrera,' he said gruffly. 'What are you doing here?'

Cat returned his glare without flinching. 'Like Erin said, I'm a friend. We're a bunch of friends sitting around talking over a bottle of wine.'

Evan stepped into the light, and Erin introduced first him, then Alex. 'And the cat is Miss Silver.' The Siamese was still growling faintly, her alarming blue eyes fixed on the newcomer. 'She's not too fond of strangers.'

Erin pulled a straight chair from the dining table, placed it between the loveseat and Cat's chair, and offered it to Carver with a gesture. He sat, loosening his tie and unbuttoning his collar.

'Wine?' she asked.

'Please,' he replied. 'Just a swallow – I'm driving.' He shot another glare at Cat, who sat with a half-empty glass in her hand. She smiled blandly back.

Erin fetched another glass and poured the last of the wine into it, making for about an inch of red liquid in the bowl. 'Looks like a swallow is all we have left.' She handed it to him, and he downed the wine in one gulp. With a raised eyebrow, Erin took the empty glass from him and set it on the coffee table, which was an inch or two out of his comfortable reach.

She resumed her seat, feeling for Evan's hand. She no longer cared about subtlety; she needed his support. He gave her hand a reassuring squeeze.

'What brings you here this evening, Detective? I assume it isn't a purely social call.'

'No.' Carver pulled himself together and sat forward, his elbows on his knees. 'I got a call this afternoon from the CBI. It sounds like you've stuck your toe in some pretty dangerous waters, young lady. I've come to give you a warning – there could be some nasty big sharks circling around.'

'You mean like the Russian mafia?' she said. 'We're already aware of them. In fact, that's why we were happy to have the case go to the CBI. Clearly everyone in this room is out of their depth dealing with those guys.' She pointed that 'everyone' directly at Carver.

He frowned. 'I'm glad you realize that. But I'm not sure you understand just how dangerous they can be.'

Erin leaned forward and skewered him with her stare. 'I realize they were dangerous enough twenty years ago to make you stop investigating my mother's disappearance. To make you fail to turn it over to the CBI, as you ought to have done as soon as you realized she was no longer in Santa Cruz.' She watched those words sink in. 'The only thing I'm not sure of is exactly how they got to you. Was it money, or threats? I'm guessing they offered my mother money first, but she'd never have taken it. So they stepped up to threats – probably against me rather than against her directly. She was a brave woman. She wouldn't have been easily intimidated.'

Carver's face turned white and sweat began to bead on his brow. He reached for his already-loosened collar.

Erin took his empty glass and filled it from a pitcher of water on the dining-room table. 'You look as if you need this, Detective.'

He grabbed it and gulped the water at one go. 'They offered me money first. I didn't want to take it, but my wife was ill – our savings were already drained, with no cure in sight. I held out until they threatened her.' He buried his face in his hands, suddenly a broken man. 'Then I gave in and took the money. She died a month later.'

Erin was momentarily silenced by empathy for his situation. But Evan broke in. 'So why didn't you turn the case over once your wife was dead?'

Carver looked up at him with shadowed eyes. 'Because they had me then,' he said, as if it should have been obvious. 'They would've put the finger on me as a crooked cop. My career would've been over.'

Erin's empathy withered as quickly as it had bloomed. 'You let my mother *die* to save your career?' Each word fell into the silence of the room like the clang of a death knell.

He held out his hands toward her, palms up. 'I didn't know they were going to kill her. I thought she'd gotten away. I thought she was safe. You and your father were safe, and what did I care about a few fake paintings? What difference does it make who did them, if they look like the real thing?'

Evan put his hand over his eyes as if in physical pain. Erin was shocked, too, but to a lesser degree. Even for her, forged paintings were nothing compared to the loss of her mother – and her childhood.

'Your career is over now,' Cat said, in a voice like steel. 'As of Friday. So why didn't you turn the case over to the CBI yourself when Erin and I brought it to you? Instead of fobbing me off with writing a useless report for the Carmel police, which I'm sure never left your inbox?'

He turned to her and straightened, as if trying to regain some vestige of his former authority. 'I want to retire. I want to be *alive* to retire and spend time with my grandchildren. I've earned that, in spite of everything.'

'You've earned nothing,' Alex spat, once again entering the conversation. 'Some public servant you've been. And anyway, once they had the report, the CBI would've offered you immunity and witness protection. Wouldn't they, Cat?'

She nodded. 'Most likely.'

'Witness protection.' Carver snorted. 'That's no life. Moved to some place I don't know, where no one knows me. Never seeing my kids or my grandkids again. No way would I subject myself to that.'

'But that's what you subjected my mother to,' Erin blurted. 'At least, that's what you're claiming you *thought* you were abandoning her to. When in fact you were condemning her to death.'

Carver's face went stony. He stood, drawing himself to his full height. 'I came here to warn you, not to be accused. I'm not answerable to any of you. If you choose not to heed my warning, on your heads be it.'

He turned and stalked to the door. No one moved to stop him.

The door closed behind him, and they all sat staring at one another. Cat was the first to break the silence. 'Not answerable! The public is precisely who he *is* answerable to. I'm turning him in. Let me know when the CBI contacts you, and I'll be there.'

Erin's concern for her friend outweighed her desire to see Carver face justice. 'Think carefully, Cat. What will happen to your career if you turn him in? Isn't it like the cardinal sin to rat on another cop?'

'It is, but Carver's not well liked, and he's on his way out anyway. His cronies have already retired. I'm willing to take the risk.' She gave a wry grin. 'I can always set up as a private dick if they force me out.'

# THIRTY

Once Carver was gone, Erin felt suddenly drained. She let Evan pick up the tale where she'd left off, telling the others about their gallery visit and being followed by Dark Suit.

Cat whistled. 'No wonder you hesitated to open the door,' she said to Erin. 'Are you safe here tonight? Maybe you should come crash at my place.'

Erin exchanged glances with Evan. 'I don't think they'll act right away. They don't know how much we know, or that the case has already gone to the CBI. As far as they're aware, we have no real evidence – and of course they're right. We have enough to convince ourselves, but not a jury.'

Cat hesitated, chewing her lip. 'Well, if you're sure . . .' She stood and moved toward the door, then beckoned Erin to come into the hall with her.

'Is he going to stay the night?' she asked, tipping her head toward Evan. 'And if so, is he any good in a pinch?'

'For the first, we haven't discussed it, but if he does, it won't be in my bed. And for the second – I think he'd have a cool head in an emergency, but he's not a fighter. It would have to be brains over brawn.'

Cat frowned. 'You've got me on speed dial, right? You'll call the second you hear or see anything suspicious?'

'Of course. And nine-one-one too.'

'I'll make a sweep of the property before I go. Keep your outside lights on, and some inside too. Don't make it obvious which room you're sleeping in.'

'Will do.'

Cat stood a moment poised to go, then gave Erin an impulsive hug. 'Take care of yourself.'

Erin teared up at this unaccustomed show of affection as she returned the hug. 'I will.'

She closed the front door behind Cat and turned back to the

living room. Alex and Evan were both standing, facing each other as if squaring off for a fight. Except that Evan was relaxed and slightly smiling, while Alex was scowling, his whole body tensed. Clearly he had no intention of leaving while Evan remained behind.

Erin's emotional capacity was already stretched to the limit by her newfound joy in Evan's love set against her growing anxiety about the looming threat represented by Dark Suit. But she stretched it a little further to include a profound compassion for Alex. If what he felt for her was anything like what she felt for Evan, he must be in agony.

'Alex,' she said from the doorway. 'A word?'

With an obvious effort, Alex broke his visual lock with Evan and came to meet her, the anger in his eyes morphing into a pain he couldn't mask.

She put a hand on his arm, but feeling its muscles tense even further under her touch, she dropped her hand. 'Alex, I'm sorry I had to spring Evan on you like this. It's not like I planned it – it all happened so fast. But he's not staying – well, maybe on the couch, because I really don't feel comfortable alone here tonight. But you know what I mean.'

His jaw muscles unclenched just enough to allow him to speak in a strangled voice. 'None of my business what you do. But I can't help worrying about you. You barely know this guy. How can you be sure you can trust him? He could even be in on the whole thing.'

How could she explain to Alex the basis of her belief in Evan? Its foundation was as gossamer, no more than an instinct. And yet that instinct was the surest thing in her world.

'I can't tell you how, but I am sure. As sure as I've ever been of anything.' She paused, searching his eyes. 'I know this is hard for you, but don't worry about me. I'll be fine.'

He blinked a few times, squeezed his eyes shut for a moment, then opened them. He stepped back and raised his hand to make the sign of the cross over her. 'The Lord protect you,' he whispered. 'From dangers inside and out.'

He was gone before she could respond. She remained dumbly staring at the door that had closed behind him.

Evan waited a minute, then came up and put his arms around her from behind. 'How long has he been in love with you?'

'I don't know. He's never said anything, and I didn't suspect until recently. But we've been friends a long time.' Her voice caught in her throat. 'I guess that's over now.'

Evan turned her to face him and pulled her close. 'I'm sorry,' he said into her hair. 'Love always demands sacrifices. From the lovers themselves, and from the people who love them. That's what makes it so precious.'

She clung to him a moment, then said, 'I'd like you to stay. But . . .'

'Not in your bed. I understand. I'll be better protection for you on the couch anyway.' He smoothed the hair back from her face and kissed her gently. 'Our time will come. Soon, I hope, but I'll wait as long as you need me to.'

A shiver of longing ran through her, almost destroying her resolve. But she knew their coming together would be all the sweeter for the wait. 'Yes. It will be soon.'

Erin awoke to sunshine streaming into the east-facing bedroom window. She blinked, scrubbed her hands over her face, glanced at her phone for the time, and groaned. Barely six o'clock. It had been close to midnight when she and Evan said goodnight.

The double bed that had once been her parents' creaked behind her. She jumped up and spun around in one movement. A rumpled copper head lay on the opposite pillow, and a man's arm flopped into the space where she had lain.

Panic flooded her, then anger. Had they made love for the first time and she didn't even remember it? How could that have happened? They'd gone to bed sober, Evan on the couch downstairs, she here. The idea that he might have deliberately violated her in her sleep could be dismissed out of hand.

She hoped.

Reason reasserted itself as she glanced down to see herself fully clothed in pajamas. Evan's arm that lay outside the covers was encased in a shirt sleeve. She glanced around the room, rounding the bed to check the floor on his side. No discarded trousers. Presumably, he was still wearing those as well.

She calmed herself with a breath and sat on the edge of the bed, turning to face him. 'Evan,' she whispered, taking his hand and bringing it to her lips. 'Good morning.'

He blinked, stirred, smiled at her, and squeezed her hand. 'You're beautiful in the morning.'

Her heart turned over at that. Finn had been the first to call her beautiful, but it hadn't carried the same meaning coming from him. She forced herself back to the issue at hand. 'Not to be unfriendly or anything, but what are you doing in my bed?'

He blinked again, looked around, then withdrew his hand in order to push himself up to sit against the headboard. 'Good question,' he said, then grinned at her. 'Wouldn't you like to know.'

'Evan. Please.'

'Sorry.' He took her hand again. 'I heard you scream. I don't know when exactly – after I'd been asleep for a while. I ran up here as fast as I could, but there was no one else here. The window was still locked. You were having a nightmare.'

He reached across and stroked her face. 'I lay down beside you to comfort you. After a while, you went back to sleep, but when I tried to get up, you kind of whimpered, so I just got under the covers and stayed. You seemed to sleep fine after that.'

A nightmare. A vague memory came back to her – a memory of terror, but with no clear images attached to it. Just a feeling of abandonment and dread.

She snuggled up under his arm. 'Thank you. I'm glad you were here.'

They sat like that for a while, luxuriating in the intimacy of the moment. Then Evan said, 'If you don't want this to turn into something else, I think we'd better get up.'

She nodded and extricated herself from his embrace. 'I'll put the coffee on.'

'No, I'll do that. You go ahead and shower or whatever. Breakfast will be ready when you come down.'

Erin marveled. Somehow she'd managed to fall in love with a man who could cook. Could it get any better than this?

Well, yes, she reminded herself, it could. This whole business around her mother's death could be over, and she and Evan could feel themselves safe. And then . . .

But she'd better not go there just yet. She straightened the covers and headed for the shower.

* * *

Evan could indeed cook. Though limited by the unimaginative ingredients available in Erin's kitchen, he'd produced a delicious repast of French toast with strawberries and whipped cream, accompanied by a side of bacon cooked to the exact crispiness Erin loved. And his coffee was to die for.

They were lingering over second cups when the doorbell rang. Erin checked the clock on the wall – seven thirty. Who could be ringing her bell so early?

'I'll go.' Evan was halfway to the front door before she could react. He looked out the peephole, then turned to her as she came up to him. 'It's two guys in dark suits. What do you think – is either of them our friend from yesterday?'

Erin looked out in her turn. The man in front was tall and blond, the other shorter and Hispanic-looking. Both appeared under forty – too young to be *the* Dark Suit. 'No. I'm betting they're CBI.'

The blond one leaned on the doorbell again. Evan opened the door enough to look out, keeping his weight against it. 'Yes?'

Blondie flashed a badge and said, 'CBI. I'm looking for Erin Washington.'

Evan stood back to reveal her. 'I'm Erin Washington,' she said. 'Come in.'

She led the way to the living room and stood in front of the loveseat. Evan moved to stand beside her. 'This is my friend Evan Gifford. He's a witness in this case as well.'

Blondie said, 'Mark Swenson. My partner, Miguel Fernandez.' The dark-haired man flashed his badge in turn, and they sat in the two armchairs facing the loveseat. Erin, who as a child had watched hours of old TV with her mother, half expected their first words to be 'Just the facts, ma'am.'

But Swenson led off instead with 'I understand you have some information about an ongoing art fraud in Carmel.'

'Yes. I believe some of the same people have been operating for twenty years or more.' Erin plunged ahead, wanting to ensure that the original and more important point of her investigation did not get lost in the more easily provable forgery case. 'And I believe it may all be connected with my mother's disappearance in 2001.'

Swenson remained stony-faced, but Fernandez allowed a flicker of astonishment to cross his features. 'Was your mother's disappearance reported to us at the time?' he asked.

'No. Though I realize now it should have been. My father reported it to the local police. They investigated – at least I assume they did, briefly – but the officer in charge confessed to me last night that he was intimidated into not passing the case on to you.'

'Intimidated by who?' Swenson said.

Erin winced at the incorrect pronoun. But after all, he wouldn't catch the bad guys with good grammar. 'The Russian mafia. They appear to be involved in the forgery ring.'

Swenson put thumb and forefinger to the bridge of his nose, then pulled out a notebook and pen. 'Maybe you'd better start from the beginning. Who was your mother, and how did she get involved with the Russian mafia?' He didn't say *how in hell*, but it was implied in his tone.

Clutching Evan's hand for moral support, Erin related the whole story, beginning with her mother's employment at Cruikshank's, her hints to Erin of something amiss at the gallery, her disappearance and Carver's non-investigation. Erin then jumped ahead to her own decision to follow the trail that had led Gina to her death. She skated over the sketchier elements of her own train of conclusions and focused on the tangible: the forged Forbes, Finn's memory of her mother's behavior at his opening, finding the sketch at Pescarelli's studio (omitting the breaking-and-entering part), Cruikshank's suspicious behavior, and, finally, her and Evan's being followed by *the* Dark Suit the day before.

Fernandez wrote down every word, while Swenson made a note here and there, stopping her occasionally to ask a question. When she finally came to a halt, they glanced at each other and then at Evan. 'And you can confirm this?' Fernandez asked him.

Evan gave Erin's hand a gentle squeeze. 'Parts of it. I haven't been around for all of it. But I did meet Gina up in Garberville twenty years ago, while she was on the run, and she hinted at a forgery ring operating in this area. I spoke to Cruikshank yesterday about the supposed Forbes, and he was extremely cagey. And I can confirm that Erin and I were followed by a man in a dark suit from the time we left Cruikshank's gallery until we drove out of Carmel.'

Erin returned his hand's pressure gratefully, knowing he was fudging a bit to say he could personally confirm their having been followed – he was taking her word for it, not having noticed Dark Suit himself before the man ducked out of sight.

Swenson drummed his pen against his notebook. 'I have to tell you, this isn't much to go on.' Erin opened her mouth to protest, but he held up a palm to stop her. 'But – and this is a big but – your story does go a fair way to confirming some things we've suspected for a while. Especially about Raymond Cruikshank and the Russian mafia connection.'

He peered at Erin. 'But this business about Gina Washington is news to us. You're convinced her disappearance had something to do with all this?'

Erin nodded, gathering her courage for the leap onto less solid ground. 'I was able to follow most of her trail after she left home. Please don't ask me how I knew where to go, but I did find people at many of the places who remembered her. She stayed at an inn in Carmel for one night shortly before she disappeared. My guess is she was trying to confirm her suspicions about Cruikshank, and what she found convinced her she and her family would be in danger if she stuck around.'

Erin paused, her throat dry. Evan read her mind and fetched her a glass of water. She took a drink and went on. 'When she left here, she went first to Oregon. She stayed the whole summer there, made friends. Those friends told me she'd talked about longing for home – for me – and finally headed back here, maybe hoping the danger had passed. That's how I know she didn't leave home because she wanted to.' She swallowed down the pain that thought had given her over the years, even though she'd never allowed herself to believe it.

'On her way back to this area, she stopped in Garberville – where Evan met her. That's my first definite indication that she suspected anything to do with forgery. After that, she stayed in Brookdale for a week or so, then moved down to Carmel. She went to Finn's – Seymour Finnegan's – opening in disguise and hinted at her suspicions to him. It's my belief she was recognized there, and she knew it. She left Carmel the next day, stayed at Asilomar for a few nights, then moved on to Seafarer's Rest in Pacific Grove. That's where the trail ends.'

Erin looked into Swenson's eyes, willing him to accept the truth of her final statement without any court-worthy evidence. 'I believe that's where they caught up with her. And killed her.'

Out of the corner of her eye, she saw Fernandez cross himself. Probably no more than a reflex left over from a Catholic upbringing, but at least one of the officers might acknowledge the validity of something beyond the palpable.

Not Swenson, however. He frowned at her. 'What makes you think that?'

She took a deep breath. Here's where she had to step out into quicksand. But at least she didn't have to mention the dream.

'This – I mean my personal investigation – all started a few weeks ago when I spent a couple of nights at Seafarer's Rest.' She saw Swenson glance at Evan and added, 'Alone. While I was there, I got a strong feeling that my mother had been there before me. The owner let me look through her registers from 2001, and I found a name written in my mother's distinctive handwriting. Not her real name, but one she would have been likely to use – one of her favorite fictional characters.'

Swenson and Fernandez exchanged glances – Swenson's resolutely skeptical, Fernandez's with a hint of *let's hear her out.*

Erin went on. 'The first part of the entry – the checking-in part – was in my mother's handwriting, as I said, but the checkout time was in a completely different hand. The numbers were formed the way Russians write them. Here, I have a photo.'

She pulled out her phone, scrolled quickly, and showed it to the two officers. Swenson's eyebrows went up in a *she's got something there* look.

'The innkeeper recognized a picture of my mother, though she didn't connect the face with a name. But she told me she remembered that around that time, some woman had failed to check out, and a man had come by in the morning, claiming to be her husband. He said she'd been taken ill in the night and he'd picked her up and driven her to the hospital, and now he'd come back for her things.' She paused for dramatic effect. 'The way she described him fits the man who followed us yesterday – what he would have looked like twenty years ago – to a T.'

Swenson frowned more deeply. 'So let me get this straight. You believe this guy – let's call him the Russian for now – somehow got into her room during the night, killed her, removed her body and disposed of it someplace where it's never been found, then went back for her luggage? And presumably disposed of it as well?'

Erin nodded with all the certainty she could muster. 'The inn is right on the coast. He could have put her in her car and sent it off a cliff into the ocean.'

Fernandez said, 'Not too likely a car would have washed out to sea. But a body could have. I'll check on whether any wrecked cars were found around that time but never identified.'

'Speaking of cars,' Swenson put in, 'if she was driving all this time, how come she was never picked up based on her license plate?'

'I don't think Carver ever put it in the system. He didn't actually want to find her, remember? Or, possibly, she could have traded the car in somewhere on the way to Oregon. With some unscrupulous seller who would agree not to report the sale.'

Swenson nodded, making notes. 'You don't remember the license number, by any chance? Or the make of the car?'

'It was a ninety-six Camry. Dark green. And I do remember the number, because it was funny – 6FRA789. You know that joke – why was six afraid of seven? Because seven ate nine.'

Swenson was clearly not amused, but he wrote it down anyway. 'We'll look into it. But I have to warn you, based on only what you've told us – with no body – there's no way we can even charge the Russian with murder, let alone get a conviction.'

Erin closed her eyes for a moment, then nodded. 'I understand. But if you can put him away for fraud, maybe intimidation, whatever – at least that will be some sort of justice. And the other people involved – Cruikshank especially. I hold him morally responsible for my mother's death, since he was running the scam under her nose and failed to protect her.'

Swenson nodded, and Fernandez permitted himself a tiny reassuring smile. 'We'll get Cruikshank. If everything you suspect pans out, I think I can promise you that.'

They stood and walked to the front door. Swenson handed Erin a business card. 'Let me know if anything else comes up. We'll be in touch.'

# THIRTY-ONE

Erin closed the door behind the officers and sagged against it. 'That really took it out of me. I think I need to go back to bed.'

Evan put an arm behind her back, holding her up. 'How about another cup of coffee instead?'

She nodded, and he walked her to the kitchen. She didn't truly need his physical support, but she was glad to have it nonetheless.

She fell into a chair and laid her head down on her arms until he placed the steaming cup in front of her. She raised her head and sipped, cradling the warm mug in both hands. The house wasn't cold, but she was chilled through. Miss Silver, who had disappeared into one of her hidey-holes when the CBI agents showed up, materialized at her feet and leapt onto her lap as an extra warming pad.

'You've had quite a morning,' Evan said. 'And it isn't even nine o'clock. What say we take it easy the rest of the day?'

Erin nodded. 'Sounds good to me.' As the coffee restored her, she began to feel a sense of lightening and release, knowing that the whole problem was now in the hands of professionals who would act rather than fobbing her off with empty promises. 'Although I'm feeling better already, just knowing those guys are on the case.'

Evan smiled. 'I vote we spend the day getting to know each other. I for one feel as if I've known you forever, but I don't know much of anything *about* you – your childhood, your interests. Heck, I don't even know what you do for a living.'

Erin gaped, then laughed. 'Oh my gosh. I guess it's never come up. I'm a research librarian. Alex works with me – that's how we met.'

He looked her over thoughtfully. 'A research librarian. I can see that. Curiosity, attention to detail. A desire to make connections, to fit things into their proper place in the world.' He nodded. 'And what do you do in your spare time?'

'Spare time? What's that?' At his quizzical look, Erin explained. 'The last few weeks have been consumed with this investigation. And before that, I spent a couple of years nursing my father through cancer. He didn't need actual nursing that whole time, of course, but he seemed to need *me* every minute I wasn't working. I'd settle him for the night and then be lucky to get half an hour to veg in front of the TV before I fell asleep.'

Evan took her hand and held her gaze, as if absorbing the pain, exhaustion, and stress of those years out of her body into his, then letting it all drain away. 'Go back to when your time was your own. What did you do then?'

She gave a rueful half-laugh. 'That would mean going back to before my mother disappeared. From that time on, when I wasn't busy with school, I was at my father's beck and call.'

He winced. 'OK, then. What were your interests as a child?'

With an effort, Erin cast her mind back to the happy days, so distant in both time and quality from what followed that they now seemed like a dream. 'My mother and I did all sorts of things together. Everything was fun when I was with her. But on my own . . .'

A memory came back to her of her child self, sitting on the window seat in her bedroom, a composition book propped on her knees, scribbling away.

'I used to write,' she said in wonderment. 'Stories, poems, plays – you name it. But after she went, I just couldn't anymore. I've kept a journal all along, but nothing else.'

Evan leaned toward her, his eyes alight. 'Do you still have any of those old stories? I'd love to see them.'

She laughed. 'My twelve-year-old scribblings? Would you want to show your sketches from that age to anyone now?'

'To you, I would.' He grimaced. 'Only to you.'

Yes, of course. She would have to get used to this – what could be shared with no one else in the world could always be shared with Evan.

'Let's go find out.' She put Miss Silver down, against loud protests, and led the way upstairs to her childhood bedroom.

The room was small, just big enough for a single bed, student desk, and dresser. Once her father had been installed downstairs for the last months of his illness, Erin had cleared out his things and moved into the master bedroom, leaving her old room untouched. Its pastel-striped wallpaper and curtains, along with the well-worn stuffed animals on the bed and Nancy Drew books on the shelf above it, bore out Erin's tale of an adolescence and young adulthood in which she had rarely had the opportunity to do anything for herself.

She stood a moment in the doorway, overwhelmed by the memories that flooded in. Then she shook herself into focus. She was looking for her old notebooks. Where had she kept them? The image of herself scribbling on the window seat returned. Of course. She'd kept them in the storage area underneath the seat.

With some trepidation, preparing herself to discover unwelcome visitors of the small four-legged or even smaller eight-legged variety, Erin creaked the lid open. Instantly Miss Silver was at her side, nose twitching. Before Erin could stop her, she leapt into the wooden under-seat, sniffing every corner. At last, she settled down on an old comforter folded up at the far end. Erin breathed more freely.

At her end of the seat were several neat stacks – one of sketches and watercolors, one of half-finished knitting projects, and one of yellowing composition books. Erin blew a layer of dust off the top book and lifted it out.

Momentarily forgetting Evan's existence as she returned to a time when he was not, she sat cross-legged on the floor and flipped through the notebook slowly, stopping to skim a poem here, the abortive beginning of a story there. All were cringeworthy in some way, though a felicitous phrase did pop out here and there. Each entry was headed with a date in June, 2001.

She turned the page marked 'June 20' and a sealed envelope fluttered to her lap. Probably some random thing she'd used for a bookmark. She turned it over and saw, in her mother's handwriting, 'To my beloved Erin.'

Dumbfounded, she held the envelope between her fingertips like a holy relic. How had she never seen this? She cast her mind back to those dreadful days in that distant June. At first she'd been too stunned and preoccupied even to think of writing anything; later on, she'd felt drained of creative ideas. She'd begun journaling that July, but had bought a fresh notebook for the purpose and kept it in her desk drawer. It was entirely possible she'd never opened the window seat from that day to this.

'What is it?' Evan asked, his gentle voice startling her into the present.

'It's a letter from my mother. One I never saw. I think she must have left it just before she went.'

She sat there on the floor staring at the envelope, uncertain why she would hesitate to rip it open and devour its contents.

Evan took her elbow and helped her up to sit beside him on the bed. 'You have to open it sometime,' he said.

'I know. But it's like eating the last piece of chocolate cake you'll ever have in your life. When it's gone, it's gone.'

'Not exactly. You can't eat the cake a second time, but you can reread a letter as often as you want.'

'Yes, but it will still be the same letter. The last one ever. I'll never hear anything new from her again.'

He put an arm around her shoulder and drew her close. 'That's true. But it comes to us all at one time or another. And you do have a lot of other new things to look forward to.'

She looked up at him, foreseeing many of those new things in his eyes. The spark of joy contained in that thought gave her the strength to tear open the flap and pull out the single sheet of stationery it contained.

She held it so that Evan could read along with her. 'My dearest Erin,' the letter began.

> *My darling girl, I hope you will find this letter before grief overwhelms you. I daren't leave it in any more obvious place, because it must never be for any eyes but yours.*
>
> *I have to go away. And I cannot take you with me. That's the gist of it. I have to go because my presence is putting you in danger, and if I took you with me, the danger would only increase. Neither can I explain all this, because if you knew the why of it, you would be a target in your own right. As it is, they are only threatening you in order to manipulate me. Once I'm gone, your danger will cease to exist. Remember this and do not be afraid.*
>
> *I hope and believe that my absence will be only for a little while. I will find a way to make it safe for us to be*

*together again. I've already tried going to the local police – a detective called Carver. Do not trust him. He's been so obstructive, I can't help suspecting he's working with them. And – yes, I think I must say this in spite of the risk. Do not trust Raymond Cruikshank either. He is in it up to his beady, lying eyes. Stay as far away from him as you can, and never let him have any of my things.*

*I can't share this with your father, and I can't tell you the why of that, either. I hope and pray that he will take good care of you while I'm gone. Perhaps you'll take care of each other. If you need anything, or if you need to get away, call your nan in England. It's sad that you don't know her well, because she is a wise woman. She will know what to do.*

*I have so much I want to say to you, my darling daughter, but there is no time. May God be with you and protect you. Always remember I love you, and everything I do, I do for you.*

*All my love,*
*Mumsie*

Erin could barely read the final paragraph through her tears. She clutched the letter to her chest and sobbed.

Evan held her, making soothing noises and rubbing her back. When at last her sobs subsided a little, he offered her a tissue, then another and another. Her face would not stop leaking.

'I must look a fright,' she said when she could speak. 'So much for maintaining the mystery in our relationship.'

'We don't need mystery. We have something far better than that.' He tilted her face toward his. 'We have trust. You letting me read that letter along with you means the world.'

She gazed at him with dawning wonder. She did trust him – as she had trusted no one since her mother disappeared. She'd made strides in that direction with Alex and with Cat, but she'd held things back from each of them, not quite knowing why. But with Evan there was no question, to reveal or not to reveal. She must lay herself open to him, or they had nothing.

But there was something she hadn't told him yet. Just as the thought crossed her mind, he said, 'One thing I wanted to ask you. You told the agents you got a feeling at Seafarer's Rest that your mother had been there. Was that the whole truth, or was it a scrubbed version for their skeptical ears?'

She sighed. He had done it again – read her mind. 'Scrubbed. What actually happened is that my first night there, I had a dream. It was as real as if I were in the room watching actual events unfold. I saw my mother getting ready for bed in the same room I was staying in, only the room had subtle differences, the way it might have been twenty years ago. I saw her go to sleep, then a man all in black climbed in the window and crept up to the bed. He grabbed a pillow and smothered her.' She shuddered, remembering. 'And then I woke up. I never saw his face.'

Evan absorbed this in silence until she went on.

'From that time on, every place I went, everything I found, I felt like my mother was guiding me. I'd get a pricking feeling in my thumbs when I came upon any sort of clue. Sometimes I've even heard her voice in my head. I feel her spirit hovering about me, urging me on. Giving me her benediction.' She looked up at him. 'Does that make me crazy?'

He squeezed her shoulder. 'No. That makes you your mother's daughter – a sensitive spirit motivated by love.' He paused, staring out the window. 'As an artist, I know there's something more to the world than what we can see or touch. I get inspirations that I am absolutely certain come from somewhere beyond myself. I can't put a name to it, but it's like Hamlet said – "There are more things in heaven and earth, Horatio . . ."'

She finished along with him, '". . . than are dreamt of in your philosophy." Yes. I feel that, too.'

After a few moments of contemplating the mysteries of the universe in companionable silence, Evan said, 'Do you think the CBI guys need to see this letter?'

Erin started. The letter was so personal, so precious, the thought of sharing it with anyone but Evan was repellent to her. But she had to admit it could be construed as evidence. And if it would help bring Carver, Cruikshank, and their cronies to justice, she must not keep it back.

Evan eased the letter from her grasp. 'I'll photograph it while you call them. OK?'

She nodded, relinquishing it reluctantly. She found Swenson's card in the pocket of her jeans and made the call.

It took only a moment. 'They're in Carmel right now, but they'll be over as soon as they can to pick it up.'

'Right.' Having taken several shots, Evan put his phone away and handed the letter back to her. Then he ran his hands over his face and hair. 'Much as I hate to be parted from you for a moment, I have to admit I am feeling the need of a shower and shave and some clothes that haven't been slept in. And I need to make some calls about my show. Would you mind if I nipped back to my hotel for an hour?'

She kissed him lightly, feeling the prickle of his beard against her skin. 'I see what you mean. I would prefer you smooth.' He grinned. 'Go ahead. I'll be fine on my own for a bit.' She glanced at the pile of composition books still waiting in the window seat. 'I might do some reading.'

# THIRTY-TWO

Erin read through one notebook after another, absorbed in revisiting her childhood. Though her scribblings did bring up memories, they felt more like stories she'd heard long ago than like things that had happened to her. The young girl she'd been had not evolved in the normal way into womanhood, but had abruptly ceased to exist the day she woke up to find her mother gone.

She was so engrossed that when the knock came at the front door, it was like a real-world sound breaking through into a dream – at first it didn't register as something that required her attention, her action. But when the knock intensified and was interspersed with prolonged rings of the doorbell, she at last woke up.

Evan must be back. She ran down the stairs to the door and pulled it open without checking the peephole.

But it wasn't Evan.

Raymond Cruikshank stood on her doorstep, wearing a navy suit, a familiar-looking blue-and-green silk scarf around his neck, and a smile that did not reach his eyes. *His beady, lying eyes.*

In the moment before her stunned brain could move her body to shut the door in his face, he pushed past her and stepped inside, closing the door behind him. He stood in the entrance hall and looked around, as if he were any normal visitor, then glanced down at the threadbare Craftsman-patterned rug under their feet.

'The place hasn't changed,' he said with a note of surprise. 'I thought surely you would have redecorated by now. Or at least replaced this worn carpet.' Even if Erin had ever had time, thought, or money to spare for redecorating, she would never have gotten rid of this rug, because her mother had loved it.

His fluid, monotonous voice was already beginning to weave a spell over her. She shook herself into full consciousness. 'What do you want, Cruikshank? I have nothing to say to you.'

The corners of his mouth turned up. 'Oh, but I have plenty to say to you, little Erin. To begin with, I've seen far too much of you and your friends lately. You need to keep your pretty little nose out of my business.' He tapped his gloved finger against the tip of said nose. Why was he wearing gloves in July?

She stepped back a full pace, out of his reach, resisting the impulse to wipe his touch off her nose. Outrage mowed down all her native caution. 'I'm afraid I can't do that. Your business includes at the very least fraud, and possibly conspiracy to murder my mother. The CBI is onto you now. You're going to see some justice at last.'

His pasty face went a shade paler, but he didn't flinch. Perhaps he already knew about the CBI's involvement. Had they just been interviewing him? And if so, how had he arrived here ahead of them?

'Justice . . .' he said in a meditative voice, walking slowly around the hall and running his gloved finger along the wainscoting as if checking for dust. 'Such an interesting word. A flexible word, don't you think? What is justice for one may be persecution for another. Or retribution for a third.' He stopped by the foot of the stairs and turned to her. 'Or, if pursued too avidly, it can mean sacrifice.'

'The sacrifice was made twenty years ago. My mother sacrificed herself to save me. And you had something to do with making that happen.'

His smile grew to split his face, while his eyes burned into her, cold as dry ice. 'I had everything to do with it. My Russian friends only cleaned up after me. I owed Gina a great debt' – his words dripped sarcasm – 'that only I could repay.'

'What debt?' Erin asked, more to keep him talking than out of any real curiosity. She moved her arm across her pocket, but the hard rectangle of her phone was missing. Damn. She must have left it on the bed after calling Swenson. It wasn't likely she could have either called 911 or set the phone to record without Cruikshank noticing, but at least she might have tried.

Without her phone, she didn't even know how much time had passed since Evan had left her house or the agents had left Carmel. Surely it was close to an hour, at least. If she could only keep him talking, someone might get there before . . . whatever he had planned.

Cruikshank sneered. It wasn't often she saw someone actually sneer. 'A debt of honor. Saint Gina made me out to be some kind of lowlife. She was always so kind, so generous, so unselfish. Always showing me up.' His voice became strangled. 'So beautiful, but never turning those bedroom eyes on me.'

His nostrils flared as his hands clenched on the ends of his scarf – a scarf Erin now realized with a jolt of mixed grief and outrage had belonged to her mother. 'And she was such a goody-goody, so damned self-righteous, she couldn't turn a blind eye to a tiny peccadillo. A little harmless sale of a beautiful painting that would immeasurably enrich the buyer's life – just because it wasn't technically painted by the person whose signature it bore. Even though neither the buyer nor anyone else was ever likely to know.'

'But you knew. You and your cronies. You made a handsome profit off a lie. That sounds pretty lowlife to me.'

His eyes narrowed. 'You're just as self-righteous as your dear, sainted mother, aren't you? I suspected as much. And now you're going to meet the same tragic end.' He gave a dry chuckle. 'With artistic variations, of course.'

Erin's stomach plummeted. She should have pretended sympathy, or at least curiosity, in order to keep him talking. Instead, with her blunt honesty, she had sealed her own fate.

He closed the space between them in two strides while pulling the scarf from his neck into both hands. She whipped around and had the doorknob in her hand, summoning a scream as she turned it, when she felt him behind her, wrapping the length of silk around her neck.

She could feel the fabric biting into her flesh, beginning to constrict her airway and the blood flow to her brain. She put her hands to her neck, scrabbling to get her fingers under the scarf, but it was already too tight for them to find purchase. She kicked out behind her with all the force she could muster and felt her bare foot connect with Cruikshank's knee. He yelled in pain and anger but only pulled the scarf tighter.

She began to gag, and dark spots appeared in her vision. This was it. The bad guys were winning. What had happened to the cavalry? This wasn't the way the story was supposed to end.

She reached once more for the doorknob, but Cruikshank had

pulled her back out of reach. She kicked out forward instead and made contact with the frosted glass panel to the side of the door, shattering it. As if from a great distance, she heard yelling and the slamming of car doors.

With her last conscious thought, she cried out silently to her mother for help. She felt the aged silk of the scarf begin to rip and crumble, loosening its hold on her neck. Then the world went black.

# THIRTY-THREE

When the world swam into focus again, a pale, freckled face topped by a shock of copper hair was bending over her, calling her name in urgent, panicked tones. She tried to answer, but no sound would emerge from her damaged throat. But Evan saw the spark of consciousness in her eyes, and relief flooded his features. He made a move as if to gather her to his breast, but another man in a paramedic's uniform gently pushed him aside and began to fuss around her, adjusting the oxygen mask she now realized she was wearing and inserting an IV line into her arm.

'Oh my God, Erin,' Evan said from his enforced distance. 'I thought I'd lost you. I'd never have forgiven myself for leaving you alone.'

Since she couldn't speak, she squeezed his hand as he held hers between both his own. She tried to say with her eyes that she loved him, there was nothing to forgive, everything had turned out all right. Her mother had saved her.

In the ambulance, Evan told her what had happened. He and the CBI agents had arrived simultaneously. Seeing the door glass shatter, they burst in and caught Cruikshank in the act of strangling her.

Evan's eyes went dark and fierce as he told her. 'It's a good thing they got to him first. I would have strangled him with his own scarf.' His grip on her hand tightened painfully, and she made a little noise. He started, raised her hand to his lips, and kissed it. 'I'm sorry, love. I can't get his face out of my mind. I don't think I've ever seen such hatred.'

Looking like her mother was not without its drawbacks, apparently. All Cruikshank's festering resentment of Gina, having survived his murder of her, had been turned against her daughter. A vivid picture came into her mind of Cruikshank striding toward her, twisting the scarf in his hands.

Her mother's scarf. The gall of the man! He'd saved that trophy all these years – and finally returned it to Gina's daughter.

'You were barely breathing when we got you away from him,' Evan said. 'And I'm lousy at first aid. I tried mouth-to-mouth, but I don't even know if it was the right thing to do. Thank God the paramedics got there as quick as they did.'

He bent over her hand again, overcome. She willed all her love, relief, and gratitude into that hand.

Once they'd arrived at the hospital and she'd been transferred to a bed in the ER, Swenson and Fernandez appeared at the entrance to her cubicle. She motioned them to come in, and they stood at the end of the bed.

'How are you doing?' Swenson asked Erin. 'Are you up to answering a few questions?'

She tried to say 'yes,' but her throat still wouldn't work. She mimed writing, and Fernandez handed her a notepad and pen. Evan reluctantly let go of her hand so she could take them.

'Did Cruikshank say anything to you before he attacked you?' Swenson asked.

She nodded and wrote, 'He confessed to killing my mother,' then held the pad up for him to see.

Swenson's eyebrows rose into his thick blond hair. 'Just like that?'

She shook her head and wrote, 'Cutting to the chase.'

The Nordic glacier of Swenson's face actually cracked into a tiny grin. 'All right. We'll get the details from you when you can talk again.'

He cleared his throat. 'And I want to apologize. We should have put a guard on your house right after we spoke to you. I didn't realize how spooked Cruikshank already was – I thought we'd have some time.'

Fernandez shot his partner a glance and added, 'Also, we didn't expect him to act on his own. We thought the Russians were the muscle in the operation and Cruikshank was the brains, directing everything but keeping his own hands clean.'

Erin shook her head again. 'We all underestimated how much he hated my mother,' she wrote, exhausting the space on the page as well as her own strength. She fell back against the pillows and let her arms drop.

Evan took the pad and pen from her hands and passed them to Fernandez, who read the message and nodded. 'I guess so.'

'We found the letter from your mother upstairs,' Swenson said. 'It doesn't say anything definite, but it should at least serve to corroborate Cruikshank's confession. We're letting him stew for a bit, but he's over the edge – he'll crack for sure. We'll have him for fraud, murder, attempted murder – the whole enchilada.' He permitted himself a tiny smile. 'You won't be seeing him again anytime soon. Except in court.'

Erin had been admitted for observation and was resting in a regular room when Cat and Alex burst in. Evan had gone in search of something to eat.

Alex rushed to her side and took her hand. 'My God, Erin, you gave us a fright! Thank God you're OK!'

Cat came up to her other side. 'Yeah, way to leave your buds out of the big moment,' she said with a grin, then sobered. 'But seriously, Erin, when Evan told us what happened – I guess it's a good thing I wasn't there, 'cause I would've shot the guy and probably been suspended.' She leaned over and planted a kiss on Erin's forehead. 'You are the bravest woman I know.'

Erin opened her mouth to protest that there was nothing particularly brave about being rescued from imminent death, but all that came out was a croak. She settled for a whispered, 'Thanks, guys.'

Evan returned with a packaged sandwich in one hand and a cup of coffee in the other. Alex waited for him to set them down, then put out his hand for Evan to shake. 'Thanks for taking care of her,' he said huskily.

The look they exchanged as they shook hands was a clear transfer of responsibility for Erin's well-being from Alex to Evan. She closed her eyes and breathed a prayer of gratitude that Alex had found the strength to step back so graciously. That might not have happened if she had not come so close to death. If that was the case, it was worth it.

Back at home the next morning, her voice having returned as a squeaky treble, Erin reclined in state on the loveseat with Miss Silver ensconced on her lap. With Cat, Alex, and Evan all gathered around her, competing to meet her slightest need, she went through the events of the last twenty-four hours. She felt like the original Miss Silver explaining to Frank Abbott all the insights and thought processes that had led her to solve the case – although Erin hadn't really solved this one. Cruikshank's confession of hands-on murder had come as a complete surprise.

Cat was able to fill in a few details of how the CBI investigation was progressing. 'They arrested Carver. I wish you could've been there, Erin. They led him out of his own office in cuffs, two days before his retirement party was set to happen. I almost felt sorry for him.' She made a face. 'But not quite. Especially since I'm now in line for his job.'

'Cat, that's wonderful!' Erin squeaked. 'It couldn't be better deserved.'

Cat bowed her head with a tiny smile, then went on. 'And the big news is they found the car! I mean, they found a record of a burned-out vehicle on the rocks near Pacific Grove from October of 2001. Carver got the report and sat on it. The VIN plate was damaged, but it matched the description of your mother's car. No license plate, of course. And no body or possessions, I'm afraid – those must have ended up in the ocean.'

Erin nodded, tearing up. She'd expected as much, but still, it would have been some comfort if they'd found remains she could have buried. To have a grave, a place she could go to talk to her mother, to say a proper goodbye.

She couldn't hold a funeral. But maybe she could do the next best thing.

# THIRTY-FOUR

An autumn chill was in the air as Erin moved about the rented hall, making sure the paintings and their labels were properly paired and hung straight and secure. She had painstakingly framed the pieces, prepared the labels, and hung them all, with Evan's help. She would not entrust this first and only show of the life's work of Gina Washington to any gallery. It would be a long time before she could trust a gallery owner again.

Evan came to her side, having spoken to the caterers and made sure everything was in readiness – trays of full champagne flutes and tempting canapés all set to go. 'It's time,' he said, putting an arm around her shoulders. 'Time to open the doors.'

Erin nodded and walked to the entrance. She unlocked the glass double doors and stood aside. Cat and Alex were the first ones through, followed quickly by Finn. He paused to give Erin a peck on the cheek before striding directly to the centerpiece of the show: his own finished portrait of Gina.

Finn had chosen a large canvas to depict his subject life-size. Erin had been almost afraid to look when he'd delivered the portrait to the hall, remembering the sketches she'd seen in his studio. But Finn had not painted an unhappy woman desperate for love. Instead, he'd somehow managed to convey every side of Gina, both those Erin had known as a child and those she had later discovered: her warmth and playfulness, her zest for life, her passionate potential, and, above all, her courage.

Erin had gazed at the portrait until her knees gave out beneath her. She'd turned to Finn with tears in her eyes. 'Thank you,' she'd said. 'Thank you for giving her back to me.'

Now the artist flicked an imaginary fleck of dust from the portrait's frame, stood back, and nodded in satisfaction. He turned to survey the rest of the exhibition.

Erin had hung the public pictures – the landscapes and portraits of her child self – on one side of the hall and the private paintings

– the surreal ones that revealed Gina's hidden despair – on the other. Gina's unfinished portrait of Finn hung at the end of the private section, facing toward the lobby. Finn ignored the public side and headed toward his own portrait, pausing to peruse the other pictures along the way.

Erin had put price tags on some of the landscapes, consulting Evan as to appropriate amounts. But the portraits and the private pictures she would never sell.

She took a flute from a passing server's tray and circulated as she sipped. She'd hardly known whom to invite to this show, beyond her own few friends – along with Jackie from Tor House Lodge and Elise from Seafarer's Rest, who were both in attendance – and a couple of old acquaintances of her mother's, including the friends she'd made in her final travels. But Evan and Finn had compiled a healthy list of people they knew from the art community, and the number of attendees was gratifying. Erin paused here and there to greet people and answer their questions before coming upon Cat and Alex, standing together before the largest and most harrowing piece on the surreal side of the hall.

Cat tore her eyes away as Erin approached. 'These are . . . I don't know what to say. It's awfully brave of you to show them.'

'I was torn about it at first. But Evan and Finn both insisted these represent her best work, the most worthy of being seen by people who are able to appreciate them. In the end, I felt like she was telling me to go ahead.' Erin gestured toward the empty space where a label should have been. 'But as you can see, I had nothing to say about them. They aren't titled or even dated. And since I'm not selling them, there was no point in giving them a number. They can just . . . be.'

Alex nodded, then turned to her. 'So you're going away after this? You and Evan?' His voice caught only a tiny bit on Evan's name.

Her face lit in spite of herself. 'Yes. We're going to travel – no plan, no itinerary, just go where the wind takes us. And then we'll settle in his place up in Point Reyes.' She fondled the vintage pearl ring on her left ring finger. 'After the wedding, that is. Cat, I hope you'll be my maid of honor.'

Cat's face split in a huge smile as she enfolded Erin in a

crushing hug. 'If you'd asked anyone else, I would've arrested her. You can count on me.'

Alex smiled at the back of Cat's head. When she released Erin, he laid a hand on Cat's shoulder. 'I don't expect to be best man or anything, but I'll be there. With bells on. To dance with the maid of honor – and the bride.'

Erin hugged Alex in his turn, releasing him as Evan came up to join them. 'Did you ask her?' Evan said to Erin.

'Yes. And they'll both be there.' She hesitated a moment, then plunged ahead. 'Alex, as my oldest friend, will you give a toast on my behalf? Since I have no family member to do it?'

He smiled broadly. 'It will be my honor.'

After a bit more chat, Cat and Alex moved on, and Erin returned to stand in front of her mother's portrait one more time, with Evan at her side. 'What ever happened to Finn's portrait of you?' he asked.

She gave a little laugh. 'He's never let me see it. Maybe he's afraid of showing it to *you*.'

'Or maybe he merged it into this one of your mother. I can see some of you in there.' He gave her shoulder a squeeze. 'Anyway, soon enough I'll be doing a portrait of my own, and it will be a masterpiece, because I see you as you truly are. Right?'

She turned and gazed at him, feeling her cup of happiness overflow. 'Right. I'm finally ready to show my face to the world.'